The
DESCARTES
HIGHLANDS

WITHDRAWN

The
DESCARTES
HIGHLANDS

a novel

Published by Akashic Books
©2014 Eric Gamalinda

Paperback ISBN-13: 978-1-61775-304-6
Library of Congress Control Number: 2014938692

The author would like to acknowledge Facets Multi-Media, Inc., for permission to reprint a quotation from "Why I Make Films" by Béla Tarr, from "The Early Films of Béla Tarr"; and Guy Picciotto, for permission to reprint lines from the Fugazi song "Last Chance for a Slow Dance." The author would also like to thank the La Napoule Art Foundation, Jonah Straus, Ubaldo Stecconi, and the staff at Akashic Books.

Front cover images: moon © Shutterstock, and cityscape © audioscience/Shutterstock.

Akashic Books
Twitter: @AkashicBooks
Facebook: AkashicBooks
info@akashicbooks.com
www.akashicbooks.com

*This book is dedicated to my family,
and especially to my mother, who taught me to write fearlessly.*

I despise stories, as they mislead people into believing that something has happened. In fact, nothing really happens as we flee from one condition to another. Because today there are only states of being—all stories have become obsolete and clichéd, and have resolved themselves. All that remains is time.

—Béla Tarr

We are held in place by gravitational forces

My mother and I used to play this game when I was growing up. Every time I had a question she couldn't answer, she made me write to my imaginary father, Mr. Brezsky, who lived on the moon. I would later learn that Mr. Brezsky was my biological father, but he could just as well have been Santa Claus for all I cared. In fact, in 1976, when Santa Claus was down with the flu, it was Mr. Brezsky who left me a mechanical train.

My letters were addressed like this:

Mr. Brezsky
The Descartes Highlands
The Moon

Mother and I always sat out in the backyard whenever the moon was full. It seemed bigger and brighter in Westchester, where there was not much else to see. Among the dark patches of the moon were the peaks of the Descartes Highlands, where the *Apollo 16* mission scooped samples of rock and soil. You could see the tracks left by the moon rover with a telescope. She told me they were left there in the year I was born. Man's tracks on the moon, she said, were like my Bethlehem star. They were going to be visible for a million years, and a million years from now they would remind people that I was once on earth.

* * *

I'm eight years old, and the school principal pulls me out of class one afternoon and says my mother has come to pick me up and take me home. Mother told them it was an emergency. They're all nice to me, thinking someone died. My English teacher slips a Hershey's bar in my hands, nodding quietly as I accept her gift, tears welling in her eyes.

Inside the car, Mother rolls the windows up, takes a deep breath, and tells me the truth: "Jordan, I am not your mother."

That's when she begins telling me about the real Mr. Brezsky.

"It was September, 1972. He was a very young man. He had no money. He sold you for thirty thousand dollars. Five months later, he wired the money back. Then he died. That was his story."

From then on she never stops talking about him. Now that she's opened up the subject, it seems like everything is all right, and she's never going to keep any secrets from me again.

Every time she retells the story, some new detail is amended, but Mr. Brezsky remains as murky as ever. I finally have to ask her why she even bothered to tell me the story in the first place. She replies, "Frank has moved to the Dominican Republic with his girlfriend. They've set up a new clinic there."

That seems to her enough of a reason, and from then on she tells me the story even more frequently, in fact way more often than necessary. Here's another version:

Andrew Brezsky died at the age of nineteen or twenty

in a military prison in Manila. She got that one from ex-Communists in Manila who had tracked her down through the Life Crusaders' hit list and wanted to talk to her for a report on human rights violations around the world. Through the years, and several more calls from them, that version acquires even more details, some incongruous, others simply incredible. In prison, anti-American students allegedly beat up Andrew Brezsky and left him for dead. In yet a later version, some petty criminal or corrupt police officer assassinated him for his money, which, if you put two and two together, he must have earlier wired to us to get them off his back. Always the ending is sudden, violent, unresolved, and likely doubtful.

In time, I catch on and realize a lot of it is probably just made up. It's as if she's trying to figure out, in the redundancy of the telling, if this Andrew Brezsky was unknowingly pivotal in her life, if that one brief encounter sparked off a karmic chain reaction whose repercussions are still felt today. And by repeating the story over and over, she will finally realize that there was some detour she failed to see, signs that could have told her where to turn.

"He was such a beautiful boy," she says. "You could tell he was going to die young."

One night, while she's in bed with Frank, the phone rings and she picks it up. The caller immediately hangs up. The same thing happens for the next three nights, and on the fourth Frank himself grabs the phone. He doesn't say a word. He keeps the receiver pressed against his ear, listening as though he's trying to catch the faintest rumor of some mysterious, important missive. And then for a fleeting moment he looks at her, and she sees something she's never seen before. Something inexpressible. Such sadness in his eyes. Not just sadness but fear. Not just fear but her fear conjoined with his, a mesmerizing mirror in which she can only see a self-reflected horror.

That is when she decides she wants to have a baby. *!?*

She's read that at forty-five a woman's biological clock is a ticking time bomb; it's now or never. The next day she visits a gynecologist, a friend of Frank's. That evening, with Frank still out in the city, she finds a message for him on the answering machine. The message is very brief, *Please call back, please*, but the desperation in that woman's voice is so immediate, so apparent, that she feels something apocalyptic churning in her guts, and the next morning, when the gynecologist tells her she is incapable of conceiving a child, she thinks for a moment, *Frank made you tell me that*, but she doesn't say anything, and the word *barren* keeps whirring tauntingly in her mind like a chain saw. *Barren barren barren.* Frank comes back that night. He's just been with a friend, a lawyer who could help them file a lawsuit against the Life Crusaders who have been harassing them to leave town. Et cetera, et cetera. *Barren barren barren.* His voice sounds disembodied, out of sync. The sooner we take care of this, the better, he says; no more mysterious calls. She says, "You've been fucking someone." She doesn't actually say it. The words fill her mouth, she can taste their bitterness, and she feels like choking. Frank asks her what's wrong. She says, "That young patient of ours, that eighteen-year-old girl who's coming from the next county, I want to keep her baby."

She is well aware that that's not going to happen. The

girl is suffering from hysterical fits and has to be sedated for the abortion. Under the drug, she has delusions that the baby is crawling through her veins, contaminating her blood, and that she will burst open at the pores, like a fruit exploding. There is no way she would ever make the hard decision and forego the procedure.

Abortion, Frank reminds her, is an act of desperation, arrived at either after agonizing deliberation, or in an emergency. In almost all cases, there is no way they can save the mother's life without sacrificing the fetus. That's what they've always tried to tell the countless Christian lunatics who frequently come to spit Jesus in their faces.

The clinic in Dobbs Ferry has had its share of troubles. Several nights, from the two-bedroom apartment above it where they live, they can hear streams of cars passing by, the drivers yelling at them to burn in hell.

Frank himself doesn't want any more children. His own haven't spoken to him in years. He hardly talks about them, and whenever he does, it's always as if he's talking about an ancient, unhealed wound. He hardly ever mentions their names. Sometimes he even seems to have forgotten he has any children.

Obviously, the only alternative is adoption. There's Romania, Russia, Sri Lanka, Thailand. But adoption is expensive, tedious, and complicated by corrupt bureaucracies of donor countries. Just to find out for sure, she applies with a couple of agencies. They immediately deny her application upon learning of the kind of work she does. There you go, says Frank; that's the kind of people you'd have to deal with.

Then she hears of a couple who've come back from the Philippines with a perfectly normal, legal, healthy Amerasian boy. They bought the baby through an underground adoption ring operating there. The baby was handed to them just a couple of days after its birth, a scrawny creature, pink and hungry and full of need.

She invites the couple over one evening. They seem to have been transformed by this new presence in their lives, and they come with all the accoutrements that signify that change, an unwieldy baby carriage and FAO Schwarz bags brimming with bottles, diapers, and silly toys. They say they feel like a closer couple now, their relationship made more meaningful by a kind of aegis, a holy trinity. They talk of themselves no longer as individuals but as a single unit, a *family*. Suddenly their lives are mapped out more clearly, with plans for the next ten, twenty, thirty years. It's cloyingly sweet and she loves it. She holds the baby in her arms. It's soft and small and breathtaking. She is unaware of the growing anxiety on Frank's face, even when she turns to him and says, "I know what I want. I know what to do."

On the Delta Air Lines flight to San Francisco, she reads a story in the *New York Times* that Frank told her about earlier that morning, before she boarded a taxi to JFK. A certain Arthur Herman Bremer shot the governor of Alabama, George Wallace. Doctors have said the governor will be paralyzed from the waist down for the rest of his life.

Neither she nor Frank cares much about the governor or his would-be assassin. But Frank says there you go: that's the kind of world we'll be bringing a baby into.

She transfers to a Japan Airlines jet in San Francisco, and as soon as the attendants start rolling dinner out she sets her watch twelve hours forward to Manila time. She realizes that by doing so she has just jumped into the future. She looks out. The moon is a flat disk of light. Just less than a month ago, two humans were out there digging dirt. She closes her eyes and tries to imagine what it must have been like, but there's a constant hum in the plane that she finds distracting. She is awake all through the sixteen-hour flight.

She has the name of a contact given by the couple who had adopted earlier. It takes a few weeks for someone from the adoption ring to call her back. The couple had told her this was normal. They would be doing a background check to make sure she wasn't just some decoy.

An "agent" meets her at the lobby of her hotel apartment in Manila. The transaction is informal. It makes her feel like she's just purchasing a line of home products from a traveling salesman. It's also simple. All she has to do is put some cash down. One of their women has already been impregnated, and it looks like the father is American. The agent hesitates at the word *impregnated*, and apologizes for not knowing a term less vulgar. He is a middle-aged man in a business suit that seems too heavy for this weather. He is constantly dabbing his forehead with an already soppy handkerchief. She feels sorry for him and offers him a drink, which he declines. He seems like he's in a hurry to get this business over with. He says the mother is expecting in a couple of months. There is obviously no way to tell if it's going to be a boy or a girl. But here is a rundown of her possible expenses:

Cost of adoption: 210,000 pesos
Processing fee (documents, etc.): 7,000 pesos

All papers, he adds, are going to be arranged through contacts with the local authorities. Mentioning this, the agent's face suddenly seems transformed by what she thinks is a hint of personal pride. "You have nothing to worry about," he says, smiling broadly. His teeth are stained red with tobacco and betel nut. "We know people. We take care of all the bribes."

She hands him the down payment, mentally calculating the equivalent in dollars. With the peso quickly sliding down nearly seven pesos to the dollar, that would be about thirty thousand dollars and an additional one thousand in fees.

After that, she waits. It's like going through an actual pregnancy herself. The next couple of months are unbearable. She calls Frank every day.

The hotel is surrounded by sweltering alleys, which fan out to the boulevard and the expanse of the bay, wide and open like a sigh of relief. This is all she can see from her apartment, the postcard-pretty sunset and the coconut trees lining the boulevard. This is all she wants to see. Cities terrify her, and Manila seems more hostile than any other. Just a few blocks away, the streets are littered with trash. Peddlers and pedicabs and commuter jeepneys fill every single space. Beggars and homeless children are everywhere, crowding around cars stalled in traffic, their passengers rolling up their tinted windows to shut out the heat and the miasma of human suffering.

The weather in Manila flips from torrid summer to torrential rain. The alleys turn into muddy rivulets, waist-deep, which some intrepid souls maneuver on makeshift rafts—planks of wood and rubber tires. A sheet of monsoon gray blurs Manila's huddled skyline—a small stretch

of midsize hotels. This is a city used to constant <u>erasure.</u>
Lives and homes are lost, but disasters come and go like
clockwork, quickly forgotten when the next one arrives.
Beneath the veneer of hospitality reserved for tourists,
she senses an overwhelming self-contempt and a simmering hatred.

In August, floods wash away several farming villages
just a few miles north of the city. A group of peasants
march to the president's palace to ask for aid. They are
met with teargas and truncheon-clubbing police. Sometimes the hostility boils over, touching even foreigners.
From her terrace overlooking the bay, she watches students lob Molotov cocktails at the American embassy
nearby.

In September, in the middle of the worst tropical
storm of the season, Frank calls to say he is having second
thoughts.

"About the baby?" she asks.

"No," he says. "About you and me." He has a hard time
trying to tell her exactly what's wrong. There's a fuzzy
sound coming from the other end. She realizes Frank is
crying. He says he feels awful, he doesn't know what to
do. He's been seeing someone else, a nurse from Monte-
fiore, down in the city. She's twenty-three.

When she hangs up, she sees something spectacularly
eerie. An entire coconut tree has been uprooted by the
storm. It's hovering just outside her ninth-floor window,
as though suspended by an invisible string.

I am delivered to my mother on a day when the entire city
goes dead.

All TV stations are off the air. Only a quivering cackle

of white noise emanates from the screen. The radio sputters an otherworldly hum. There is an unnerving quiet in the streets. The students have stopped marching down the boulevards. No bombs are being thrown at embassies and hotels. It is a warm, bright late-September morning.

Someone knocks on the door. A young American looking for Mrs. Elizabeth Yeats is holding a bundle in his arms. He hands it to her. I am seven days old.

The quickness and informality of the exchange confuses her. She fumbles in her purse for the exact cash amount she's set aside, the balance that has to be paid. The young man stuffs the money in the front pocket of his Levi's. She asks where the agent she met has gone—she needs to have the legal papers he promised.

The young man smacks his forehead and says sorry. He looks extremely boyish and awkward. He has dark-blond hair and eyes somewhat an indeterminate shade between blue and gray. (She may be mixing this information up. In the redundancy of the telling, the story's details get incrementally embellished, and I would not take anything at face value, especially as that description fits me.) The papers are in his back pocket. They're all there, he assures her. The people she had talked to have other matters to attend to. He sounds vague about it. He has nothing more to say. He looks like he's in a hurry himself.

As he turns to go, she can't resist asking, "Are you the father of this child?"

He replies, "Get out with your son as soon as you can. This country is going to blow up."

You have the blood of many nations in you, she always says, to remind me of my unusual origins. The Spanish and the Berbers, the Jews and the Arabs, Europe and China and the Malaysian islands. A self-contained universe, the sound of the sea, of winter, of equatorial storms. The glorious reign of Charles, ruler of the Holy Roman Empire, and his son Philip, duke of Burgundy and emperor of half the known world. Galleons that skirted the oceans, looking for souls and gold. America and its vanished tribes. And the brave ones who built upon their absence these cities, towers, bridges, highways, and all manner of preparation to make way for your coming.

She says those words to lull me to sleep. To assure me that even though Frank left her, I have always been wanted; she always wanted me. To remind me that life still offers much good, and I am chosen.

Too bad she never believed it herself.

"If you never actually saw him again after he brought me, how did Mr. Brezsky know what my name was? Why did he wire the money specifically for Jordan Yeats?"

"You'll have to write to Mr. Brezsky to find out."

Mr. Brezsky never answers that one, but it's all right. I grow up with one singular talent: the uncanny ability to detect a lie. Brezsky is our Holy Ghost, the missing angle in our unlikely trinity. He is our religion, the beautiful lie that she has to believe in—and, for her sake, so do I.

On my twelfth birthday, Mr. Brezsky sends me a telescope. For the first time I can clearly see the craters of the highlands where he lives. I write him a letter.

Dear Mr. Brezsky: I know you don't exist. But thanks a lot anyway.

WSOWOB

Two weeks after my parents' accident, I'm back at their apartment in La Napoule, and I discover a boxful of eight- and sixteen-millimeter films. They're the home movies my parents accumulated throughout their lives.

Separately bundled with masking tape are reels of movies of a little boy. For a minute there's a disconnect. I think it's me. I look out the window, remembering. The Mediterranean is blue as a computer screen, flat and calm, punctuated only by a speck of gray tearing a thin line toward the horizon, a ferry chugging its way to the Îles de Lérins. I check the dates on the reels, and I realize the boy was two years old by the time I was born.

I call a couple of aunts in Fréjus to ask if they know anything about these mysterious films. They tell me Sylvain and Annette had never meant for me to find out.

It was the son they lost a few weeks before I was born. His name was Mathieu, just like mine. It was the boy who I replaced.

This is one of the first things I reveal to Janya when I first meet her. The place is Bangkok, the year is 2002.

She's hanging out in a bar with a bunch of friends. One of them is my editor, Philippe, who's just arrived from

Paris. Phil and I are working on a documentary on the effects of globalization on indigenous communities. He calls me over to join them. Phil is drinking Singha beer, an American is drinking a mojito, and another Thai girl a mai tai. Janya's drinking something made of seaweed jelly. It looks like green slime. I ask for the same. She has a Sony DCR-TRV900 on the seat beside her. I ask her if she's a documentary filmmaker herself. She says she's employed by this nonprofit based in Massachusetts that monitors multinational sweatshops all over the world. Phil says she and I are going to work together, and that she will arrange some interviews for me.

Everyone's getting drunk except her and me. By the end of the evening I find out that the American is a stringer for CNN and the Thai girl is a dancer at one of the local clubs. He's married; she's fucking him. The place has a jukebox blasting '80s hard rock all night. After a while my throat gets hoarse from having to shout just to be heard across the table. I turn to Janya instead, and we wind up talking to each other alone. She likes saying my last name over and over.

"Aubert, Aubert. Sounds like Flaubert," she says. "I wonder if you're as obsessive-compulsive."

I tell her I haven't really thought about it, but maybe I am. I ask her how she likes her job. She replies, putting her lips close to my ear, "Imagine that: a Thai girl who's not being paid to fuck."

After a couple more rounds, Phil and the stringer and the Thai girl want to hop on to another bar. I'm feeling jet-lagged and want to call it a night. Phil protests. After all, I've been here close to a week now. Janya walks to my hotel with me. On the way, she tells me she's glad I came along. The American and the Thai girl are so into each other they're annoying, and she thinks Phil is gay.

"Which means . . . ?" I ask her.

"You're welcome to come over."

On her bed there's a copy of *No Logo*, *Globalization and Its Discontents*, and *The End of Poverty*. "A rainbow coalition of the liberal," she says as she swipes them aside to make room.

I sit on the bed and pull my Nikes off.

"You're wearing the enemy," she says.

I lie back and close my eyes.

"Are you okay?"

"Vertigo," I say. "Too much mai tai."

"You didn't have any."

"No, but the sight of it makes me sick." Silence. Long silence. I open my eyes. "How long have I been out?"

"Oh, about ten minutes."

"I'm sorry. My head just went spinning and all of sudden—"

She puts a finger to my lips. "I was watching you the whole time. Watching your face. You looked so serene, like you were having a beautiful dream."

I pull her down gently toward me. "I like you. You're cute."

"Cute?"

"Yeah."

"That's what *fa-rung-sayt* call the prostitutes."

"Who?"

"White guys."

"No, I didn't mean—"

"I know." She starts to unzip my jeans. "Does that happen a lot? The vertigo?"

"Not since I was a kid. I was a very frail kid."

"You look quite hefty to me now."

"Cute and hefty. We make an interesting pair."

We're tearing each other's clothes quickly, fumbling like a pair of horny teenagers. I pull out a condom from my jeans pocket. She takes it from my hand and throws it aside.

"Bareback," she says.

"You sure?"

"Seems kind of like Russian roulette, doesn't it, but talking to you at the bar revealed a lot about you."

"I wasn't aware I said anything revealing at all, except that I hated doing the tourist thing—drugs, hookers, rock and roll."

"That's precisely what I like about you."

A few days later, I call to set an appointment so we can start working on our interviews. She doesn't return my calls. I don't see her for another week. The next weekend I see her at the same bar with the same people. The first thing she notices is that I'm no longer wearing Nikes.

"Yeah," I tell her. "A very subtle way of comradeship."

"I didn't know you felt so strongly about it," she says.

We sleep together every night and still hang out with the same bunch of people on weekends, pretending there's nothing going on. We sit far apart. We hardly even talk to each other. The secrecy of our relationship makes it more exciting, like we're playing a private game of coded gestures and hidden messages. This secrecy becomes the core of our relationship, a kind of mental Viagra. We keep fucking bareback, me barely able to pull out at the last minute. I ask her if she's not scared.

"Of what? You protect yourself against those with whom you share nothing but mutual indifference."

I can't help an amused smile.

"That's the closest I'll ever get to saying I love you," she says.

"Are you saying you love me?"

"Close."

She says she wants a language only she and I can understand. Not French, not English, not even Thai, but a series of signs so simple no second-guessing is necessary. Text messaging, she says, is the ideal evolution of language— communication distilled to the level of *basic necessity*. She invents a private text message, a kind of private joke, to convey this: WSOWOB, we speak only with our bodies. This way the artificial boundaries of human interaction are blurred between us.

This gives me another idea. I suggest that we reveal ourselves completely to each other, that we reveal everything. "Everything, that is, that we wouldn't normally share with anyone else," I add. "Then our private barriers break down, and we make ourselves totally vulnerable to the other."

"Is that what you want? To be vulnerable?"

"No, it's what I fantasize. Kind of like a mental striptease."

"Hmm. But in a striptease, it's the stripper who actually has power over the spectator."

"Good point. But that's the challenge, to be able to resist the animalistic drive to dominate and subjugate. To be able to trust the other while one is weak."

"So by revealing ourselves, we make the other weak?"

"Then the dynamics are redefined. We become a

world of just us two. We are united more profoundly than any two people can be. Because trust subverts the urge for power."

"Sounds like a theory that needs to be tested," she says. "Under laboratory conditions."

"Wanna give it a try?"

"Okay."

"Tell me something."

"Like what?"

"Something devilish."

"Hmm. Since this is your idea, you go first."

I tell her I would like to share the story of the lost boy. But in order to do that, she would have to come with me to my parents' home.

"Okay," she says. "So you want me to meet your parents."

"No, my parents are dead. I want you to see the films they shot of the boy."

"Oh, sorry."

"No, that's okay."

"Okay."

"Okay what?"

"Show me."

The next morning we are on the flight to La Napoule.

The brittle film flutters through the projector's sprockets. It makes lapping sounds as it hits the framing aperture, like a dog drinking from a bowl.

His image magnified on the wall, the little boy looks just like any other two-year-old, a paper hat on his head, the crumpled brim falling over his eyes. He toddles toward the camera with a plastic pistol held aloft, like some undersized Belmondo staggering away from the cops.

There are about a dozen reels. Not a lot, strangely, considering my parents shot practically everything in their lives. Little Mathieu waddles across the frame, trips, falls, smears his face with cake—ordinary gestures from what could have been an ordinary life. There's Annette coming into frame. Then it's Sylvain, who's just passed the camera shakily to her. Now Annette's holding the camera at arm's length to get them both inside the frame. The colors are washed out; everything's a faded, purplish monochrome.

Now Sylvain's taken the camera and has focused it on the little boy. The boy's pointing the toy pistol at the camera. It must be his second birthday: two flickering candles on a cake trace ribbons of light across the moving frame.

Annette pulls the boy away: now he's hitting the camera with his gun. She's laughing loud. You can almost hear it even without the sound. She's saying something else now. *Take a shot of him as he blows the candles out.* But the camera zooms in on her instead. She holds a hand against the lens and says, *Go on, take a shot of him.*

She glances toward the boy, then back at the camera to see if it's been turned away. Her mouth says, *Stop.* But the camera is still focused on her, lingering for just a few more seconds. Her face is radiant. She looks incredibly young. The film's so overexposed it seems there was much more light back then.

"Even now," I tell Janya, "I find it hard to believe that this two-year-old disappeared one summer during a squall on the coast of the South China Sea, and was never found again."

"How did that happen?" she asks.

"Nobody knows."

"How could nobody know?"

"He fell in the water and disappeared."

"That's crazy. That's impossible."

"I know."

"And what did your parents do?"

"Well, that's the part of the story that's been missing, and for the last twelve years I've been looking for it among these films."

Truth to tell, I've always been afraid to ask the questions Janya is asking now. Film has this mythic quality we can't resist. The image defies what we really are—transient and ephemeral. It's like what physicists call *relic light*, those spectral traces of radiation emanated by objects that once existed. No other medium, in that sense, captures our indestructible material remains.

I guess Sylvain and Annette did all they could to cope with the loss. The image makes the object persistent, if not immortal—it makes its absence imperfect. But by hiding the reels and sealing them in an interoffice envelope, they declared that particular absence completed.

And this, I guess, is where I come in. I imagine my being here was meant to create some continuity, a bridge over the gulf of grief. As long as we kept on crossing and didn't look down, time would appear uninterrupted. In other words, little Mathieu was never lost, he just morphed a bit. Grief was never required.

"Have you ever wanted to go there and find out?" Janya asks.

"It's crossed my mind."

"But you never gave it any serious thought."

"Well, actually, it's been kind of an obsession."

"Aha."

"I watch the films over and over. I watch them so much sometimes I confuse what I've seen in them and what I imagine may have happened. Film and memory get mixed up, in a slow dissolve."

"Sounds like a concept for an experimental film."

"Forget it, somebody's probably already done it. But yes, sometimes I strip off the masking tapes marking the dates of the films. Then I can imagine that the boy with the plastic gun is me."

"And you do that because . . . ?"

"Well, I can imagine the years before I existed. I've always wondered what it was like not to exist. Like I browse used bookstores and look at those postcards from the 1950s. And I feel wonder mixed with dread or panic—because, you know, I'm looking back at a time when I was nothing, when I was just, you know, part of the void or something."

"A kind of ontological experience."

"Yeah."

"And have we learned anything from this story?"

"Maybe. By some inexplicable equation, some karmic tit-for-tat, I can see that my life must have snuffed out the other."

"That's depressing. And illogical."

"I know."

She pulls me down to the sofa and unbuttons my shirt. "I don't want you thinking like that."

"Sure."

She clamps her teeth gently on my nipple. I get hard immediately. The last reel is over, and I've paused the projector so that the image of the young boy is staring straight at me, his paper hat falling over his eyes, his plastic gun pointed at my heart.

Janya has unzipped me and then she pulls her skirt and panties down and hops over and straddles me. She deftly slips my cock in and when she wiggles her hips around, the sensation makes me groan with pleasure.

"Oh, fuck, Janya, I like that."

I accidentally knock my elbow against the projector, which makes a weird flapping noise. I reach out to pause it, but Janya grabs my hand and slips it inside her blouse and makes me squeeze her breast. She gives a soft moan.

The projector sputters—in my haste to pause I must have set it to slo-mo. Janya has her back to the image projected on the wall. As I suckle her nipple I can see the boy's close-up behind her. I can see his eyes from under the brim of the hat as he slowly lifts his head. I have an eerie sensation that he's staring straight at me, his lips curling into a knowing, fiendish smile.

the little toil of love

—because this time of day the crows leave them alone. Nothing else is moving, except these two dogs. Been watching them trying to get it on for the last half hour, me & the guy with the Uzi & Eddie the rapist. The bitch finally gives in. The male's got his dick locked inside her now. They're like conjoined, spastic twins. Eddie bets a peso it's going to take another 30 minutes before the male can pull out. The head of a dog's dick pops open like an umbrella when it's fucking, he says. Once he's in, it's even harder to get out. We're supposed to be picking vegetables some guy planted last summer. Then the guy was shot in the back of the head & he's been fertilizing them since. The eggplants & bitter melons are scrawny but the tomatoes are ripe & about to burst. It's November. The air is cool. It's one of those days when you feel so doped out you don't even want to move.

Now Eddie's dropped his spade & starts heckling the dogs. The guy with the Uzi's getting bored. The lieutenant bellows a stream of curses from inside the barracks. He's been taking a siesta to sleep off a hangover. Even he is in no mood to keep order around here.

The guy with the Uzi gets up, a machete dangling from his hand. The dogs are in too much heat to notice him approaching. The male's tongue is hanging out, a thick red flap. He's drooling all over the bitch's back, yellow spume dribbling on tufts of mangy brown fur. The guy with the Uzi yanks the male by the scruff. With one swift stroke he cuts its dick from the bitch. There's a long, ear-splitting squeal. The dogs scamper apart. Jets of blood spurt from the male's mutilated dick. He doesn't know what's happened to him. He runs amok, howling helplessly. He stops & curls up to lick his balls. Now he's spinning round & round, now he's dragging his butt on the ground, yelping madly, leaving a black circle of mud on the earth.

The guy with the Uzi is laughing & yelling curses at the dog. Eddie's cheering wildly, shouting to make it spin faster, howl louder. He picks up a rock, hurls it at the dog. It misses, landing in a small explosion of dust just an inch away.

It's 1972. It has been for the longest fucking time.

There are roughly 3.86 billion people living on the planet. Five of them are caught trying to bug the Democratic National Committee headquarters at a place called Watergate in DC. Another 8 have killed 11 athletes at the Munich Olympics. And 8,000 others in Uganda are being deported by 1 person, a fuck-up job called Idi Amin.

My name is Andrew Brezsky. My name. Andy. A. A plus. Or A minus, depending on who you talk to. I have to remember my name. I have to remember what year it is. What happened before I got here, the dark heart of nowhere, some hardscrabble ghost town on an island in the Central Philippines, Archipelago of the Absurd, Little Brown Brother of Big Old Uncle Sam. Must. Remember. Everything. If I don't I'll forget that I'm still here. Still hoping, like everyone else in this Pearl of the Fucking Orient Seas, still looking for a way out.

* * *

There's me, & Eddie, & a student who's been here a couple weeks earlier than me & Eddie, & who refuses to reveal his name. Every day the lieutenant & the guy with the Uzi take him away. When he comes back, something imperceptible has been damaged in him. It's as if his body's being annihilated, one part at a time, with the ultimate aim not of death, but a long, drawn-out <u>disabling</u>.

Last week they burned his nipples with a cigarette. A couple days later they stuck a barbecue skewer through the hole of his dick. Last night they attached live electric wires to his testicles. No evidence is visible unless he's naked. No one can tell unless he talks about it. But Eddie & I, we can tell.

They don't want anything from him now. Even his name's no longer relevant. He's told them about as much as they can use. But they've done it so many times, over & over, Eddie thinks it's pointless to ask why anymore. Even the student, when Eddie does ask about it, always gives the same reply—that's just the way it is. He seems hostile to any show of concern from Eddie or me. Once he staggered to the toilet bowl & pissed blood. Eddie pretended to look away.

There's another reason he doesn't want to talk about it, but it's pretty obvious. Always the act is sick & dark & sexual. What normally gives pleasure is nothing now but a source not just of pain, but of shame. The more sexual the punishment is, the less likely he'll talk about it. Torture deprives the body of making sense of itself. Eddie says it's the same thing with people you rape. He's gotten off the hook so many times because no one just damn wants to talk about it.

You see it happen all the time. Pretty soon you realize that's just the way it is. They have a phrase for it: <u>Bahala na.</u> God willing. Even the freaking Communists believe this. God can drive a stick up your ass, & you'll bleed, but God knows what's good for you. Trust him. <u>Bahala na.</u>

There's one window in the cell, high above where no one can reach it. If I stand at an angle a couple of feet off the wall, I can see the sky checkered against the steel bars. The full moon passes right through it in a nearly vertical arc.

Eddie's on his steel-spring cot, lying on a black stain of sweat on a mat of woven palm. He says he finds me strange, writing all night & never seeming to sleep.

The cot sags & forms a hammock, I tell him. It makes my back sore.

He wants to know what I find so fascinating about the moon.

I tell him it never turns its back on us. You only see one side of it, anywhere you go.

It's kind of like people, then, he says. I bet the good side is on the far side, the one you never see. But if you can't see it, who the hell cares?

I tell him it's much brighter in this part of the world. Bigger and brighter.

It's the only one I've ever seen, he says. I wouldn't know the difference.

By the time they're brought here, Eddie & the student have already been tempered earlier, passed on from camp to camp. We're in the middle of nowhere, a ghost town, the fields scorched black, burnt spears of bamboo jutting out of the ground where a few huts used to be. At night bats swoop from a mountain cave close by, clouding the sky like a storm & filling the air with the stench of guano. They're bloodsuckers, they'll tear apart anything in their path. Even the lieutenant stays indoors when they wake, rabid with an ancient & vicious hunger.

Eventually we'll be shipped to Manila, where Eddie says the privileged ones go. In Manila they won't touch you so much, because people will know. Reporters, Amnesty International, that whole shit.

I've seen scars where other soldiers cut them up or burned them, bumps in their arms & legs where bones have broken & healed. At some point they've confessed everything these guys want them to confess.

Things are slower now. They're no longer useful. Nothing more will be taken from them.

Neither one talks about it much, but the damage has been done: they've already betrayed a father, a brother, a friend.

Once in a while Eddie's jacking off & we can hear it & the student whispers, Knock it off, & Eddie whispers, Why don't you try it, faggot.

I think they're both about as old as I am. The student was picked up the day the president declared martial law. Before he came here, his life was pretty normal, cramming for an exam, going to a movie, getting to first base with a girl. He & Eddie talk about it all the time. The stories are all the same after a while. They've run out of new things to say. When something new happens, like the dog & the bitch & the soldier hacking the dog's dick off, they talk about it for days. Pretty soon the story gets exhausted, neither of them wants to hear about it anymore. They don't say it, but I think they know that in the act of telling, something is always given up. Something withers away.

Rain patters everywhere, drumming on the tin roof of the barracks. It sounds like something enormous has crashed through the atmosphere, & its wrecks are falling over our heads.

"And life is not so ample."

I've been trying to remember that poem but the rain jumbles the words in my head. If only I can remember it, I'll be all right. Tomorrow, this afternoon, in a couple of hours, someone will come. This is not happening. & suddenly I'm okay. My entire body is changed. I feel a kind of lightness I can't explain.

Then the hours pass, the days pass, & I dread the prospect of tomorrow. I force myself to recover that buoyancy. Sometimes I succeed. I'm also aware that this emotion is tenuous, even phony. One single word, one unguarded moment, will send me crashing back to earth.

Some newfangled thing called the compact disc is predicted to change the way we listen to music.

Somebody's invented "electronic mail," but whether people will actually use it remains to be seen.

A first-class postage stamp is still necessary, & costs 8 cents. That's how much it cost the US government to serve John Lennon & Yoko Ono their deportation papers in New York City.

John & Yoko, no one's going to step all over you. You will live forever. We are not all fucked-up assholes. Trust me.

"We've got a few things to learn about the Philippines, lads. First of all is how to get out."

That's John Lennon in 1966. The Beatles had a rough time here that year. Lennon said he wanted to drop a hydrogen bomb on it.

But 6 years on, nobody talks about how bad the Beatles had it. Not here. There's a constant effort to erase memory. No day is connected to the next. No event is caused by another. Everything is taken as it comes.

<u>Bahala na.</u> It is God's will. This is how everyone survives.

All through the scorched fields the wind sends a long, inconsolable howling. No ammunition, no dictator, can challenge a typhoon. You sit out its rage for as long as it takes. You stay still while the entire world spends its fury. You respect what is stronger than you.

The typhoon's trampled everything in the vegetable plots. The guy with the Uzi brings our food, a muck of rice & salted fish dumped in a pail, from which we scoop our share. We drink tap water brought in a plastic bucket. Flies float on the water. Eddie can endure anything, but not this kind of shit. They beat the crap out of him until he simmers down. Eddie's tantrums always work. After he calms down the guy with the Uzi shares some of their food. Eddie gobbles it greedily, & with his cheeks stuffed with food he mumbles, We're not dogs, we're people just like you.

Bobby Fischer has defeated Boris Spassky for the world chess title. Remember this.

Pink Floyd has started recording their 8th album. It's going to be called The Dark Side of the Moon.

Apollo 16 has brought back rock samples from the Descartes Highlands.

Remember, remember.

Because no winds blow on the moon, the tracks left by Apollo 16 are going to be visible for another million years.

Eddie doesn't know that his people fought us at the turn of the century. All he knows is that we liberated them from the Japanese, & that Americans have lots of money.

The student tries to educate him. We share the same space, at least for now, but we're still divided by our histories, our countries' politics, everything that would have divided us even as free men. It's no use.

Eddie picks up a few big words from the student but he has no idea what they mean. He tells me, candidly: It's good to know even imperialists can be jailed by our president. What do you know, Americans aren't so special after all.

It's not always hostile. The student wants to know what I'm doing here, where I come from. He wants to know what kids are really doing in America. If people really like Nixon. If we really think we're going to win the war in Vietnam. He wants to know what I'm scribbling all day & all night in my notebook, what I say about them. For all his suspicion & vitriol against me & what I represent, he's still concerned that what I say about them <u>doesn't make them look bad</u>.

May 1970, demonstration to protest the draft, 4 students killed at Kent State University.

June 1970, the US sets voting age at 18.

End of June 1970, I arrive in Manila. I've just turned 18.

Soon after, a typhoon hits the country, flooding rice paddies & villages & killing thousands of residents. Aid is sluggish & slowed by government corruption. Hundreds die of hunger & disease. Students storm the president's palace. Police arrest demonstrators during riots in Manila. Things get so fucked Marcos & his family are forced to flee in a helicopter, only to come back when the army finally gets everybody out of the way.

If things go well around here, credit is given to God. If things go bad, a lot of people get blamed, but lately it's us Americans. They don't really say it to your face, & even the Communists follow certain rules of courtesy. Americans are an abstract concept, like God. But I've learned one thing living here for the last 2 years. Everything I say has to be sugarcoated, a form of flattery. Anything less will be too American, therefore offensive.

So this is what I tell Eddie & the student. What we the youth in the US failed to do, the students in Manila are about to achieve. This country is on the brink of a full-scale revolution.

The student stops bugging me after I say that. My words have created a temporary truce.

When I think about it now, I think I really meant it. Only Eddie, who doesn't give a damn, remains unimpressed.

I'm standing naked in the middle of the room. The lieutenant's sitting at a table, sucking on a cigar. He's had this one cigar for weeks, but he doesn't ever light it. He just sucks on it. He has this beady stare, a junkyard dog stare.

The guy with the Uzi's inspecting my jeans, T-shirt,

sneakers. There's a long, uneasy quiet as he scrutinizes every inch of my clothing.

The lieutenant puts his booted feet up on the table. Finally, he lights the cigar. He blows the smoke out in one steady stream, his lips puckered, his eyes shut to savor the sensation. He's got a large dark face & his skin is tough & greasy, like the skin of roast pork. He looks at me in a way that seems both bored & snide. I'm one more in a list of endless chores.

You, Yankee boy, touch your cock.

I don't understand what he says. So he says it again. Show us how big it can get. Americans have big dicks, right? You proud of that, right? Go on, touch it, masturbate.

You a homo? I ask him.

The lieutenant's face turns red. His eyes bulge. He looks like he's going to explode. He glances at the guy with the Uzi, who looks away. But he tries to help the lieutenant save face. He says, There's plenty of time to deal with that, he's not going anywhere.

The lieutenant isn't letting it go. He's decided they're keeping my clothes. Then some kind of argument begins. They fight over who keeps the jeans, who takes the T-shirt, who gets the sneakers.

The lieutenant takes his feet off the table, unlaces his boots, & yanks them off. Then he stands up & takes his T-shirt off. There's a tattoo of a crown of thorns on his chest, right over his heart. He pulls his fatigue pants down. He throws the T-shirt & pants at me. They stink like shit.

We like Americans, he says. You & us, we're friends for life. No matter how much you fuck us, we still like you.

I put his T-shirt & fatigues on & the guy with the Uzi leads me out of the room.

As I leave, the lieutenant says, In this country, revolution is a bad word. You say it again & you're going to get really fucked.

We are held in place by gravitational forces

Humans are the only creatures who can tell a lie, to others and to themselves. Mother once told me that. Obviously she set herself as a perfect example.

A lie: Mother quickly forgets about Frank. Dubious proof: a rapid succession of unlikely lovers. But to be brutally honest, at her age, her only options are young Latino and African immigrants who take advantage of her, then move on. This is her latest relationship, and it's going to be her last. Newly arrived from Brazil, probably twenty-five years old. A walking stereotype, a Carioca with six-pack abs and the insouciance of one who knows he is young and beautiful and desired.

I catch him sucking her nipple in the kitchen one afternoon. I watch them in silence, observing how his lips perfectly pucker over the rosy aureole, the expert way in which he flicks his tongue over the tip of the nipple and sends her swooning, giddy with pleasure.

They fuck boisterously, their moans so painful they seem in the throes of death. My room is just next to hers. I can hear everything, even the sullen, throaty endearments after sex, the obligatory shower, the furtive departure so as not to wake the kid.

Sometimes we go out to places that he likes. He doesn't know much. He's been in the country only a few months.

Mother always tries to show how much she appreciates everything he suggests. We go to half-price movie matinees in rundown theaters uptown in the city, where cockroaches crawl over the stale popcorn people dropped on the greasy floor.

Sometimes we sit till sunset at the Cloisters. Whenever Mother goes to the bathroom, her boyfriend and I sit in silence, staring at the river. Once he tries to break the ice and says, "You hate me, don't you?"

"I don't feel anything for you," I reply.

When Mother comes back she asks how we two are getting along. He says, "He's a very *precoscient* kid."

"Yes," Mother agrees. "That's what he is."

They buy food and stuff and share it like conjugal property. He never stays too long, but his visits always transform her. She moves gracefully, as though she's picking up the last gestures of a dance. She smells different, always a scent of almonds and musk.

I never find out what his name is, and never ask. (That's not entirely true. She may have told me his name. I may have chosen to forget.) He is writing all over the blank slate that she used to be, recreating something foreign out of the emptiness that she has become. A creature whose voice has acquired an unfamiliar lilt, whose smile evokes joys so private they shut everything out. One of these days, he is going to stop creating her. That's what I think. And when that happens, she might disappear without a trace.

Instead he's the one who disappears. He finds someone with less age and more money. He stops coming over. There is no way for an affair like that to end except the way it does—hackneyed and predictable as a primetime telenovela on Univision.

Then she goes crashing back to earth and becomes the one I have known all along. And once again, somber with loneliness, sitting by my bed at night, she enchants me with her lies: the blood of Europe and Asia and Africa in you, and the ships swaying on the open sea.

Another lie: Mother loves her job.

She neither loves it nor hates it, and I feel the same way. It is simply the only kind of work she knows she's good at, having had a lot of experience working with Frank.

When my mother comes back from Manila, she finds all of Frank's personal belongings gone, his half of the closets empty. The only reminder of his presence is a series of phone messages, a bright red 8 blinking on the answering machine. She doesn't want to play them back, thinking they'll be that helpless woman's voice again, or the usual anonymous nonmessages. But she takes a deep breath and presses the button, and listens to eight consecutive messages from the Life Crusaders who have finally decided to speak up, threatening to blow up the clinic. Poor Frank, she says to herself, run out of town by a bunch of crazies.

With Frank out of her life, she realizes this one thing about herself: she doesn't know anything except what she's learned from him. She is his shadow, and where does a shadow go when what casts it has gone?

But she picks up the work when she comes back. She can do it on autopilot. Years later I realize why. She was hoping that when he came back, everything would be as he had left it. The break in their narrative would be seamless.

I stand beside her, beaming a light into the cavern of a

young woman's uterus. Mother cuts up the fetus and with a forceps slowly plucks the pieces out. I hold up a tray for her to deposit the mangled bits.

It's an emergency, Mother's part-time assistant can't come in, and I'm the only one around. I turn out to be an excellent nurse. I ask only the right questions. I know when to hand her the right instrument. I am fastidious and efficient, distant but not indifferent: the terrified young mother finds my presence surreal, but also somehow soothing, like a little angel.

When it's over, I collect the pieces in a trash bag to throw in a furnace in the back of the clinic. I peer inside the bag before I do so. There are tiny, barely discernible parts that seem not quite human. The lacerated prototype of a hand, the impossibly minuscule fingers, still conjoined by a slimy web. And a small skull, squished like the head of a fish and marbled with blood and mucus.

I pick up the skull and examine it against the light of the fire. There are small veins showing through the translucent bone, like the beautiful imperfections one finds in certain stones.

Feast of the Assumption. In certain gnostic scriptures, God fucks Mary through one ear and her child is born out the other.

My mother always told me a virgin birth was possible, and she was living proof. I'm not stupid. Being Mother's angelic assistant at the clinic has dispelled any romantic notions I might have had about fucking, or how babies are born. As I grow older I realize that statement was supposed to be a joke. Then I get it, and Mother and I have a good laugh.

I get it, and her lullaby of fictitious origins has become no more than that, a foolish childhood song. As I grow older the stories take a U-turn and Mother feels it is time to explain how someone like me really came into the world. Not in a test tube, which has some kind of futuristic glamour to it, but through a baby factory in some hardscrabble barrio halfway across the world. My birth helped pay off someone's debts. On that account there weren't going to be any secrets.

"Did someone want to get rid of me?"

"What do you mean, Jordan?"

"Did my mother want to abort me?"

"That wasn't going to happen. Because you were meant to be mine."

"But it could have happened, right?"

"No. Because you were special."

"How?"

"I came to get you. I came at the right time. We were meant for each other. That's why your birth was marked by man's footprints on the moon. A million years from now—"

"There must have been a million babies born that year. Are we all special?"

"Yes."

"Are we related?"

"No. But maybe in spirit."

"Were some of them meant to be aborted?"

"Maybe."

"So they weren't so special after all."

"But the important thing is *you* are. You are here. We are here together."

"I wish you'd do something else."

"What do you mean?"

"People hate what you do."

"Some people don't understand."

"It could have been me."

"But it wasn't. And I wouldn't do that to you."

"But how would you have known it was me?"

"I would have known. We are connected."

"Like an umbilical cord?"

"Like an umbilical cord. Yes."

"I wish you'd do something else."

"We are being helpful."

"Nobody likes us."

"I like you."

"I have no friends."

"I'm your best friend."

Let me say this about my mother: we are very close, yet we are total strangers to one another. She had read all the how-to books on raising an adopted child, she knew all the rules. Don't hide the truth, be straightforward, show them you love them, remind them they are not unwanted, they only had to be given away due to compelling, inescapable reasons. Let them grow up whole, and confident, and sane.

She knows the entire rigmarole, and she's done her best. In truth, I have a niggling, maddening need to probe everything that remains unanswered—about myself, about Brezsky, about how I wound up not in that barrio but here, halfway across the world. Once you start thinking like that, every single thing in the world becomes obstinately imbued with mystery. And that's a dangerous thing. I know that and Mother knows that. Even the books tell her so.

So, since the child psychiatry manuals have very little to offer (I have been reading them without her knowledge), I'm convinced that, in the grand scheme of things, something like my life—our lives—is largely karmic. Furtively, I even collect the pamphlets left by the Life Crusaders on our door—words literally scorched with fire and brimstone, pockmarked with copious passages from the Old Testament—wondering if maybe they have answers Mother and I should really know about, and guiltily hiding them under my bed the way other boys hide copies of *Penthouse*. And when Mother discovers them, she reacts like she's just found her little boy whacking off to Miss July.

"Someday you'll find the real thing, and all this will be trash."

"Mother, why does God hate us so much?"

"A God that hates is not true."

Which leads me to this. According to Tibetan Buddhism, God is all creatures, and all creatures were once our mothers. Presuming we have been reincarnated millions of times, it's likely that someone out there, the cop at the corner, the Korean greengrocer, the coked-up homeless bag lady, could have given birth to us at some point in time. This idea is supposed to evoke in us compassion for all beings. And once in a while, if you try it, I suppose it does.

But that doesn't explain much either. This is my idea of reincarnation: at death, our molecules, atoms, quarks, and gravitons disperse, spread into thin air, and realign and recompose somewhere else, mixing randomly with a million other particles to create entirely new organisms. At death, Jordan Yeats can become a fern, a groundhog, the next president of the United States, or all of the above. This, I've read, is my mind clinging to its materialist fixations. My mind refusing to let go. I am a Buddha's nightmare.

Mother always tells me mine was a virgin birth, that I came into the world miraculously, and I am unique and special. That's what I am, a fucking baby Jesus. Eventually I understand that this isn't meant to be taken literally. Although I never met Frank, and only spoke to him briefly once or twice on the phone, she always talks to me about him as "your Dad." But she also makes it clear, in no uncertain terms, that Dad fucked up and ran off with a cocksucking slut from the Dominican Republic.

The years drift by, and strangely I have no clear memory of them, except that everyone I meet in school drives me to bouts of torpor. Year after year my teachers write to my mother expressing their concern about my "reticence," which in today's world is a disorder as alarming as, say, bulimia. In my junior year in college, after a long and nerve-racking argument with my mother who refuses to give me her blessing, I undertake a bold experiment and live in a dorm off the Columbia campus. I've taken a long time to decide what I'm going to major in but this time I settle on film studies, a course easy enough to endure, in my estimation. It's also becoming of interest to me, I mean the distance and immediacy of film, which happen simultaneously, its uncanny ability to immerse you in a world that it merely *reflects*. I decide that I have a lot to say about the subject. I might someday become a filmmaker myself. I will work alone, without a crew and without a studio; the thought of having to deal with so many people for a single work bothers me a little, but in time I will figure it out. In a few weeks, of course, the dilemma of wanting to create a film and not wanting to work with other people makes me doubt if this is the right course for me.

During my sixth week my roommate sets me up with an English major from Barnard who, no doubt offended when I pass on her offer to spend the night, spreads rumors that I am a "homo." My roommate asks to be moved to another hall, but I do receive a warm invitation to join the LGBT soiree.

A week later I get mugged by two black teenagers on Amsterdam Avenue at four p.m., have to have four stitches to close the cut above my left eyebrow, and, still dazed with painkillers, I pack my bags and head back home. My mother says nothing when she sees me at the door. We are never going to part again.

And so I keep her company, and I grow older. We grow old together, as boring and complacent as a married couple, content in the safety of our lies. I read her some books at night, beside the fire. She makes me a cup of chamomile tea before bed. That's what the world is like, and we live as best we can. The stories are there to make us feel better. A lie is an act of complicity between the one who tells it and the one who chooses to believe.

WSOWOB

I'm in a time warp.

An elderly woman has been standing outside the post office in La Napoule for an hour, waiting for it to open. Walking with Janya past her, along the slope behind my parents' apartment, I find myself in a bizarre flashback. When I was a young boy, I would always see an old woman who looked just like the one waiting there, and who kept forgetting that the post office wasn't open on Saturday. She would spend hours outside the door, ignoring people's advice to come back the next week. Standing under the searing sun, or sometimes in the rain, she seemed to believe her defiance alone would prove everyone wrong, that this was in fact not Saturday, that a small miracle was going to happen, and the doors would open soon.

That could be the same woman, exactly as she was some thirty years ago. She is wearing the same black billowing skirt that once terrified me, the same scarf wrapped loosely around her head, its butter-yellow print dulled by repeated washing.

I tell her the post office isn't open today.

"Eh," she rasps. "Don't believe everything they say." She turns around and walks away, muttering curses to herself.

This is a day when everything is significant. Everything is a sign. I'm thinking of a story by Nabokov that Janya had me read on the plane, about a boy suffering from referential mania. Maybe it's time for a little referential mania of my own. This, for the moment, is important and necessary. I have a very good excuse.

Across the rotunda, at the *librairie* managed by the same Italian family that moved here from Ventimiglia when I was a kid, Janya stops to buy a pack of cigarettes.

A lady from Florida, an anorexic *grande dame* with blindingly bleached hair, has been chatting with the manager and interrupts their conversation to ask me if Janya and I are a couple.

I tell her we've just met in Bangkok, and, pulling her aside, I confide that I've decided last night to ask Janya to move in with me. I've been trying to find the right moment to say it.

She's overjoyed by the news and, confident that we have made a connection, she tells me that the most amazing thing happened to her this morning: her husband turned the radio dial to some local station airing an old American pop tune—Irving Caesar's "Tea for Two"—the very same song he sang to her on the day they moved here thirty years ago.

"I can tell he was listening with me," she says.

"Who?"

"My husband. He died last April, but this morning, when the song was playing, it was as if he was back, listening with me."

I look to see where Janya's gone, hoping she'll rescue me. She's chatting with the manager's son, whose pregnant wife is waiting silently at the door.

The lady from Florida whispers in my ear, "There's

something about your girlfriend." She's leaning very close to me, her dark red lips all but smudging my ear. "Something new," she says. "Something about to begin."

I ask her if she means Janya's going to be okay about moving in, and she gives me a wink. I add that she's terribly sweet and her husband must miss her a lot.

"Oh, no," she says. "He's right here, as we speak."

Janya joins us and I wrap my arm around her waist. She's purchased a pocket-size journal and wants to show it to me. The pages are lined with grids and held together by one large staple, like a metal navel. The cover is a shade of blue exactly like the sea, which can be seen from here. She holds it up against the blue horizon to compare. She's right, it is the exact same shade, the notebook seems to disappear against the Mediterranean, and her hand appears to be holding nothing but the staple. Somehow that discovery seems so important, so touching, and I clasp her hand as we walk out.

I glance back and see the lady from Florida following us with her gaze, her lips moving as she silently hums a tune.

Farther down the block, the weekend market is already open. A dozen tables have taken over a small parking lot, displaying a modest if rather pathetic array of local vegetables and kitschy souvenirs. La Napoule is a weird town, one of those intermediate places that people don't really stop for, overshadowed by its larger, grander cousin, Cannes. My parents moved here to work in Cannes. Its anonymity has always appealed to me, and I never saw any reason to give up their apartment.

Janya's been looking at a bunch of souvenirs. One of

them is a clay figurine of a little boy, a little imp poised to take a leak, its little hand wrapped around its penis. Beside it is a replica of a grinning gargoyle, an elongated tongue sticking out of its wide mouth. Both were designed by the late eccentric American millionaire Henry Clews, whose outlandish chateau by the shore is probably the town's most prominent attraction.

"Don't tell me you're going to get that," I tease her.

"The peeing boy or the gargoyle?"

"Doesn't matter. They're equally disgusting."

"I think the boy's pretty cute. Reminds me of the boy in your films." She holds it up to the light. "Kind of looks like him too."

"All little boys look the same."

"I want to look at the real thing. Let's go there."

"The chateau?"

"It's right across the street, right?"

I agree to go reluctantly. I've been inside the place just once, when I was a kid. It didn't really impress me much. Walking toward the chateau, I ask her, "What about your story? I've told you a lot of things nobody else in the world would ever know. What dark, delicious secret will you share with me?"

"Nothing," she says.

"Not fair."

"Compared to yours, my life story is really dull. I'm almost ashamed to even talk about it."

"Try."

"Okay. I have eight brothers, and twelve uncles, and I've always wanted to be a boy."

"Hmm. Interesting."

"I'm not a lesbian."

"Okay, just a passing thought."

"You're my first real relationship."

"Hmm. And the others were, what, unreal?"

"False starts."

We reach the chateau's gates and walk around the garden. The castle itself is closed. Janya's disappointed. I lure her farther into the gardens, beside the shore. There's a moss-covered sundial surrounded by a topiary garden of odd-shaped trees whose chopped-off branches, she says, remind her of the upraised hands of the screamer in Munch's *The Scream*. We can see the outlying islands from here. No one else is around.

"I want to suck your cock," she says.

"Right here?"

"Al fresco."

I look around, hoping not to see any other visitors. There's a Japanese couple walking toward the castle, seemingly lost in the garden's maze. Janya's mouth feels soft and warm.

"Oh, Janya."

"Call me Vasin."

"What?"

"It's a man's name."

"Uh, okay."

The sound of the waves is both harsh and soothing, drowning the loud moans that I can't help from coming out of my mouth. I try to pull out when I come, but Janya grips my butt and presses me closer. The sensation of pleasure and pain as she keeps sucking overwhelms me. My knees buckle. When it's over, she's looking up at me, smiling.

"I want you to move in with me," I tell her, gasping heavily.

"Thought you'd never ask," she says.

I am alone in the apartment. That much I know. Janya's headed out to go back to the market before it closes. She wants to get the figurine of the little boy for me.

I can see the entire apartment as if through a wide-angle lens, the corners distorted, the walls coming up toward me. I am floating above everything. It seems to me like I'm dying, or dead. Yet I am conscious of the fact that this is *an event*, that I am in the midst of something happening. Everything is still. Time stops.

There are small, almost imperceptible signals at first. It's like what happens when a DVD gets stuck, and the image freezes for just a fleeting, disorienting second. Then, in a series of stroboscopic images, I see things as their opposite: trees are red, the sky is yellow, my hand, held before me with a mix of shock and wonder, appears as in a film negative, a shadow, the skin translucent and the bones showing through.

Now I can see Janya coming in. She stops at the door, frozen in shock. Something, maybe a cry, comes out of her mouth, but all I hear is a fuzzy sound, like a drawl. She drops the paper bag she's been carrying. There's a dull crack as it hits the floor, like something splitting inside my head.

I don't see what's happening as much as I feel it. I'm in her arms. She grabs a pencil and holds it between my teeth to prevent me from biting off my tongue. The pencil cracks in two. I've stopped convulsing. My body goes limp. I'm breathing slowly. My eyes are wide open. I'm gazing blankly at the ceiling, gazing, it seems, at me. She holds my head up, dabbing her scarf on the sweat that's beaded on my forehead.

I don't want to move. I fear that the slightest movement, the slightest noise, will dispel such a clear, unmistakable *vision*.

"Something's happened," I tell her. "Someone's spoken to me."

"Who?"

"Mathieu."

"The lost boy?"

"The same fucking one."

"Was that what the vertigo was all about?" Janya asks me.

"What vertigo?"

"Bangkok. My apartment. Mai tai."

"No. I don't know. This hasn't happened in a while."

"When was the last time it happened?"

"Not sure. Months before my parents' accident. Since then, I've been completely well."

"How did you get well?"

"I was in a monastery."

"What?"

"My parents put me in a monastery. They asked the monks if they could, you know, heal me."

"This is getting really bizarre, Mathieu."

"It's right there, half an hour by ferry from Cannes. You can see it from here. I often wondered if they ever remembered me, and asked themselves if I was okay."

"And does that have something to do with the lost boy?"

"It's got everything to do with the lost boy."

She's looking very distressed.

"I feel like telling you the whole story, but I'm not sure I want to."

"No boundaries," she says.

"You sure?"

"We made an agreement."

"There are dozens of other reels left by Sylvain and Annette—discarded films of an aborted project that took them from Normandy to the Philippines. They contain the rest of the story."

"You said you think the boy's spoken to you. What could he have possibly said?"

"I don't know. He said everything's already been revealed. I think."

"I don't get it."

"I don't either. I think it's something to do with his being lost. Maybe he's trying to tell me what really happened."

"That's so Stephen King."

"I know. Yet I didn't feel spooked at all. I wanted to know."

"Did you, like, you know, speak to him?"

"I think I tried. But I was kind of frozen. My words were coming out weird, like what happens during a nightmare, when you want to do something but can't."

"So that's all he said, that everything's been revealed?"

"One boy will be lost and another will be saved."

"What?"

"That's what else I remember him saying."

"What does that mean?"

"It's something from one of my parents' films. It was a prediction some mystic in Normandy told Annette."

"Maybe it's your mind, Mathieu. That happens, you know. Maybe it's you recalling your mother's film."

"You know what? I think you're right. Of course that's

what it is. It just sounded so real. The voice, I mean. Like it was whispering close to my ear."

"I'd like to see them."

"The other films?"

"Yeah."

"There's a whole bunch of them."

"We have a whole bunch of time."

"Okay. Get yourself comfortable."

"Are you going to be all right?"

"I'm perfectly fine."

"You sure?"

"Don't worry about it. It's absolutely nothing. A little wine would be nice."

She goes to the kitchen to open a bottle. Along the way, she picks up the paper bag she had dropped coming in, to throw it in the trash. I haul the boxes out and lay out the reels in as chronological an order as possible. As I spool the first reel, I hear the sound of glass crashing, and a loud gasp from Janya.

I rush to the kitchen to see what's happened. A dark red puddle has spread around her feet. At first I think she's hurt, but it's the wine from the bottle that slipped from her hand. She's staring at the trash can, where she's just emptied the bag. At the bottom of the can, instead of the figurine of the little boy she thought she'd purchased, the grinning gargoyle has been smashed to smithereens, hardly recognizable except for its perfectly intact face, its long, pointed tongue sticking out.

It begins in Oslo, in 1981. A copy of Carl Theodor Dreyer's *La Passion de Jeanne d'Arc* is found in a closet of a mental institution. No one's seen a print as well preserved in over fifty years. When the film is shown to patients at the institution, several reportedly suffer epileptic seizures. A few others reportedly get healed, and are released some months later.

Completed in 1927, the film's original negatives were destroyed in a fire at the UFA studio in Berlin the following year. Dreyer reassembled the film using alternate shots, but nothing compared to the original version. Surviving copies deteriorated through the next few years. No one would see Dreyer's masterpiece again until the discovery in the Oslo sanatorium.

In that same year, Annette is working on a documentary on popular hysteria and psychic phenomena. She has just gotten married, and Sylvain has just begun working with the Centre national de la cinématographie. She wants to become a film archivist, to ride the crest of the Nouvelle Vague. Sylvain helps her get a grant to investigate a strange incident in Dozulé, Normandy. Some whacked-out church worker named Madeleine Aumont claims to have seen an image of the cross one morning and to have spoken to God. This is the time of Medjugorje, and Mother Mary has been packing crowds in that obscure Yugoslavian village. It's a good time to be God. Needless to say, even the bishop of Bayeux takes her case seriously:

"Madame Aumont has been quoting from the Scriptures and the liturgy. As far as we can tell, she knows neither Latin nor the gospels. She speaks only French and has a lisp. When she repeats the messages, her lisp is gone, her Latin is perfect."

And this is what Annette says to herself (also on film) after that interview: "I don't think I believe in these things, but it does make an interesting subject for a documentary. I think it's the mind that makes you see things. The mind can even make you hear the voice of God. And it's the mind that convinces you it's all true. We'll see what she says about that."

When she finally gets to meet Madame Aumont, she asks if the voice from the cross had personal messages for individuals. Madame Aumont says it has none. "God deals with creation in universal terms. His relationships with individuals are private, unique, and cannot be shared."

And then, just when Annette is about to run out of film, Madame Aumont adds: "One boy will be lost, another will be saved."

Flash-forward: Annette's just had a son, and her documentary project has grown bigger. As soon as the boy is old enough, the three of them travel to San Crisostomo, in the cluster of islands in northern Philippines, where Annette wants to report on the growing international popularity of faith healing in that country.

This is where the gaps in the story happen, because no other footage of that trip survives, except this:

Annette's in a canoe with little Mathieu. She's using a paddle to push the canoe away from the craggy shore. It's hard to keep them both in the frame. The water's rough. The canoe bobs up and down. She's saying something difficult to hear against the crash of the waves. She's trying to paddle back now. She's having a hard time. You can hear Sylvain's voice behind the camera: *Oh my God, oh my God*. The camera's dropped, and now all you see is the water sideways. All you hear is Sylvain's voice grown faint, drowned out by the sound of waves.

* * *

What follows is a series of jerky footage apparently shot on the run, as Marcos declares martial law and the country descends into chaos. What you see gives the impression that Sylvain may have had the camera on randomly, continuously—an unedited journal of the next few days.

Everything happens quickly. Shortly after they return from the island to catch a flight out of Manila, Sylvain comes back to their hotel with a newborn baby in his arms. He's just heard a horrific story. There are newborn Amerasian babies for sale in the country—children abandoned by GIs in the US base towns. It's an illegal but relatively easy transaction. None of the usual red tape, none of those pesky social workers Vietnamese babies come with. The babies have to be sold. Unsold ones are thrown back into the litter of mixed-race orphans and wind up as street kids or child prostitutes. In other words, there's a perfectly humane reason for being an accomplice to the crime.

Here is that clip again. Annette's holding me in her arms. There's an indescribable expression of relief and anxiety on her face. You can hear Sylvain's voice telling her they can use Mathieu's passport—*These monkeys wouldn't know the difference.* She wants to say something, *What if they find out it's not him?* Her lips move but something's wrong with the sound, and no words come out. She seems unable to figure out what to make of this situation. She appears gaunt, bewildered. She lifts her eyes to look at the camera. Her eyes are swollen, like she's lost a lot of sleep.

Then there's a brief and ghostly shot of a TV screen. Marcos is announcing the reasons he's placed the country under martial law.

Jump cut to Annette nervously boarding the plane, the baby in her arms. She's bobbing in and out of the frame. Everything's jerky, and it's obvious the camera's being kept on surreptitiously. Soldiers are everywhere, on the streets, at airport security, in the plane before takeoff. A tense moment, off-camera, as we stare at nothing, at what looks like the floor of some room somewhere, and we hear the voice of a customs security officer asking for Annette's papers, and then Sylvain's, and then the baby's.

Months later, they hear that the dictator has dealt decisively with crime. There's a newspaper clip tucked into the box of this reel. For some reason Sylvain and Annette may have thought the story was important. Quoting the Philippines' government-run press, the story says that every member of the adoption ring has either been jailed or executed.

Flash-forward. Clips of my parents' apartment on rue Cazotte, in Montmarte. Stacks of film everywhere. An editing console looming over one side of the living room. Images of Dreyer's *La Passion de Jeanne d'Arc* flickering on the monitor.

Sylvain and Annette have been commissioned by the Service des Archives du Film et du Dépôt Légal to digitally restore the recovered print of the film. The images in the video copy are muddy. The light that made Dreyer's work famously transcendent is barely discernible. But the situation isn't hopeless. One scene is exceptionally preserved. It's the one where the monk Massieu, played by Antonin Artaud, warns Jeanne that the tribunal's question is going to entrap her, and advises her to remain silent.

The question is this: "Are you in a state of grace?"

Jeanne takes a long time to respond. Finally, ignoring the monk's warning, she replies: "If I am, may God keep me there. If I am not, may God grant it to me."

I'm watching the scene behind my parents' backs. The suspense of those fourteen interminable cuts between question and response is too much for me to bear. Something in me shuts down.

When I come to, I find myself lying in my mother's arms. My father is still on the phone, calling for an ambulance. I've drooled all over my shirt. My body feels weak and numb. I look toward the freeze-frame on the monitor. The ghostly, tortured close-up of Renée Maria Falconetti looks down on the three of us. I'm hoping I'm dead, and this is all there is to it: I have, at the age of nine, what you might call a revelation.

As work on the restoration progresses, Annette and Sylvain take turns looking after me. Improbable causes seem to provoke the seizures: aspirin, milk, even Darjeeling tea. Equally improbable remedies seem to calm me down: the sound of the mistral, the presence of water.

On the rare free weekend, we spend hours walking along the promenade, idly watching the nodding yachts. Even just bowls of water soothe me, which Annette, having quickly read a book on feng shui, places uncomprehendingly each night beside my bed.

Nothing makes sense. My condition challenges everything they believe in. Everything outside of reason is coincidence, illusion, mystery—like chicken entrails that faith healers pull out of sick bodies, Annette says; like Madame Aumont's visions of the holy cross.

Street scenes, Cannes. Rue d'Antibes, packed with cars and pedestrians. One morning, en route to the lab, Annette asks Sylvain to park for just a few minutes. She wants to get out and call home, to make sure the Moroccan nanny they've hired doesn't forget to place the bowl of water beside my bed.

There's nowhere to park. Sylvain lets her out and keeps the motor running. She dashes into a tobacco shop, frantically places a call, and for some reason has a hard time explaining to the nanny exactly what to do.

A traffic cop tells Sylvain to move on. Sylvain has already backed up traffic all through the street. He honks, she glances quickly, a look of panic in her eyes.

The cop has lost his patience now, slams his fist against the roof of the car, and suddenly Sylvain is yelling at him, telling him this is an emergency and he shouldn't slam the car so strongly like that, because it will leave a dent. He gets a ticket, drives around the block, hoping to catch Annette by the time she's done.

When he reaches the same spot, after a grueling cruise around three or four jam-packed blocks, Annette is nowhere in sight. He heads slowly past the tobacco shop (the same cop is eyeing him with suspicion), then moves on, taking the same congested route, and drives back again. Annette is still missing. He drives on.

Finally, in the rearview mirror, he sees her running after the car. She catches up, breathlessly opens the door, and slips in, annoyed that she has been walking round and round the block, looking for him. Caught in the morning's interminable traffic, the car hardly moving from the same spot, they argue heatedly, their voices heard all across the street.

By the time they reach the lab, they are exhausted, unable to even think of work. Sylvain finally says what they've been trying not to say. The options are clear. For the sake of the boy, they will have to abandon the restoration altogether.

In the summer before I turn fifteen, my parents take me on a short cruise to Île Saint-Honorat. In the chapel, I keep my eyes shut as the Cistercian monks chant the liturgical service. Sylvain and Annette quickly usher me out, thinking I'm about to have another seizure.

It's impossible to explain what has happened. I feel as if my entire being has been turned inside out, and every part of my body is susceptible to the slightest sound, to softness, to this wonderful mystery that is assaulting me, for which I can think of no other word but *beauty*. My eyes brim with tears, my body trembles all over. I have begun to feel the first pangs of love. But this love is directed toward something abstract and ungraspable—almost, in a way, inhuman. And I realize, also for the first time, the sorrow that such a love can bring. Because it can never be expressed or shared, it condemns those it has ensorcelled to a lifetime of solitude.

From then on I can bear to go nowhere else. Here are clips of the chapel. Bare and austere, the walls a pristine white, the stained-glass windows unspectacular, the altar a single slab of ancient wood, bare-bones and ascetic. There is nothing to hold a visitor in thrall, but like a paramour who has idealized his lover to the point that no imperfection is possible or admissible, I am hopeless, deranged by the fervor of my desire. There is no way to placate me but to keep bringing me back to the place where that fever began, to let me sit through the entire service, which to me is as exquisite as it is torturing. To leave me, in short, mesmerized by my infatuation. CDs are no good. They're only as good as a lover's photograph—it evokes the lover's memory, maybe some remembered happiness. But it also underscores the absence, and creates a deeper melancholy for the beloved.

Over time Sylvain and Annette conclude, against all logic, that the chanting produces a startling effect on me: I am starting to heal. They begin to look for signs that things are turning providential, that everything good is going our way. They want to believe it so much they're willing to accept anything. Forced to accept what they can't explain, for them everything has become serendipitous.

It so happens that at this time the monastery is in dire straits and has been sending out calls for support. They have begun to offer board and lodging to people who want to escape from the bustle of the Côte d'Azur, for a minimal fee. Sylvain and Annette offer them substantial financial support if the monks will watch over me and expose me to a healthy dose of daily chanting.

It's supposed to be for just one summer. I stay three years, the time they need to finish restoring the film.

One afternoon, a novice catches me lying prostrate before the Eucharist in the chapel. It doesn't mean anything. It's just something I suddenly feel like doing. I tell him I've been replaying in my mind the final scene from Dreyer's *Ordet*, a film I once found in my parents' library. I've been projecting that scene, through my mind, to God. I want to get God's opinion, to ask if that scene was, in God's view, credible. It's a joke, a kind of serious joke. But the novice doesn't get it. His mind has been dulled by faith, the unconditional surrender of reason that God demands. He walks away, shaking his head.

I check my watch and notice that quite some time has elapsed. Sylvain and Annette should have been here an hour ago. In another hour, it will be sext, lunch will be communal in the dining hall, and the rule of silence will mean we can't talk till sometime before nones, when I'll be asked to clean the barns. At vespers, they're still not around, and by the end of the day, all I can think of is the novice who caught me lying prostrate in the chapel, and how, walking away, I heard him mutter, "You better shape up soon or they'll send you back to Cambodia."

Sylvain and Annette do come, but not till the following morning. Yesterday's conference took longer than expected, and they missed the last ferry. Highly in demand in the digital restoration business, they already have a backlog of about half a dozen films. They tell me how happy they are, how great their work is going.

Nothing registers in my head. I am consumed by an emotion that floods my entire body, so potent I feel it coursing through my veins. I taste something bitter lingering in my mouth. I want something that can't happen— that everything be turned back to the day before we first took the trip to the island, back to the point before all this truculent, sickening happiness began.

And so, abruptly, as Annette talks about yet another new project (her voice fades in and out, ". . . might have to go away," "in Paris for another couple of weeks . . ."), I tell them exactly what I feel.

"I don't give a fuck. You don't have to come see me again."

These words have the intended effect: both my parents burst in tears. Inelegant as my few well-chosen words may seem, I am satisfied that I have made myself clear.

But Sylvain tries to placate me and says he has an idea. He suggests to Annette that they transfer me to a couple of aunts in Fréjus who can look after me. They drive directly to Fréjus to make arrangements. I can imagine them snaking through the sinuous roads of the Massif de l'Estérel, which they loved to shoot, over and over, mounting the camera on the car's dashboard, the reckless daredevils zipping past in their open convertibles. The southern air must have become suddenly more soothing, the view even more breathtaking. The mistral, a brief squall of gloom, is lifting off the Mediterranean. The road is wet and slippery. They are driving fast, unable to control their exhilaration, knowing their problem at last is virtually solved. As they maneuver a hairpin turn through the rocky outcrops past Saint-Raphaël, they don't see another car speeding from the other direction. Sylvain loses control. The car skids and shoots off the cliff, landing on the jagged rocks below.

There are more reels and more boxes, but we've finished an entire bottle and, not surprisingly, Janya and I are both exhausted.

The next morning, Janya suggests that we take the ferry to Île Saint-Honorat. There's not much to see there, especially at this time of the year. We walk around the island and linger at the ruins of the tower, where we have a 360-degree view of the bay. Below, we can see the back of the abbey's barn. A monk comes out, stands against a wall, lifts the skirt of his soutane, and takes a piss.

"Well, this is it," I tell her. "This is where the story ends."

"Or begins," she says.

"Now that I've told you my life story, I'm afraid to lose you."

"What do you mean?"

"Weird to think about it, but it would be like losing a part of myself."

"Well, isn't that what this game is all about?"

"I wish we wouldn't call it a game anymore."

"Well, it's certainly beyond that now."

"I wish I hadn't told you so much, but we do have this agreement. I wish you'd tell me something as outlandish or as intimate from your own life. Then I wouldn't feel so, well, vulnerable."

"I could make something up."

"That's cheating."

"Or I could start something outlandish right now."

"Hmm. What did you have in mind?" I slip my hand inside her blouse. The wind has picked up and is getting icy cold. Her nipples are hard. I pull her other hand down to my crotch.

"Not here," she says.

"Why not?"

She points to the stone slab behind me. There's a carved inscription of the Twenty-Third Psalm written in Provençal. She reads it aloud. "Bewitching," she says. "I don't get it, but it almost makes me want to believe."

I check to see that the pissing monk is not in sight. It's late afternoon. Cannes is all lit up now, a gaudy jewel. "I want to fuck right next to the Twenty-Third Psalm, Janya. I want to do something really, really bad. Let's fuck right here."

She presses close to me. I can smell her skin, a scent like orange blossoms which always reminds me of Bangkok.

"Don't ever leave me," I whisper in her ear. "I'd go nuts if you did."

She looks at me in the eye, smiling, wondering.

"What?" I ask her.

"You are so full of surprises. Maybe I should pull one of my own."

"No, don't. I hate surprises."

"Not fair."

"Okay, but make it nice. Like Christmas or a birthday."

"Or a baby."

"No, no babies. Babies scare me. They're loathsome and full of themselves. Egomaniacs."

"We were all babies once. Some of us still are."

"Hmm. Broad hint."

She presses her lips to mine. "Shut up, baby. Close your eyes and open your heart." And then she mumbles something strange, and I realize she is reading the psalm again. *"Surely goodness and mercy will follow me all the days of my life. I will fear no evil."*

the little toil of love

His first words to me are: You don't look like shit.

His next words are: Liana hasn't been asking about you.

I have no idea what he's talking about. I stare blankly at him. He passes his hand across my face.

Jesus fuck, Andy, he says. It's me. It's fucking Nick. I've come to get you out.

The 3 most important things in life are marijuana, getting laid, & rock music. That's what you always said. So what the fuck are you doing in there with a bunch of Commies?

Nick's words bounce off me & make no sense. He's brought me coffee in a thermos jug. I haven't had decent coffee in months. The liquid scalds my tongue. It feels good. It feels good to feel something.

We've traveled days on foot to get to this town. I don't know its name, I don't know where we are. It's a small army barracks with a visiting area packed with people looking for guys like me & the student & Eddie. There's no one else here, but they're staying just the same, as though the sheer persistence of their presence will make the missing materialize before their eyes. They're wives, mothers, fathers, children, & babies—lots of squealing, besotted babies. Every time somebody's brought in, they come here, thinking it's someone they know.

I tell Nick these guys have a lot to learn from Mao. What?

Mao. You know. The babies & shit. Only one child per household. That's the way to get your shit straight.

He looks relieved. Welcome back, you old mother-fucker, he says. Thought I lost you there for a while.

Nick's just got a job scraping corneas off dead people. He says it's some kind of transplant experiment that's going to be standard in a few years. He works late-night shifts, alone in a lab in Manila with a bunch of dead bodies. Some of them come all badly messed up from accidents or shoot-outs with the Communists, but their corneas are still perfect. It pays good money.

Nick's never had any medical experience, much less held a degree. He's already passed himself off as a day-time soap actor, a journalist, & an exiled aristocrat. Nick says it's easy to fuck these guys when they think of you as white. Greeks technically aren't white but he can be white if that's what it takes to get things moving. He's learned to be anything since he escaped Papadopoulos's dictatorship back in Greece. White guys can do anything, he says. Give us a dead body, & we'll goddamn scrape any eye off like it's nobody's business.

Where are we?

You're back in Manila, man. Just outside the city. Fucking suburban boonies. Back where you started from.

Nick stares at me with a mixture of sympathy & horror, like I've risen from the dead. You look 10 years younger without your hair, he says. You look like a fuck-ing teenager.

He's trying to make me feel good. I know I look like shit.

Why'd you do it? he asks. I think Nick is playing the guilt thing again, & he senses it, & he says, Your hair, why did you cut your hair?

I tell him I had to look inconspicuous. Like I was already enlisted. Like I was just on furlough.

Good thing, he says. The government's banned long hair.

I know all about it. The lieutenant says it all the time, says long hair is a sign of decadence. The Beatles are messengers of the Antichrist. Rock is the music of the devil. Hippies are souls that have gone astray. There's a strong message of divine righteousness in dictatorships. Every megalomaniac has to believe his actions are sanctioned by God.

Long dark-blond hair, Nick says wistfully. You looked like James Taylor in Two-Lane Blacktop.

James Taylor had darker hair, I tell him.

You know what I mean. Now you're just damn skinny. What the fuck got you here anyway?

Here we go. I knew it was coming. To do that, I tell Nick, we'll have to talk mojo.

Talk mojo, noun, or verb, or whatever: a language of negatives, purely intended as a private joke. Nick & I invented it, one stoned & drunken night at a bar or something. Hard to remember where.

Examples: I'm never getting high again. I'm not so going to fuck that girl. I'm never horny. We used to banter it around in the red-light district & got all the putas puzzled or pissed & afterward Nick & I had a good laugh. & of course sometimes it backfired. She's so not good look-

ing is something no girl wants to hear. & Nick liked it
when it backfired because he didn't like it that the girls
liked me & just sort of liked him, because he was a doctor
or a baron or some kind of important person from the US
consulate & that's supposed to turn them on.

Talk mojo. I knew that shit was going to be useful
someday.

I haven't been avoiding the other American residents in
the city. I don't hang out with the few backpacking dharma
bums just passing through. They don't tell me to lie low,
to go somewhere else. They don't tell me it's too risky
here. The army's not going to conscript every fucking one
of us, no matter where we are. I don't follow their advice.
I don't disappear somewhere myself. I haven't been living
in the south, on the island of Cebu.

& absolutely none of this can be blamed on Liana.

The language of negatives poses some problems. How do I
tell Liana to stop asking about me? How do I tell Nick not
to mention her ever again?

Here is what Andy did, in real language.

Follow Liana to Manila, where she has found work as
a Peace Corps volunteer. Don't ask why. Filipina American UC Berkeley activist wanting to go back and do something for her country. Immediately finds a local boyfriend,
a friend of the family, whatever. Me alone with Nick,
that's the only friend I have left. The girls. Anna, most of
all. Liana gets insanely jealous, but what the fuck? She's
fucking someone else, I get to do the same thing, right?
Draft happens; I receive a notice to report to base headquarters in Olongapo. Anna knows how to get me out,

use a fake passport. I fly south, to her town, the only one I know. Fucking stupid mistake. Wind up like Anna & her friends, owe these people money for passport, other things. Drugs. Nirvana. Owe too much. Have to pay them back. Everybody is for sale. Big business. Big money. Everyone involved. Cops, military, politicians, maybe even the president. Then people warning me the government is planning a big-time cleanup, everyone's got to clean up his act. Get out while you can. Rumors in town that Manila is under siege. Gang bosses get arrested. All gone. Babies are born, Anna & family need money not babies. Beg me to take them home to US, otherwise they will become child prostitutes. That's all they'll be good for. Half-breed gooks are nice to fuck. Arrive in Manila the night martial law is declared. Stay with this American woman for a night. I go back to Anna, tell her I've sold the kid, she runs away. Look all over for her. The lieutenant has been waiting for me, greasy pork smile, fascist pig throws me in provincial jail. This is where I've been. This is how I found the long, thorny road to hell.

How do you talk mojo & say all that? Impossible. I will never be able to tell my story.

I explain to Nick that I can't tell him anything, not even if I talk mojo.

What the fuck? he says. I'm here to help. What the flying fuck?

Double negatives are long & awkward. It's not math, you can't negate what you've already (-) & get a (+). It doesn't work that way. What you've broken apart can't become whole again.

Nonformula: $(-) \pm (-) \neq (+)$.

Remember this. Always remember.

We are held in place by gravitational forces

Then the Life Crusaders blow our place up.

It begins that afternoon, when Mother and I come back from the supermarket. As we unload the bags from the trunk, a car speeds by, and somebody hurls a couple of beer bottles straight at us. One grazes my shoulder, and smashes against the hood of the trunk. The other hits Mother on the forehead. She reels, puts one foot back to steady herself. The car has already sped away, someone poking a dirty finger at us.

I help Mother in and as soon as I sit her down I notice the blood dripping down the gash on her forehead.

"Fuck, Mother, I'm calling the cops."

"Don't." She walks into the clinic and comes out minutes later with her wound sealed with a thick wad of gauze, a small bright spot of red the only sign of her ordeal.

"I'll take you to hospital."

"No need."

"What did you do?"

"I'm not letting them hurt me."

I lift the gauze a little. The stitches she's done are fine and tight. "You could have asked me to help you."

"No need." She unloads the bags and starts putting the groceries in the fridge. Then she falters, stands dazed for a few seconds. I rush to her and catch her just before she hits the ground.

* * *

"How long was I out?"

"Two hours." The steaming bowl of soup by her bed is starting to form an ugly crust of grease. "Bad soup. We should have gotten the other brand."

She gets up. "I feel fine." She walks out of the room.

"What are you doing?"

"Tea. Want some?"

I follow her to the kitchen. She's scrounging around for the pot. I pull it out from under the sink. "Mother, we have to do something."

"You show them you're scared, that only makes them stronger."

"I *am* scared. And they *are* strong. People who think they have the full support of God, any god, think they've invincible. They will do anything and not even think twice about it."

"They should read Freud."

I keep staring at her.

"You know, *Civilization and Its Discontents*. Religion is an infantile neurosis—"

"I know, Mother."

"I feel sorry for them. Stupid people are helpless creatures. They live all their lives stupid, and they die stupid. What a waste. Of life. Of all the possibilities of life. I feel very, very sorry for them."

"Well, they don't feel sorry for you."

"That's Christian love for you."

"I wish it would stop."

"What?"

"This. Everything they're doing."

"Try telling them that. Try telling that to their stupid

god, or their stupid church."

"I don't see why we have to keep doing what we're doing."

"Don't give me that again, Jordan. You know why we're doing what we're doing."

"No, I don't."

"Because those girls need us."

"Because you don't want to stop."

"Why don't I want to stop?"

"Frank."

"Oh, for Christ's sake."

"You have enough to retire on."

"No."

"I hate living like this."

The kettle is whistling. Neither of us pays attention. She is holding the tea bags in her hand. She has crushed them in her fist.

"I hate living like this," I say again.

"You want me to surrender."

"I wish something would happen that would make you want to stop."

"Be careful what you wish for."

"I want you to realize that you can stop. No more of this. No more of Frank. Time to move on, Mother. It's time."

"You don't tell me what to do." Her hands are shaking. "You don't know what I want."

I'm wide awake, unable to sleep from the heat of the humid summer night. Mother comes in my room.

"There's a noise downstairs." She hasn't spoken anything else to me all night.

"I'll go down and look." I put a shirt on.

"Don't bother. I think I left the exhaust fans on." She walks out.

"Mother, I'm sorry."

"About what?"

"What I said earlier."

"I don't remember what you said."

"Okay. You sure you don't want me to go check?"

She is heading down when a flash of light bursts from the stairs. It seems to last for a long time, although it takes no more than a few seconds. It blazes up toward her from below, so that all I see, for what seems like a motionless eternity, is the skeletal silhouette of her body against her nightdress, an X-ray of her in the reddish glow. Then there's a quick pop, like a bottle uncorked. A thunderous explosion shakes the apartment and jolts me out of bed. A searing heat rips through my room. I shout to her, but all I hear is the clangor of the fire alarm as the sprinklers turn on. The water hisses as it hits the crackling flames.

I find her sprawled on the stairs. She's cut up and bleeding in many places. I carry her out a fire exit in the back. She's staring at me, her mouth moving without words, her eyes wide with shock and gratefulness and relief.

How to build a pipe bomb. Take a steel pipe, stuff it with gunpowder, and bore it with a fuse hole on one side. Insert a cherry bomb inside the pipe as a five-to-ten-minute detonator. Add a few slivers of steel for greater impact, and like the bomb dropped at our clinic, throw it inside the ventilation shaft for maximum effect: an enclosed area like that converts a crude, homemade device into a bigger, more lethal explosive.

That's all it takes, a device so simple and low-tech any amateur terrorist can assemble it. A thoroughly persuasive weapon nonetheless: the bomb wrecks the clinic entirely. There is not much for the fire department to save. The job, I must say, has been well done. Of course I still wish some bungling rookie apostle had fucked up and lit the fuse at the wrong moment, blowing up himself and his fellow terrorists for Jesus. Blowing them to kingdom come. That didn't happen, obviously. And somewhere out there the same zealots are still looking to assassinate people like us in the name of love.

Several pieces of shrapnel pierced Mother's arms, back, and lungs. Doctors are able to pluck out most of them, except for a small triangular piece, the size of a guitar pick, that landed so close to her heart it's risky to even touch it.

With the insurance money, I have the clinic rebuilt and furnish it with new equipment. Mother comes home from the hospital to a place that's barely changed, except for the fresh-out-the-box smell of new machines.

Her recovery is quick and easy. Or so it seems, at first. Then late one morning I find her still in bed, her eyes wide open, staring blankly at the ceiling.

"You all right?"

"I can't move."

I open her canister of painkillers. "You'll have to eat something first," I remind her.

"It's in there."

"What?"

"The thing that wants to kill me."

"Don't worry, Mother. It won't do that. The doctors gave their word."

"It's going to rain soon."

I look out. The sky is overcast, a big gray blur is inching its way toward us.

"I feel cold."

I pull her blanket up and feel her forehead. "You're okay. You want me to call the doctor just in case?"

"I don't like the cold."

"Me neither."

"It's going to make me burst."

"Just rest awhile. You're just having a bad day. We knew you would get bad days now and then. It's all right."

"I smell something."

"What?"

"Sulfur. Nitrate. There's a bomb inside me. It's inside my soul."

It's weeks later, and I find her on her knees, rag in hand, scrubbing the kitchen floor.

"Mother, you don't have to do that. Let me do it."

"It's not going away," she says, standing up. She lifts her arms. "It's coming out of my skin."

"What is?"

"That rotting smell. That old-people smell. That stench of formaldehyde that makes them smell as though they're dying from within."

I take her hand and raise it close to my nose.

"Don't patronize me."

"I don't smell anything, Mother. Just soap. I always liked the smell of your soap."

Late that night I find her still awake in bed. All the lights are on. She has the radio humming softly, an old Frank Sinatra favorite.

"You'll be all right?"

"I don't want to sleep."

"Don't force yourself. Read, do something. Let your body tell you when it's ready to sleep."

"I don't want to sleep."

"Okay."

"Because if I do, I'll never wake again. And you know what that means?"

I pull a chair over and sit next to her bed.

"It means I never survived the bomb. It means, at last, that I'm dead."

"Oh, Mother. Please don't say that. Please."

"Am I dead?"

"No. Not at all. Don't let them do this to you."

"I can't feel anything."

I poke her arm lightly with my finger. She twitches, pulls away. "You're okay," I tell her.

"I didn't feel a thing."

Days later the caravans come. They must be people from the next county, driving by several times a day and shouting, *BABY KILLERS GO TO HELL!* When it becomes obvious that, under my supervision, it's going to be business as usual at the clinic, they use more covert, and more annoying, tactics. I find our door locks stuck with glue, the car tires punctured, the phone wires cut. Fake clients keep calling to set appointments and book us for weeks, and we have to turn away patients who really need our services. Someone spray paints, *MOMMY DON'T KILL ME,* on our front door.

Right before Thanksgiving, Mother's name appears on the Life Crusaders' online hit list, just below Frank's; the list is alphabetical.

I decide to move Mother out of the place. It isn't a hard decision to make. Her delusions soon overwhelm all sense of reality. In time I have to admit that she is never going to work again.

I pack our things in a U-Haul. As I heave the last of our stuff in the back of the truck, the neighbors stare at us, peering from behind curtains or through slightly open doors.

Just before we move, the Life Crusaders have one last thing to say. They send Mother a letter with a line from the Book of Hebrews. This is what it says:

For our God is a consuming fire.

We move down to the city, where I can have her close to specialists who can keep her under observation. She is diagnosed with a rare disorder called Cotard's syndrome. In Cotard's syndrome, all senses become disconnected from emotions. Everything in the world ceases to have any emotional significance. The only way a patient explains this is that she's dead. Anything that contradicts that conviction is distorted to fit the delusion.

I have never heard of anything like it before. Despite the specialists' careful though arcane explanation, it sounds too weird, too sci-fi, and I argue that all Mother needs is a little rest and a little time. I find a two-bedroom apartment on West --, five flights in a walk-up above a truck garage. Every night when the trucks come in, the building shudders like an island sitting on a tectonic plate. We hardly see anyone else, except for a young Korean couple on the first floor who walk a yapping terrier late at night and don't like to chat much.

In the apartment below, someone plays a cello every

morning. For several weeks after we move in, the same Brahms andante floats up to our apartment as I make coffee. I am desperate for signs that I have done the right thing. This seems as good as any. It gives me, at least, some reassurance that Mother and I can now safely disappear.

The apartment has enough room for some of the stuff I saved from the bombing, useless junk that she and Frank once shared, some CDs and books. Not one photograph of our life in Dobbs Ferry has survived the fire.

"Who are you?"

The first time she asks that question, I realize no proof of our existence remains. I don't know how to respond.

There is no better place to move her to than New York City. It is the only place where we can avoid caravans of indignant Christians and be safe from their threats and pranks. It isn't going to get her name off their hit list, but at least no one is going to lob another pipe bomb at us around here.

In my need for providential signs, our move seems significant at that time. The city is the opposite of what she is. It is her image in reverse, magnified and multiplied. She is alive and believes she is dead. The city is by all appearances alive, and only when you look closely, not up at the lights and towering high-rises but down in the gutters and tunnels, do you realize it's in an advanced state of decomposition. It's propped up by a life-support system of billboards, shops, train tracks, tourists, money, noise, and seemingly purposeful mayhem. But it's a lost cause. It's rotting in its bones, its innards infested with cockroaches, mosquitoes, and rats, its services inept, its dissonant ghettoes teeming with the refuse of the human race, the homeless, the crazy, and the poor. It's a city sewn together from many cities, people from all over the world bring their shit here and call it a life: a Franken-stein's monster of a city, born without a soul and doomed to die, if not already dead. No wonder Lorca's impression of it was morbid:

> *Por los barrios hay gentes que vacilan insomnes*
> *como recién salidas de un naufragio de sangre.*

> *In the neighborhoods sleepless people stagger*
> *like survivors of a shipwreck of blood.*

I am happy to stay home with her all day. The city discombobulates me. Its farrago of everything causes my head to spin. Just the idea of having to go out already makes me feel nauseous. The shortest trip to a Rite Aid three blocks away, where I have to get her medication, feels like I'm walking through a gauntlet, past the rebellious gun-toting teenagers streaming out of Martin Luther King High School, the hawkers of fake Gucci bags, the Chinese takeout cyclists who will run you down for no reason. Anything within three feet of the building's front door only makes me want to slink back home.

Wild animals seek some place of solitude when they're injured. They wait out patiently for nature to take its course, for the body to heal itself. I am certain Mother's body will do the same thing.

Either that, or she and I will have to blend into the shipwreck. She and I will have to disappear.

❈ ❈ ❈

In 1889, Jules Cotard, a neurologist and former military surgeon, finds out that his daughter has contracted diphtheria. He has been living in Vanves for fifteen years and is already famous for having first described what will be known as the Cotard delusion, the belief that you are dead, don't exist, or don't have bodily organs. Cotard refuses to believe that his daughter is dying, and doesn't leave her bedside for fifteen days. Eventually she does recover, an event that, though no records show it, I imagine Cotard may have interpreted as proof that disease is at bottom a manifestation of the mind. Ironically, he contracts the illness himself and dies a few days later.

I take copious notes about the disease, but to what end I can't imagine. I come up with a story. Cotard, through some demonic, Faustian transaction, saves his daughter by exchanging his life for hers. It appears to me that, in the small universe in which we operate not through will but ultimately through patterns, I will eventually have to do the same thing for my mother. The idea of such a sacrifice fills me with a sense of purpose, a destiny, but also with dread and a simmering resentment toward her stubborn refusal to heal. In short, my mind is getting really fucked.

It takes me days to unpack. Boxes choke the apartment, and I eat my dinner on them, write my journal on them, masturbate on them. When I finally find the energy to open them, I discover a bunch of folders from mother's files, records of patients, deeds of sale, tax returns—and a browned and crisped document that will, if this didn't sound too dramatic, change the course of my life.

It is a typewritten bequest prepared by a notary public whose scrawl I can barely read. It is tucked among the documents she drew up before the Life Crusaders destroyed the clinic. It specifies the money that Andrew Breszky wired back to Mother, a few months after I was born: fifteen thousand and five hundred dollars, half the amount Mother told me she paid to adopt me. By to-day's standards I reckon that has appreciated and must be worth twice as much, maybe even more. So I guess Mother did get a full refund.

Then it occurs to me that this is evidence that Mr. Breszky did in fact exist, and maybe still does. That he is indeed my father, and that all her incredible stories about Manila, the storm, the dead air on the day I was delivered, aren't just embellishments to an otherwise in-credible history. But I really don't care whether it is fact or fiction; history, as far as I'm concerned, is dead matter. What I never knew, and discover only when I read the document, is that Andrew Brezsky also bequeathed the exact same amount to another son, who, it seems, was born on the same day that I was.

His name is Mathieu Aubert. Grew up in Paris, or the south of France, or the Philippines, or all of the above.

He is, it seems, the only family I have left.

WSOWOB

Janya's in the bedroom packing a suitcase. Tomorrow she leaves for Vietnam. It's been a couple of weeks since we came back to Bangkok from La Napoule and moved in together. I can hear the slightest move she makes, though she packs quietly, surreptitiously. I tell her she packs as if she's stealing away from an inescapable situation, or a crime.

"Yeah," she says. "One of these days, you'll find that you've been living with a fugitive. Then you'll have what the industry calls *a story you can pitch.*"

I've decided to bring Sylvain and Annette's films with me. A box of ghosts. Janya says I carry them like ashes. I don't know why I decided to bring them, but after revealing the story to Janya, I need to look at them all over again. Now, for some reason, I feel there's something there I might have missed.

Here's that clip where Annette's in the canoe with the little boy. She's using a paddle to push away from the craggy shore. It's difficult to keep them both in the frame. She's saying something hard to hear against the crash of the waves. She's trying to paddle back. A white wave rises behind her, like the dorsal fin of a breaching whale. Sylvain's voice behind the camera: *Oh my God, oh my God.*

And at that moment, when I think I *know*, when I think

I get it, the signals come again, the waves freeze, and the voice begins to speak.

I have made a startling discovery. When I pass out, I don't really *pass out*. I am aware that my mind is somewhere above my body, an unbelievably separate thing. Disengaged, my mind is always lucid, always calm. And I feel sorry for my body, for the bodies around me, for everything I've left behind. I never want to come back.

I know what to anticipate now. I expect the same grueling, ecstatic lift. I don't resist it. I know it's easier to just let go. I let my body succumb to its own malfunctions.

But this time it's different. The longer I stay in that dreamlike world, the less I feel that soothing, intermediate limbo in which all connection with the world of suffering is severed. Instead, I'm pushed further toward a brink beyond which is a bottomless emptiness. I stand precariously, steeling myself against a storm wind that any minute will tip me over. This is the point that I find hard to endure, this sensation that I am, at last, on the verge of dissolution.

And then I hear the voice. It bends close to my ear, whispering. I can barely hear the words. I can only sense the hot breath warming my ear.

I don't know how long it lasts. Once again I find Janya rushing to my side, once again she holds my head up and wipes the sweat off my face. Her tenderness feels achingly sincere. And she says something I can barely understand, a low whisper: *"Sleep, little brother. The other will be saved."*

"There seems to be a minor defect in your brain that could

correct itself over time," the doctor tells me. "It has something to do with the anterior cingulate, which is part of the frontal lobe. Whenever it becomes extremely active, it inhibits or temporarily shuts down the amygdala and other limbic emotional centers."

"What's that supposed to mean?" I ask him.

"This is the way the brain suppresses potentially disabling emotions like anxiety or fear."

"So you're saying there are things that my brain wants to suppress."

"All brains do that. That's one of the things they're supposed to do. The result of an extreme condition like this is what people in the incipient field of cognitive science call *derealization* and *depersonalization*. There are moments when you think you're not real, or the world isn't real, and everything is a dream."

"Will hypnosis help?"

"Probably, but it's not necessary."

"Drugs?"

"Drugs will very likely make it worse. All you need is time. And a lot of rest."

"I'm working on a documentary."

"Well, take it easy. Can you find someone to take over or assist you?"

"No."

"You'll have to. With a little rest, you'll be good as new. Take a vacation."

"I just did."

"Relax. Do nothing. Take it easy on yourself."

"So that's all it is, then. Just a slightly fucked-up brain."

"That's all it is."

* * *

I tell Janya that I'm following the doctor's advice to get some rest. She seems relieved.

"Phil's not going to like this," I remind her.

"It's not as if you're giving up the project. You just have to pace yourself a little."

"I tried to tell the doctor about the boy."

"And?"

"He says these episodes usually produce visions like that. A lot of the saints who claimed to have spoken to God were epileptics."

"Okay. So now we know. You're a saint."

"Or Smerdyakov."

"Karamazov?"

"The weirdest of the lot. The most defective."

"Oh boy. Hope not."

"It's funny. It feels like there's some impostor preying on the junk in my brain. And the longer I deny it, the stronger it overpowers me. And yet I know it's just stuff hidden in my brain, junk that my brain digs up and throws back at me. But when I fight it, it fights back. The voice gets louder, and my head feels like it's going to burst. Like I'm caught in Polanski's *Repulsion* or something, the walls caving in, limbs morphing out of nowhere. And he keeps saying that message over and over. *One boy will be lost, another will be saved.*"

"Your brain produces those, oh, I don't know, dreams or something. You don't really think your dreams are real, do you? This is pretty much the same thing."

"It's the dreaming that fucks me. I have to stay awake. It's the only way I can shut him up."

"Come on, Mathieu."

"No, seriously. I don't think this will stop until I find out what really happened to the lost boy."

"How do you suppose you can do that?"

"The answer is in those films. I know if I look hard enough, I'll find something."

"Like what?"

"I don't know. Something."

She stares at me, and doesn't say anything more. I am aware, all of a sudden, of everything she feels. I sense it with an unnerving clarity. She's in the dark, she has nowhere to turn, for the first time she has no idea what to do. Her confusion terrifies me. Her silence fills me with alarm. And against my will, I tell her what I've stopped myself from saying since we came back. "I'm sorry."

"Don't," she says.

"I'm sorry I told you that story. You didn't have to know."

"Stop," she says. "I *know*. We can't change that now."

In *The Doors of Perception*, Aldous Huxley mentions a theory lavishly endorsed by the Cambridge philosopher Dr. C.D. Broad, regarding the connection between memory and sense perception. The function of the brain, the nervous system, and the sense organs, he says, are *eliminative*. Each person is theoretically capable of remembering everything that has ever happened to him, and of perceiving everything that is happening everywhere in the universe. The function of the brain and nervous system is "to protect us from being overwhelmed and confused by this mass of largely useless and irrelevant knowledge," by shutting out information and leaving only a small, specially selected, and practically useful few.

"According to such a theory," says Huxley, "each one of us is potentially Mind at Large. But in so far as we are animals, our business is at all costs to survive. To make biological survival possible, Mind at Large has to be funneled through the reducing valve of the brain and nervous system. What comes out at the end is a measly trickle of the kind of consciousness which will help us to stay alive on the surface of this particular planet."

Janya's been reading a number of books to help explain what's going on. Aldous Huxley is our latest guest of honor. She's made up her mind to work this out with me. No one's ever taken the trouble to do so. Whenever I think about it, I feel so much tenderness I want to cry.

She worries a lot every time she has to travel. That's the part I don't like. I tell her I'm okay, nothing's wrong, Huxley makes a lot of sense. She's already cancelled Vietnam and several other assignments. Her director has been on her case for a while now. I've finally convinced her to go to Cambodia for a few days. The Gap has opened new sweatshops there and has finally agreed to let in a monitor. In the sweatshop-monitoring world, that's like brokering an end to conflict in the Gaza Strip.

She's in the kitchen brewing some tea. I hear the kettle whistle. It keeps going for a while, one long insistent siren's note, and finally I have to get up to see what's happening. She's standing by the kettle, watching the thin jet of steam blowing out of the spout. In her hand are two bags of jasmine tea. On the tray, beside the cups, lies her plane ticket, torn in two.

"Water's boiling," I state the obvious. "You've ripped your ticket."

She pulls the lid off and drops the bags, two at a time, absently, dropping the paper tags as well. She realizes her mistake, tries to scoop them out with a spoon, and drops the spoon on the stove as a mushroom cloud of white-hot steam scalds her hand. I hold her hand under the cold-water tap.

"You okay?" I ask her.

"Let's solve this mystery once and for all," she says. "Let's go there."

"Where?"

"There. Where your parents lost the boy."

On the plane to Manila, she tells me she has one more secret she can share only with me.

"Uh-oh. Is this about your being a boy?"

"I found your stepbrother."

"What?"

"There's a guy in New York who claims to be some relation. Something about your supposedly biological father."

"Is he, like, asking you to deposit some money in a Nigerian bank?"

"Well, assuming the e-mails I've been getting are reliable, your real father apparently sowed some very wild oats in Manila. Ran short of cash as most hippies island-hopping in Southeast Asia did in those days. Got involved in some kind of local racket, and produced a nice clutch of sons to sell."

"Great. My dad was a bimbo."

"A surrogate father."

"A himbo. Whatever."

"And this guy from New York says he's one of the sons."

"Like puppies in a puppy mill."

screwed up, if Sylvain and Annette had not come to take me, I would have ended up as somebody else. I would have been one of these people. Wretched as rats, still waiting for someone to save me."

"You okay?"

"Yeah. No. Last night I had a dream. I was in some kind of time warp. I was trapped here, like everyone else. Helpless and doomed. And I hated him. I hated him so much I wanted to kill him."

"Who?"

"My father. The guy who left me here. He should have ust aborted me or something. But to leave me in a hell-ole like this, that was real shit."

"FYI, abortion would have been out of the question. s illegal here. Always has been. This is paradise for the ristian Right."

"Yeah, that fucker had no choice. He had to have me. er. You know what, though? Maybe Sylvain and An- te knew he was—a loser, I mean. Maybe, you know, thought, when I started getting, you know, *defective*, , you know what, it's the loser gene showing up. knew this was going to happen someday. Maybe s why they just gave up on me. Damaged goods . . . ?"

r voice breaks in and out of static.

id you hear a word I said?"

tic.

don't want to know. I don't want to know why he up. I don't want to know what happened to him a?"

thieu, speak up. Oh shit."

, Janya?"

"Didn't you ever want to know?"

"No."

"It could tell you something about your condition."

"My condition?"

"Your seizures. I mean, isn't that hereditary or something?"

"What would finding out do?"

"I don't know, Mathieu. Maybe some research has already been done that could, you know, help."

"Yeah, like they can snip some nasty gene and I'd be good as new."

"Okay. End of conversation."

"A stepbrother, for Christ's sake. In New York, my God. The epicenter of con artists. Is he in a Ponzi scheme or something?"

"All right already."

"I mean, really, Janya. Where did you find this wacko?"

"In some message posted on some website. I was googling you."

"Why?"

"I was looking to see if there was anything, some archive or something, about accidents involving tourists in San Crisostomo. An exercise in futility, of course. No news from that island ever went out until fairly recently."

"Okay, let me just warn you that A, there are thousands of scams lurking on the Internet. And B, close to 75 percent of material you find there is unreliable. Not to forget C: there are probably thousands of other losers with the same freaking story."

"Just indulge me, okay? Indulge the investigative nosy in me."

"I told you. The answer is in the films. Besides, it's

been so long. We won't find anything there. This is nothing but a sentimental journey."

"We're doing this for you. Say thank you."

"Thank you."

"Think of it as a vacation."

"Whatever."

"A sort of honeymoon. *Life and Leisure* ranks the country as one of the top ten beach destinations of the world, you know. "

"Hmm. We've never fucked on the beach. Isn't that weird? We've never done, you know, the Burt Lancaster thing."

"The Burt Lancaster thing?"

"You know, *From Here to Eternity.* Don't deny it. I've caught you watching it a lot of times."

"Stop it, you're incorrigible."

"I brought my Speedo with me. Will you be my Deborah Kerr?"

Well, as it turns out, we have to spend some time apart soon after we land in the Philippines. She takes a few days monitoring the export-processing zones north of Manila, an excuse to placate her director who wants to know why she is here instead of Cambodia. I wind up watching *From Here to Eternity* on pay-per-view for two nights in a row, masturbating to the beach scene while I lie naked and sweating on the hotel bed.

On day two, she calls to tell me to use my time creatively.

"Like how?"

"Research. About your hippie dad."

"I don't think so."

An hour later she sends me a text message: *FWIW,* for what it's worth.

SSINF, I text back: so stupid it's not funny.

Just so I can say I tried, I bribe every son of a bitch in city to get some leads. Not surprisingly, no one has he of anyone doing the sort of thing my hippie dad alleg did thirty-two years ago, something that I discover, mit, not without some relief.

But a local official hears of my inquiry. He's those lackeys working for some senator or some small-time warlord with his own posse of slum- thugs, underpaid cops, and drug pushers. He take me around the city's low-income neigh but not even he really understands what I'm l He thinks I'm trying to adopt a kid. Some fa me their children. Sick children, starving ch worse off than dogs. And when I say I'm n adopt one, they offer them just the same, sa certain terms that the kids are okay for me t dollars, fifty dollars, and I can fuck any ki

Janya suggests that I go to city hall ar looking for my biological mother. Her fol sage says, *ICBW:* it could be worse; *TTTT* time. Two days later twenty-five peopl one wants to claim me. Everyone has ness, a story to tell. Everyone will do

I call Janya again. She's still som ping up her last assignment before have to say is something no text me

"Any new clues?" she asks.

"I give up."

"Oh, Mathieu."

"Listen, I just realized sor

Static, echo, and finally she says, "He did me a favor by letting you live. Does that make you feel better?"

That night I wake up in a sweat. I lie in the dark, catching my breath. I turn the TV on. All the local stations are still signed off, but I surf to American cable, CNN, porn. I lie mesmerized by the numbing reassurance of their presence, a soothing reminder that outside of this apartment, away from this country, a world unlike this one still exists, and there's a way out. It takes me several minutes of mindless channel surfing to assure myself that I'm not caught in the trap. I'm only passing through.

The following morning I shoot a crowd of women at Baclaran, a church popular among the destitute and despairing, because it's said to grant even the most impossible of wishes. The women are walking to the altar on their knees, candles dripping on their fingers. In a place where no help can be expected from fellow humans, God by default is their last hope. I envy their obstinacy, their capacity to endure. I refuse to believe in God, but I think I understand why some people have to. I don't know who among us are the least fortunate.

From Manila, San Crisostomo is an hour's flight into hurricane country. The island is one of a tiny cluster that's practically invisible to the naked eye. Perpetually shrouded by mist and rain, it's caught in the crosshairs of the monsoons that pummel through the South China Sea. During the monsoon season, ferocious typhoons rip ancient trees from their roots and send them flying across the water. Cabins are hunched and burrowed in trenches, their thatch roofs held down with nets of thick hemp rope tied to stakes in the ground. Their walls are three feet thick, carved from massive limestone rocks that have turned, with age, to the color of bones.

So remote is this part of the country that anything halfway plausible is taken as fact—unconfirmed stories that have been retold so often they acquire the polish of truth, like the rosary beads people here carry in their pockets and pull out whenever the need for reassurance arises, the fragrant wood rubbed smooth by constant use.

Rumor has it that one of the islands, Sampetro, is populated by descendants of Portuguese mariners ship-wrecked in the 1600s. Because of the inhospitable weather, they have been largely secluded all these centuries. They look more Eurasian than Filipino, with all the genetic quirkiness that comes from inbreeding. People here say they are descended from angels—beautiful but out of this world, or, in real-world language, "special" or "mentally challenged."

Janya's fascinated by it—by the juxtaposition of Western folktale and local hearsay. She's done all the research, of course. In San Crisostomo, people say the surface of the northern Pacific Ocean circulates clockwise in a vortex every seven years. This, surprisingly, has been proven to be a scientific fact: oceanographers have shown that the movement, the same phenomenon that causes the doldrums, is caused by the spinning of the earth. The natives believe that the ocean is a living creature with a logic of its own, and, in an uncanny echo of the eternal return (uncanny because it is unintended), they say that what was lost at sea is bound to return every seven years. One must be ready for such encounters.

The flight from Manila feels like we're barreling through

a wind tunnel. The turboprop is packed with natives loaded with crates of groceries from the mainland, not to mention piglets squealing and chickens squawking in the back, like Noah's ark. Janya grips my arm and digs her nails in every time the plane swoops into an air pocket.

By the time we land in San Crisostomo—the plane skidding down a short runway, barely missing the edge that would have plunged us into a deep volcanic trench— Janya and I are sick as hell, barely able to lug our bags to our rented house by the shore. We try to sleep through the rest of the day, holding each other up as we take turns vomiting in the tiny untiled bathroom.

The next morning, I wake up early to discover brilliant, limpid sunlight all around. The house we've rented is modest, the facade painted sky blue. Its ancient wooden door, rotted by wind and rain, is desiccated so that the wood looks like a giant strip of brittle bark, an old chain looped in two holes where the handles used to be. An iron cross hangs from a pair of rusty nails on the door, the nails pierced right where they should be, through the hands of an embossed Christ. The rust on it looks like dried blood. Three starfish, bleached and dried, adorn the top of the doorway.

The house is a two-room affair: a mahogany table, no doubt imported from the mainland, since even mahogany is no match for the natural forces that lacerate the island; two benches, in disrepair, made of fragile local wood; a bamboo sofa with old, lumpy cushions covered in frayed Thai silk; a rattan shelf with several shells, stones, and flat dried seaweed like the veined remains of leaves, found objects that someone else must have lovingly collected, and for whom they held some private, personal importance.

From the front door, I can see the South China Sea down below, where giant waves crash against submarine, volcanic rock, forcing geysers to spew above the surface, three stories high. Behind the house, streams seep out of the volcano's slopes. Waterfalls pour from unexplored summits.

It's close to Holy Week, the Lenten season when the rains begrudge an uneasy reprieve. What was a stifling, colorless bubble of rain has opened to an omnipresent blue. This respite is as welcome as it is short-lived, starting in April and lasting for just seven weeks, until shortly after Easter.

I can hear Janya throwing up in the bathroom.

"Come out, Janya," I call to her. "It's the weirdest, most beautiful place on earth."

By midday Janya's still ill, and we walk to the town center to seek out a doctor. The locals tell us to look for a guy named Gino, who happens to be the next best thing: he's the island's herbalist. At his house, a lady meets us to say that Gino will take a few more minutes—he's in the back loading his station wagon to go out to sea.

"He's a fisherman too?" I ask the lady.

"Every man on this island is," she replies.

"What the heck does *herbalist* mean?" I whisper to Janya. "Is he even licensed to do this sort of thing?"

"Don't worry, it's probably all homeopathic," she assures me. "Go take a walk. I won't be long."

"Don't let him do anything. Don't let him cut you up or stick a needle in you."

"Oh, for heaven's sake. I'm not a baby. Go get something to eat."

"No sharp or pointed instruments."

"All right already. Go."

I kill time around the small plaza. A recent earthquake has left a jagged crenellation along the remaining walls of the squat stone church. It looks as if a giant shark has taken a bite off it. The church is a hunkered, disproportionate version of medieval European cathedrals, the kind you see in small towns in Umbria. Its walls must be at least five feet thick, a crumbling relic of the Spanish colonial government's effort to defy the elements. Just outside it, women are decking the statue of the Mater Dolorosa with white orchids. The grieving Madonna is perched on a dais, draped in a cloak of black velvet embroidered with gold thread, her lacquer heart pierced by a dozen silver daggers.

The women recognize me, the guy who got really sick on the plane. An unfamiliar face is easily remembered in such a small town. I decide to take advantage of this to tell them the reason Janya and I have come. I ask them if anyone remembers an accident that happened long ago, a two-year-old French boy who got lost at sea and was never found.

The older among them, their faces shrouded in black lace veils, nod and say something to a younger one, who translates in English for me.

"That was the time of the big typhoons," she says. "They came with the boy, and left without him."

"Is that it?"

The young woman asks the older ones and says, "That's all they remember. Many others have been lost at sea."

I should have known that's all I was going to get. It's a wonder anyone even remembers it at all. Maybe they were talking about a completely different boy, a completely different accident. I wonder what the accident rate here must be. I'd be lucky if I found any records, any statistics.

So there it is. No rituals of grieving followed the accident, no remembering, and therefore no pain. Death, after all, is a phenomenon experienced by the living. I wonder if this had made it easier for Sylvain and Annette. Unimpeded by their emotions, the passage from life to death, from memory to forgetting, must have happened more quickly.

I go back to fetch Janya, but the lady at the house tells me she's been brought to the clinic. She gives me very vague directions on how to find it, saying merely that "it's right there."

Following the general direction of her pointed finger, I walk through an alley whose windows overflow with orchids. I'm lost in this profusion of carmine and white, colors incongruous in a landscape so desolate and gray, so that I hardly notice someone dashing out of one of the houses in a confused panic, stopping momentarily, looking absently toward the sea.

It's Janya. She hurries away in the opposite direction, her hand held against her mouth, the terror in her face so unmistakable that even I, at this distance, can feel it. She doesn't see me but keeps walking toward the sea.

A few moments later I see a man coming out. He seems to be running after her, but stops at the door, watching her move away. He goes back in and minutes later comes out again, his arms now loaded with spears, tackle, and nets, which he dumps in the back of a station wagon.

He turns the vehicle around and drives past me, and as he does he stares straight at me, as though he's known all along that I've been standing there. The station wagon heads toward the pier. I can tell he's looking in the rearview mirror at me. Children are pouring out of the school, running in all directions, crossing his path and waving to him. His concentration is divided between me and the narrow road to the pier, his eyes darting from one object to the other, as though he is being pulled in two directions, away from me and toward me, so that his vehicle, ancient and rusty, sputters and stops, backfires and sputters on again, moving out of my sight at a slow, funereal pace.

The children pass by, raucously greeting me in the slow, polite English they've just learned in school. I ask them about the man in the station wagon. Everyone knows it's Gino.

"He's the doctor, right?" I ask them.

They try to find the word for it, but haven't learned it yet. A girl attempts to explain: "He prepares the dead for burying. Everyone needs him."

I finally find Janya back at the house. She looks distraught, and I'm bracing for bad news: malaria, dengue, whatever. Instead she smiles wanly and says, "I'm all right."

"I saw you coming out of the clinic. You got me worried."

"He says I'll be much better in a few days. I feel okay."

"So apparently this guy is not just the local herbalist-slash-doctor, but is also some kind of mortician. And a fisherman, to boot."

"Yeah. Not too many people around here. They have to wear many hats. I asked him about the boy."

"So he's the official historian too?"

"Just thought he might know. Since he's, you know, kind of late-middle-aged. He says that must have happened when he was eighteen or so. He doesn't remember much, except that there was talk of it for a while."

"The women at the plaza said pretty much the same thing."

"He also said there's a myth around here, about people who are lost at sea. It's horrible. I don't want to talk about it."

"Was that why you seemed so upset?"

She doesn't reply.

"Tell me. Get it off your chest."

"Okay. They say those who are lost at sea try to come back every seven years."

"Like ghosts, you mean? Or zombies?"

"I don't know. Like reincarnation, I guess. They try to come back any way they can. And sometimes, if they can't, or if people prevent them from doing so, they get violent."

"Whoa, creepy. Like how?"

"Like pulling other people out to sea. That's why so many others drown. It's a recurring cycle."

"Well, if that's the case, this place is a going to be a ghost town soon."

"Yeah, it's really bizarre. So Third World."

"Well, to be fair, everyone has their crazy myths. When I was growing up, I used to hear a lot about the Cathars, the original people of Provence. They had priests, the *bon gens*, who believed that the act of conception is the worst form of cruelty."

"Life is suffering and all that shit?"

"Yeah. They believed the physical world is an illusion created by the devil Satanael. The world was created to lure people away from the divine. A newborn is one more spark of light trapped in earthly matter, one more soul condemned to human suffering."

"And?"

"And we must do everything we can to prevent them from being born."

"How?"

"I don't know. Contraception? Abortion? In any case, it's a good argument, right? For not having kids. Those double-income-no-kids yuppies in the '80s were on to something."

"So you don't ever want to have kids. In a Cathar sort of way."

"I don't think I'd ever be a good father anyway."

"Guys always say that. Then they become fathers and they change."

"And what if you're right? What if this thing is hereditary? This *condition*."

"I didn't say that. I was just asking."

"What if it were?"

"We don't know that. And it shouldn't bother you so much."

"It does bother me. I'll probably mess up my kid so bad he'll wind up hating me. No, the Cathars made a lot of sense, if you ask me."

"And what would happen if people all thought like that? The extinction of the human race?"

"Ah, the world would be so much better without us, no? No war, no racism, no global warming."

She still seems distraught. I push her hair behind her

ear. She's sweating like crazy. "Anything else that guy told you?"

"No," she says, resolutely. "That's about it."

The next afternoon, I bring back a coconut crab sold to me by a bunch of kids at the plaza. Janya's much better, and I figure it's time we try the local fare.

She's shocked to see it. It's a bizarre, humongous thing, with one claw as large as its body to crack coconuts open. It's been said to have snapped off a human hand or two. But this isn't the reason she's repelled by it.

"That guy told me there's some kind of taboo against eating this creature," she says.

"What guy? What taboo?"

"Gino."

"The medicine man–slash-mortician?"

"He told me that crab's been known to devour the bodies of the drowned. So people here refuse to eat it."

"Come on. It doesn't eat human flesh. And in other parts of the country, it's a rare delicacy."

"Not here. That's why those kids sold it to you. They can't do anything with it."

"Well, no use wasting a perfectly good crab."

I boil a pot of water for it. I lift the crab and hold it over the pot.

"What an awful creature," Janya says. "What an awful death."

"We can throw it back in the water, if you want."

"Okay."

"Sure?"

"You want it, I can tell. That creature is doomed."

I slip the crab in. It turns pale in the boiling water,

thrashes around in the pot, then quickly turns a bright tangerine. In just a few minutes, dinner is done. I place the crab on the table. I twist off the giant claw and smash it with a hammer. The claw oozes a slimy, purple muck. The house is suddenly filled with a sickening, sulfuric stench. She takes the hammer from me and cracks the carapace open.

"What the fuck," she says. The mangled crab is a mush of purple, putrescent ooze. She scoops it in a plastic bag and takes it out.

A vehicle rumbles past the house. She recognizes it. So do I. It's Gino's station wagon. She pretends not to see it, drops the bag in the trash. The station wagon stops briefly in front of the house, the motor sputtering. Gino's looking at her intently, and when he sees me coming out behind her, he steps on the gas and drives away.

I stand by the road, watching the vehicle head off. The hatch open. It's stacked with swordfish, their glistening spears sticking out. I keep on looking until the car rumbles up the road toward the other side of the island.

I look her way. She's standing behind the door, watching me.

"What the fuck was that all about?" I ask her.

"Maybe he wanted to sell his fish. We're the only tourists on the island. We're prime targets."

"He didn't look like he wanted to sell shit to me."

"I don't know, Mathieu. Who knows what these people are up to?"

On the sandy road, there's a bright red scrawl where the station wagon has passed, a vivid trail of blood.

She walks alone to the sea. When she reaches the lunar

crags of volcanic rock she walks barefoot, picking out craters of white sand, shards of coral cutting her soles. At the edge of the water there's a flat bed of porous rock that looks like a hard black sponge.

The water rushes in. A foaming spurt shoots out of a hole about a foot wide. She stands close to it, letting the water drench her.

She notices that I've followed her. She pays no attention but remains standing there. The water keeps pulling out and rushing in, shooting one geyser after another.

Then she turns around to head back home, and as she passes me she says, "I'm going to the dance at the plaza tonight."

"Who with?" I ask. But she's already walked away.

It's the night before Holy Week begins, and rose-colored lights are strung all over the plaza, incandescent bulbs cocooned in paper lanterns, an extravagance on an island with scant electricity to spare.

This is as wild as the residents get before Holy Week. No carnival here, but they've stocked up on *miñavajeng,* which is the only thing they have plenty of, a sweet wine fermented from palm that tonight flows freely.

She left early this evening ahead of me, though I had earlier insisted I wanted to go together. I find her in the plaza. She's wearing a long silk skirt I've never seen. It makes her look foreign to me, more so because with her features, she can blend right in with these people. She's sitting in a corner of the square, on a slab of weathered stone that must have once been part of a wall.

In the center of the plaza, a young girl is dancing a slow dance, her movements simulating the motion of water, accompanied by the high-pitched caterwaul of a violin.

Janya's watching her, mesmerized. Under the rose lights I notice that she's already starting to look older, which first shows in the eyes. She's completely melded with the dancer, and her identity has been willingly annihilated by the presence of one so young.

I stay behind the crowd along the edge of the plaza. I just want to observe her in that state that's unknown to me, in which I don't exist.

I notice a man staring at her from the other side of the plaza and realize it's Gino. He's dressed more formally than the other residents, in a white shirt and bow tie. Imagine that, a bow tie in a place like this. His hair is streaked with gray, sleeked back with pomade. He's smoking a pipe, silver smoke billowing in the air.

She's still watching the young girl. Gino briefly turns his attention to the dancer, watching her move. But this doesn't interest him. His gaze goes back to Janya. She shifts her attention briefly toward him, no more than a fleeting glance, and smiles.

And in that evanescent moment, for some reason I know something inescapable has begun, something I have seen coming but had pointedly refused to acknowledge.

I walk toward her and sit by her side. She doesn't even notice me, or if she does, she doesn't want to be distracted from this trance. Gino is still watching her. He keeps his eyes on her even as I ask, "You know that man is staring at you, right?"

"At her," she says, meaning the girl. "Not me."

"Who is she?"

"*Patec,*" she replies, without even looking my way.

She's using the local dialect, one of hundreds in this archipelago, and spoken only on this island. She has always picked up languages fast, which never fails to surprise me. "That's his daughter. *Patec*, cocoon, someone who's about to grow wings."

That night, after the dance, lying by her side, I hear a strange sound coming from somewhere very close, as close as my heart. Then I realize it's me, I've been talking in my sleep. I turn over to her side to see if she's awake, if she's heard. I'm hoping she hasn't.

"I don't like this place," I whisper. "I wish we hadn't come."

She's lying on her side, facing me, staring at me blankly. She lifts her hand to touch me, then changes her mind. Her hand hangs in midair, then she pulls it away and turns her back to me.

I force my eyes open. Darkness. The roar bursting out of my heart, like a series of explosions, a rapid fire that shakes me out of bed.

Janya follows me out of the room. The wooden shutters are slamming in the wind. A flash of lightning illuminates the shuddering walls. We rush around the house, latching the bars against the shutters. They seem to heave and swell, as though the wood has become pliant.

The storm has come suddenly, without warning. The wind howls, spinning round and round the house, so close and so alive we can follow its sound encircling us, like an animal finding a way in.

One of the shutters breaks open. A spray of water, like a boat that has sprung a leak. And then a fluttering cloud of wings, a distressed flock of sparrows, bursts in and fills the room.

The next morning we survey the damage done by the storm. She picks up the shattered remains of shells, studies them intently, and finally casts them aside.

"We can move to another house," I tell her. "It's no big deal."

"It's time to go," she says.

"You forget why we came here."

"No one remembers anything. It makes no sense to stay."

We take a jeep to the island's airport, the old army barracks a short distance from the square. Today the short stretch of grassy field that serves as its runway has been taken over by ducks and goats. Another, larger storm has been spotted over the South China Sea, a swirling, germinating nebula blinking on the local meteorological station's radar screen. She peers at the monitor silently for a long time, unaware of the amused stares of the locals who peek in. They've seen hundreds of tourists stranded before.

Outside, I can see the runway stretching on one end toward the sea, and on the other toward the dormant volcano. The volcano's slope is a deep emerald green, streaked with silver rivulets of water that course from still undiscovered sources, primitive and pure.

The wind starts to pick up again. Acacia trees quiver. I can hear the murmuring rustle of their branches as they brace for yet another typhoon. We are trapped in all this beauty.

* * *

We finally manage to catch a flight out three days later, changing planes in Tuguegarao, at another rundown airport. It looks like the site of a military coup with its barracks and guards bearing M16s.

An antiquated DC-10 takes us back to Manila. All through the hour's flight we are hammered by the storm, which seems intent on pursuing us, giving up only when we're halfway south to the city, growling like a mad dog that's just victoriously defended its territory, foaming at the mouth, catching its breath, still barking an occasional thunder or two just to make sure the intruders continue scuttling away.

We arrive in the city that afternoon in niggling but less ferocious rain. In the taxi to the hotel, I blurt out the question that's been nagging me: "What happened between you and that guy?"

"What guy?"

"That Gino."

"I don't know what you mean."

"Then what the fuck is wrong?"

"Nothing's wrong. I'm tired. Going there was a stupid thing to do."

At a stoplight, I roll the window down and buy strands of jasmine from a homeless girl peddling them along the road. The girl must be no more than ten or eleven, her tattered dress soaked with rain and torn in many places, revealing patches of dark, glistening skin that she makes no effort to hide.

"That's two cents for every strand," Janya says. "That's all she lives on."

The girl holds out her hand to accept my peso. The city's blurred landscape is a mess of shanties and high-rises. And endless crowds, bodies without faces. There are many more of these young girls in the city but they're just bodies among other bodies, mere objects, temporary and corruptible, plenteous and replaceable. The supply is inexhaustible. The long trip back has made me queasy and weak. The rain patters into the cab. I roll the window up. The taxi is filled with the flowers' cloying perfume.

One boy will be lost, another will be saved.

It was either his life or mine.

The law of equations is simple and astonishing.

the little toil of love

The lieutenant catches Eddie jacking off. He & the guy with the Uzi drag him out of his cot, make him jack off in front of them. They make it interesting for him. They burn him with cigarettes, hit his arms & thighs with the butt of the Uzi, stick a wax candle up his ass. Make him lick his shit off the candle, eat his come off the floor.

The next night the steel springs of Eddie's cot are squeaking again. Outside the cell, the guy with the Uzi's making the same noise, fucking his own cot. The body's infinite dangers, its incessant needs.

After my grandfather left her, my grandmother was rumored to have burned all his pictures in a bonfire that lasted for 3 days. She explained later that she did it not out of rancor, but simply because that's what you do. You release the dead & you move on.

Why am I remembering this?

Nobody remembers what he looked like, but I've always presumed he looked like me. People carry some remnant of their predecessors in them, some sleeping dream inside their proteins.

Sometimes I wonder if there's some hidden instinct inside our bodies that prompts us to continue what's been done before, just like Nietzsche said—if our bodies are destined to undergo the same histories, the same failures, the same joys, & we are unable to wrestle ourselves away from them because of some inherited gene, a built-in flaw, a technical kink.

If so, is life then a persistent & futile effort to improve on what has failed before?

This is me, or my best attempt at a likeness of me.

My name is Andrew Brezsky. Several generations of my family, I've been told, migrated from England & Poland through Holland, Canada, & finally the United States. I think I am a father. I think I have a son. Two. Maybe. I wonder if I can be a good father. Or will my picture burn in a 3-day bonfire, so they will never remember me. Maybe one day a wife & 2 kids, for real, maybe.

My name is Andrew Brezsky. I am an American, & though I'm aware that this shouldn't be so, my being American is all I need to get by in this part of the world.

We rule. Nick believes this like it's the word of God. They'll never harm an American, he says. They know they need every single one of us. Only America can save a country as fucked up as this.

The student's starting to bug me. He keeps asking me what I'm here for. That an American citizen should be detained for so long is unheard of. I tell him anything, Nick's new job, my grandmother's story, I tell him anything just to get him off my back.

I know what you're here for, he tells me. Don't think we're ever going to be friends.

The student believes he has a mission to save his country, if not the world. That's what he's been trying to tell Eddie. But Eddie doesn't understand or give a damn. Eddie: toothless, skinny, severely fucked up by acid, wood glue, & crack. He doesn't even have to hide his name. That means in the scheme of things, he's a nobody. He's got nothing to protect.

The student asks me what I'm fighting for.

Nothing, I tell him. He may be fighting to save the world, but I trust nobody around here.

Then you're useless, he says. One must always fight.

Why do I have to fight for <u>something</u>? You do things your way, buddy, & I do them my way. Even if I cared about the world's hungry & poor, what's the use of my caring? We use it to move things a little bit, but nothing's ever enough. How do I tell him that? It's crazy to think anyone can save the world. It's vanity & megalomania. Even dictators become dictators because somehow, deep in their hearts, they believe they've been chosen to save the world. Everyone is chosen. There lies the problem. Everyone wants to do something. Everyone thinks his, & no other's, is the only way. Everyone is <u>deranged with purpose</u>.

The student watches me all the time. He wears plastic spectacles held together at the joints by rubber bands. He's severely myopic & the lenses make him look like he's squinting & scrutinizing everything. I've learned that Marcos issued a warrant for his arrest on the very night Marcos declared martial law. That means that on the government's watch list, he's probably up there with the big honchos, the senators & Communists. He fled to Cebu straight out of class & was caught a month later when some stool pigeon told the lieutenant he was hiding in a Catholic seminary in the city.

He insists on finding out who Andrew Brezsky really is. I know what he's thinking: Every American is a spook. Every one of us works for the CIA. He & Eddie say it to my face, but they say it like it's a kind of joke, like they know my being here is a kind of joke. They get very personal with me. I've gotten used to that. In this country they want to know every intimate detail about you, & only by knowing you that close can they get comfortable with you.

Andrew Brezsky has no family, no siblings. He's rootless & homeless. He has no country. He's lost touch with the handful of friends who've immigrated to Canada & left him no forwarding address. The only time he felt really homesick was in February 1971, when he heard that an earthquake hit the San Fernando Valley. 64 people died. His parents among them. He was 19 & living in fucking fucked-up Manila & couldn't even fucking go home.

Is that personal enough for you?

My mother, age 18, talking about the occupation of Krakow.

Looking down over the bridge, among the teeming streets of the ghetto, she saw 2 little girls, age 4 or 5, holding hands. They were dressed in filthy rags, threadbare hoods over their heads. They were rocking to & fro, first on one leg & then the other, not letting go of each other, aimlessly swaying, as though they couldn't help it, they were animated by something other than themselves. Winter was over. They were looking up at her. They were smiling. The sun was bright behind her, it must have been blinding, but they kept looking, dazzled by it, by the flood of light everywhere.

My mother had never been to Krakow. But she always

said people were more interesting if they had a history. You must remember, Andy, & you must live with your story. Because that is who you are. That is what makes you you.

& for years, if you asked her what she remembered most when she was 18, she would say the exact same story. 2 little girls, holding hands. They were rocking to & fro, first on one leg, & then the other, & never letting go.

Eddie's just had a dream.

He's on a boat gliding down a river. Everything is dark around him. Suddenly the boat sinks to the bottom. He struggles to swim to the surface. Someone reaches out to grab him. It's Jesus.

Eddie rises, pulled out of the water by the hand of Jesus, & wakes up. For days thereafter he feels physically uplifted, lighter, buoyant, saved.

I'm the only one who listens to Eddie. He knows that even in an equal world, the world the student talks about, he's pegged a little lower than anyone else. So he hangs on to me like I'm his only friend. One evening he dumps half his portion of rice on my plate.

> I had no time to hate, because
> the grave would hinder me,
> and life was not so ample I
> could finish enmity.

Eddie looks over my shoulder & wants to know why I have to remember the entire poem, every syllable, every punctuation.

I tell him it's for my son.

You have a son??

I tell him I have two.

He can't believe it. He says I'm just a kid myself. Now he wants to know more, & I have to make something up for him. I tell him they're living with their mother in New York. Is that close to California? he asks. Yes, sort of. They're in New York but I think the other one is somewhere else, maybe Paris. Or Strasbourg. Or whatever. Then it gets too complicated & now Eddie thinks I'm a slut with two wives living in two different parts of the world. No wonder you're in jail, he says. You're practically a rapist, like me. Or a son-of-a-bitch Muslim.

Eddie likes me. He thinks I'm his best friend. But he can't make heads or tails of the poem, which I show him to change the topic.

So how are your sons going to figure it out? he asks. Are they geniuses or something?

Good question. I don't even know if they'll read this. I don't even know who they are, or where they are. I don't tell Eddie this. I have to keep up the story. Eddie's like that. He has to have a story.

So I tell him it's just a kind of puzzle for me, to see if my memory's in good shape.

Eddie: That's fine, but what's the point of memory if you'd rather forget?

Eddie, he can be pretty sharp sometimes. I'm the only one who knows about his dream. Eddie thinks God is trying to tell him something, but He does so in a language like the poem, a language Eddie doesn't understand. Eddie says Jesus died on the cross because only God can endure the suffering that humans must go through. To endure human suffering, you must be like God. And this, my Yankee friend, is never going to happen.

Juan Perón has been elected president of Argentina.

Twenty-six bombs explode in Belfast on what people are starting to call Bloody Friday.

The Vietcong have formed a revolutionary government in Quàng Tri, South Vietnam.

~~Revolution~~ is everywhere. Bad word. Strike that out.

I hear the news on the radio that the guy with the Uzi plays all day long. He doesn't care about the news. He just likes the noise. I think he just likes to hear the sound of a human voice. When the news gets too annoying, as it always does, he turns the dial to some local station playing sentimental love songs in Tagalog.

The world is happening everywhere. But it has come to a standstill here, where I am.

Am I to be thankful, then, that my world has become so still?

But it is not so still. It is crouching in the dark, waiting to pounce, waiting for the first moving target that comes its way.

No, I will not have these thoughts.

Change your mind, change your mind, change your mind.

Don't get fucked.

Don't let anybody get you fucked.

Eddie wants me to write him a story.

He wants it to be something no one's ever told before. Which means it has to be about something out of this world.

Like science fiction, I tell him.

But he doesn't know what that means. He just wants the story to be moving & short enough for him to remember it, so he can tell it to his sister when he's released from prison. It'll be the best thing he can bring back to her, since he's got nothing else: a story no one's ever heard before, written specially for him by a Yankee who trusted that he'd understand & remember.

Christmas Eve.

I've been here a month & ten days. A priest arrives to say Mass at the precinct. He's an old man who looks like he's just come down from another world. There are other people I've never seen before, officers from other precincts & their families. How ordinary they look, wives & children like any other.

The lieutenant & the guy with the Uzi are kneeling on the front pew, their eyes shut, only their lips moving. At Communion they all pass by in a single file, their heads bowed, their hands clasped before them. It doesn't look right. But I guess it doesn't really matter. Even torturers pray to God & take Holy Communion.

God, in His infinite mercy, merely looks away.

The lieutenant confiscates my notebook & forbids me to write anything else. He says he just wants to take a look at it. He returns it a couple of days later. There are black marker lines all across some pages. Several others have been torn off.

You & I are friends, he says, but don't abuse our friendship.

That doesn't bother me so much. It's irritating though

that the notebook now springs open by itself, because the missing pages have weakened the binding, & I have to hold it close all the time or press it down with a heavy object, like a shoe.

Who's she fucking now?

Same old, Nick says. It's Sunday again, visiting day. Nick's brought me coffee & a letter from Liana. I lay it on the table but I don't open it.

She says just say so, says Nick, & we'll call the embassy.

I tell him don't fucking call the embassy. He knows what's going to happen when they call.

She knows people now, he says.

I fucking know she fucking knows people. She's fucking with these people, that's how much she knows them. She's damn fucking the same people who got me in here. Tell her to fucking leave me alone.

All right, he says. She's just trying to help.

I tell him sending me to shoot the gooks isn't going to help. We're distracted by the sound of a baby squealing at a table next to ours. As usual, families have come to see if new people or new bodies have been brought in. They stay on even when the guy with the Uzi tells them to go home. The room is more packed than usual. I think it's because Christmas is when people worry about whether other people are unhappy. That makes no sense. Human concern has never alleviated human unhappiness. I decide I shouldn't tell this to Nick. The visitors have brought food, blankets, clothes, cigarettes, & one mother even brought some booze, which is good for the guy with the Uzi, who confiscates it & will guzzle it later.

You all right in there? Nick asks. Have they been fucking with you? It sounds like the proper thing to ask anyone who's in prison, although I've never thought of a proper response till now.

No, I say, they don't fuck with me, not really, I don't think they'll hurt me or anything. That doesn't sound very interesting. I decide maybe I shouldn't sound cheerful or hopeful. So I tell him, They know everything. They know what I've done.

What the fuck have you done anyway?

Stuff. They're all in the missing pages of my notebook. It's all there. They're keeping them all.

For what?

I don't know. But I guess they need it for my confession. They're going to use it as my admission of guilt.

What guilt, Andy? What the fuck have you done?

Well, you know, stuff. It's very annoying, I tell him, because much as I hate to admit it, sometimes I'm afraid. I'm not, really, but I've decided that's what Nick expects to hear. I get bored & irritated & even angry sometimes, but I've never really felt afraid, at least not for myself. I feel I have to qualify my answer. So I tell him I'm afraid I'll forget everything, & then I'll realize I'm just like everyone else in this place, erasing everything, slowly chipping away at memory, thinking that's the only way to survive.

Stop talking shit, Nick says. I can't help you if you don't tell me what the fuck got you in here.

I tell him I'm going to give him everything I write from now on. He'll have to keep them for me. & if they confiscate anything else, I'll just have to tell him everything when he comes & visits. He'll have to remember everything for me.

We got to get you out soon, says Nick. This place

is really making you nuts. You're going to be all right?

Fucking no, Nick. I insist that he spirit away whatever I write each time he comes to visit me. I tell him I have this strange, sickening feeling that this is all I am. Nothing else will remain of me. He'll have to do as I say. & as soon as I say it, I have a funny feeling that I mean it, that it really is important to me.

It's all that acid, Nick says. It's all those ludes, man, they really messed you up.

I tell Nick I got money. Lots of money.

How? he asks.

I got hooked up with this mob, kind of.

Jesus fuck, he says, slapping his forehead.

I have all their money.

What's it for?

Payback money. I sold something. Someone. A boy. My boy. I had a fucking boy, Nick. Maybe two. I did it for them. I sold them. I got the money. These guys, they're all part of it. Everyone is involved.

Nick's rolling his eyes up. He wants to know more, but visiting time is over. I can't believe this, Andy, he tells me. This is way too crazy even for me.

I tell him he has to promise. He has to remember everything I say.

All right, he answers. But FYI, I'm not like you. I'm not the one who can memorize all those lists. All those freaking poems. I don't know how you do it. I can't even remember who I fucked last night.

We are held in place by gravitational forces

M other, I've found my brother."

She is staring at the TV screen, staring at nothing. It's a replay of the 9/11 memorial at Ground Zero, bagpipes in the background, names being listed by a couple of readers, a lot of Garcias and Gonzalezes.

"What is it, Mother?"

"I'm waiting for my name. They're taking a long time to read my name."

"They won't read your name, Mother."

"They're only in the G's."

"I'll open the window a little. It's a beautiful day."

"Like the day I died. I saw the plane coming in, straight at me. The heat enveloped me. At first it was a warmth like an embrace, and then it stung every nerve in me. I burned instantly."

She sounds like she's being beaten up.

In the apartment down below I can hear things crashing against the wall. A plate, something made of glass. I press my ear against the floor. She is crying. She is saying, *Oh my God, oh my God.* Her voice is stifled, a cry caught in the throat. *No, stop, it hurts, oh my God.* Then everything is quiet, and there is no other sound but her whispering. I get up and turn the lights off and open the blinds a little.

An amber light shines from down below. I can see

part of their kitchen, the sink and the black-and-white-checkered linoleum. Everything is quiet now. I hold my breath.

Then she is talking calmly, quietly, to someone. I lie on the floor again and press my ear against it. I can hear the hum of a fan. She is talking about getting something to eat. A deep voice, a man's, asks her what she wants. I can hear the beeping sound of the phone, and her voice, lower this time, saying how he's hurt her arm, how her nipple smarts. *You bit mine too*, he says. She sounds like she's laughing. *I want real food*, she says. *That's too much to swallow*. A pause, silence, just the whir of the fan. Then her long, slow moaning again, *No, stop*. I close my eyes and imagine how soft she is, her lips open a little as she whispers those words, her nails digging lunettes of blood into my back.

The next morning she has a UPS parcel left at the front door. I take a few minutes pondering what to do, then I pick it up and take it to her apartment. I leave it at her door and walk away. Then I start worrying that someone will come by and steal it. I turn back, knock once. Long pause. The click of the peephole cover. Another pause. She opens the door. I tell her I'm looking for "Y. Fischer." She stares at me, wondering. I pick up the parcel. "It was downstairs. I think it's yours."

"Oh," she says, hardly surprised.

"I thought it was for a guy. The Y, I mean."

"It's Yuki," she says.

"You don't look Japanese."

"I'm not. I'm only half Japanese. That's the part I like the least."

"I'm half something else myself."

"Everyone in New York is half something else. You don't look it. Half something, I mean."

"My mother said my father was white. My real mother was Filipino. I was adopted."

"Ah."

She's wearing a terry cloth bathrobe that's loosely tied at the waist. She smells like she's just stepped out of the shower, like Irish Spring. She catches me staring.

"Sorry, I didn't realize I was disturbing you," I say.

"Thanks for bringing the package up. That was nice of you. Wanna come in? Have some tea. It's *Japanese*." Her laugh sounds like water bubbling.

She says she knows I have just moved into the apartment above. She saw me moving in, and adds that I'm probably the quietest neighbor she has ever had. I hesitate at the door.

"Oh, it's all right," she says. "My boyfriend's not around."

"And it's not all right if he's around?"

"No. But he's not around."

Her apartment looks exactly like ours. The same layout, the same pink tiles in the bathroom, whose door she shuts quickly when she catches me looking in. She says something funny about it. "An interior-design casualty from the '50s." Her bedroom is right below mine. Her bed is exactly where I have mine. There is a cello beside the bed. She asks me what I'm looking for.

"A cello," I say.

"Why?"

"It's a beautiful instrument. I mean, it's like, you know, a sensuous object. I mean, you know, it touches the senses, more than any other instrument. That's what I meant. You embrace it, you stroke it, you lean your head against its neck, and it gives a low, sorrowful sound, like someone moaning with pleasure. I hear you playing it every day."

I turn to face her. She is standing close to me, looking straight into my eyes. Her eyes are a deep black, and they seem like they have no pupils, just a deep, solid black. "I guess you found it," she says.

"What?"

"The cello."

"Oh."

"Sorry if it bothered you."

"No. I like it. I like listening to you. I always wondered what you looked like. I mean, someone who played so beautifully must be, you know, beautiful. Inside, I mean. And outside too, of course."

"Not necessarily."

I make my way out but in the awkward shuffle I almost slip, or she almost slips, and I hold on to her, supporting her by the waist. She smiles.

"It's nice," I tell her. "To, you know . . ."

"What?"

"It's nice to talk to someone."

"You like to talk?"

"Yeah. Sorry." I pull my hand away.

She holds my hand down. "Abs," she says.

"What?"

"I've been working on my abs. Musicians have to be fit. It's a grueling job."

Her waist is very small, like a cello's. She takes my hand and slips it inside her robe. When I touch her skin the shock sends a jolt through my body and she feels it, I can tell, because her body gives a slight shiver.

"It's nice," I say. "Your abs."

"Maybe she was lying."

"Who?"

"Your mother."

"About what?"

"About your being half white."

"But I am. There's no mistaking it. Just like you. Why would she do that?"

"To make you feel special. It's nice to be half white and half something else. We all have reasons. To lie, that is. I like being half and half. Best of both worlds, you might say. Exotic and, well, powerful. Yeah, that's it. It makes me feel more powerful. Do you like me being half white?"

"Yes."

"Tell me you like me."

"I like you."

I rub my fingers lightly against her belly. I can feel her goose bumps.

"Tell me I'm beautiful," she says.

"You're beautiful. I like you."

"Liar."

She opens her robe and I lean down and place my lips on her nipple. I think of Mother's Brazilian boyfriend. Her nipple is small and pink and delicately pointed. There is a barely discernible cut below the aureole where it was bitten the night before. She tastes like salt, like blood, like sleep.

The Russian soldier wakes up on a hospital bed only to find that his legs and genitals have been amputated. Then there's another story. A pregnant woman checks into a hospital in Florida and wakes up with both her legs and arms sawed off.

She watches nothing but the news. Over and over. The six o'clock recaps, the late-night summaries. Everything is horrifying. She can't take her eyes off the screen. The mutilated bodies. The scabbed, wrecked souls.

She can't stop thinking of the Russian soldier and the chopped-up mother. That's what they do when they put you to sleep. They hover around you, snickering at your flaccid body. Your chicken body. The sagging skin, the anal cavity yawning wide open, ready to receive a fistful of stuffing. They toss a coin and decide which part to cut off. The thigh or the wing? You lie half awake, in a dream-like stupor, alive but completely paralyzed, and all you can do is listen as they make lurid jokes about your face, your stomach, your pubic hair. The blade cuts through your bones. Your mouth opens and a strange noise comes out, like wind funneling through a hole in the sky. You are helpless against this whirring, grinding metamorphosis.

I tell her television is full of shit. Like radiation, it slowly eats away at your brain.

"The world is full of shit," she says. "What you see there is what the world is. Television is truth."

I try to open the window to let some air in.

"Leave it closed," she says. "The noise hurts my soul."

"Stop watching the news. It'll make you sick." I help her up. I pour her tea.

"Who are you?"

"You know who I am."

"Leave me alone," she says. "What's that noise?"

I turn the lock. The window gives a deep-bellied grunt.

Everything in the room is suddenly still. It is an unnerving silence, the silence of an incubator, and all I can hear
is the bulb in her night lamp sputtering, as if a moth were
hitting against it fatally. I try to open the window again,
but it's stuck. I try to force it open. It won't budge. I will
forget about it and only remember it months later, when
she is gone, and Simone, her caregiver, will insist that I
open the window and let some air in, and I will bend my
thumb backward trying to do so.

All that time, while she is in that room, the window
will never be opened again. I remember thinking about
that later, although I don't know why or what it's supposed to mean. Sometimes the most ordinary of moments, opening or not opening a window, begins a series
of events that will culminate in the terrible future that we
so fear. I never stop looking for signs.

The doctors have asked me to try and jog Mother's memory. Talk about the past. My childhood. Our house in
Westchester. Give her some brain exercise, give that gray
matter a good workout. It's not proven, though it might
just help.

But she remembers nothing except what her delusions
have implanted in her brain. In her dreams the Russian
boy appears again and again, his fatigues soaked in blood.
Or the mother with sewed-up stubs where her arms and
legs used to be, thumping dully on the floor as she skitters
under the bed, small and scared like Kafka's cockroach.

I tell her about the doctor's suggestion. She is convinced the doctors have sneaked in one night and cut her
up and taken her stomach out. She has only one lung left.
Her liver has been sliced in half and refuses to regener-

ate, as normal livers should. Doctors can't be trusted.

"But look at these X-rays. All your organs are there."

"They were there yesterday. They're not there today."
She's sitting in an armchair and thumps her fingers on her
belly, producing a hollow sound, like a drum. "And look,
they even took my soul."

I tell her there is no such thing. No such thing as a
soul. You can't take away what doesn't exist.

"But that Russian boy . . . that young mother in
Florida—"

"Okay, enough. I made some pasta."

"I'm not hungry."

"You haven't eaten all day."

"The dead don't need to eat. We know there's nothing
anyone can do. Death is irreversible. Once you're dead,
you're dead. You can't negotiate about it."

She has already grown thin, pale, ghostly. "How easy
it is to die," she says. "All you have to do is close your eyes
and let go."

"But you're still with me, Mother. You're talking to
me. Those are clear signs that you're not dead. You're not
dead, Mother. Please."

She's staring at the TV screen. Something trickles
down the floor, a slow, steady stream coming from underneath her feet.

I grab a rag in the kitchen and when I come back
there's a big yellow puddle under the chair.

"Don't let them defeat you," I tell her.

"Who?"

"Don't let the bastards grind you down."

"Who are you?"

"Jordan."

"You asked them to come."

I stop and look up. "What?"

"You wanted something to happen. It did."

"You know that's not true."

"I remember. You wanted them to come."

I finish mopping her piss and throw the rag in the bathroom trash. I can hear the TV and something else, something buzzing in my brain, something incoherent.

I slip a CD in the boom box in the living room and play it loud enough for her to hear. I walk back into her room. She has turned the TV off and is listening.

"Brahms," I tell her. "You like Brahms."

"Yes."

I sit with her and listen for a long time until she falls asleep. "I'm sorry, Mother. I never wanted them to come. That wasn't what I meant."

I lift her back to bed. I am surprised to discover how small she is, how light as a bird.

One night I dream that I am visiting her grave. I find it in a muddy nook of the Chinese cemetery in Manila. Not far off is a thicket of gaudy mausoleums, pagodas painted in Big Mac colors, summer yellow and bloodred.

I've never been to Manila. The only thing I know about it is that there are many areas in the city that Americans are advised not to go to, and that people are kidnapping anyone with so much as a couple dollars in their pocket. I have only heard her talk about it, derisively, bitterly. She once said they didn't have cemeteries but drainage holes where the useless dead were flushed out of sight. (That image, buried deep in my memory, was perhaps what triggered my dream.) She used to call it the black hole of

Asia, so utterly hopeless and without enough imagination to pull itself out of the sinkhole it's become.

"I saved you," she told me once, so long ago I am surprised to remember it today. "I saved you from the black hole."

Cotard's syndrome normally lasts only about three months. Mother keeps getting sicker for over a year. At some point I try to contact someone who could possibly be her closest living relative, a cousin named Wayne Brogan Yeats of Park Slope. He is listed among the few Yeatses in the white pages simply as WB, which seems to me a good sign: literate, sensitive, spiritual. But cousin WB turns out to be a Republican who believes that *Roe v. Wade* is the handiwork of the devil. He cut off ties with Mother a long time ago.

Mother's disorder gets worse. The doctors practically give up on her. Or, what is the same, we give up on them. The shrapnel beside her heart gives her ever more pain. It becomes intolerable for me to watch her suffer, to watch her as though she were, in fact, truly dead or dying.

The worst of it is, like television, like the news, I can't look away.

I tell Yuki what's going on.

"They hurt her pretty bad, didn't they?" she says.

"She's doing okay. You can come up and meet her."

"No."

"Why not?"

"I'm not good with sympathy. Never been. I'm a cold-hearted bitch."

"No, you're not." I tell her about the game Mother and

I used to play when I was growing up, how she made me write to my real father, Andrew Brezsky, who lived on the moon.

"And did you write to him?"

"Yes, all the time."

"And did he respond?"

"No. But it felt good to ask. So last night I wrote to Brezsky to ask if Mother is ever going to get better again."

"And there's no answer."

"No. I didn't expect any. Her painkillers aren't working anymore. I'm not sure I know what to do."

"My boyfriend knows someone. He can get you the real thing."

"I'm not sure I want to give Mother anything stronger. I don't think it'll help. It's her mind that's fucking her up . . . I wish Andrew Brezsky was real. I really need some answers from him, wherever he is."

"The answer is simple. In a situation like this, you either do nothing, or you look for a way out. You can't save those who refuse to be saved."

"I'm hoping Mother will snap out of it and be her old self again, and all this is just a nightmare. And nightmares always end."

"Let me tell you one thing: hope is a fiction of the mind. It's like Cremora. It's always nice to have a little around. It makes coffee taste less bitter. It makes you think you're drinking cream, but it's all chemicals and additives. And one of these days it's probably going to kill you."

"That's a cruel thing to say."

"I want to be honest. Brutal, but honest. Don't live in a dream world, Jordan. Face the facts. It's the only way you can help her."

No one else has spoken to me so candidly. I have come to rely on her every word.

Yuki always smokes in bed after sex, the way people used to do in movies, which made them appear elegantly languorous, with just a touch of ennui. We lie side by side, not talking until she finishes the cigarette, tapping the ash now and then on an ashtray beside the bed, which she often misses, the smoldering clump of ash, still aglow from within, floating like a small meteor onto the sheets.

Tonight, after she stubs the cigarette out, she gets up and plays the cello. Her bare arms wrap around it amorously as she rehearses the prelude of Bach's first suite for violoncello. She attacks the first few bars over and over, until Bach becomes not celestial but redundant, neurotic, sinister. She stops and tells me to get dressed.

"What time is he coming back?" I ask.

"In an hour. Give me the keys. Those are his keys."

I reach for my jeans, fumble in the pocket, and toss them to her. "How long is he gonna stay?"

"For as long as he wants." She watches me get dressed. "Every time I fuck you, I feel lonely after."

"Is it the same with him?"

"No. Just with you."

"Why are you cheating on him then?"

She stops in midbar. Long pause. "You know why."

"Tell me."

"He fucks around when he's on tour."

"How do you know that?"

"I know."

"How?"

"Anybody who's as beautiful as that is bound to be

fucking around. He doesn't have to find love. Love finds
him. Every fucking woman, every fucking man. Every
fucking place he goes."

"And that's where I come in?"

She starts Bach all over again. I walk to the door.

"Love finds you too," I tell her. "I found you."

She's not paying attention.

"I rely on your every word. You are my—"

"You pass your loneliness on to other people," she
says. "Like a virus."

"I'm not lonely. I never thought I was, until I met you."

I close the door. I hear her playing the cello again,
the same bars over and over, the sound following me as I
walk back to my apartment.

There are agencies all over the web that can track a missing person through public records. Birth certificates,
school reports, traffic violations, criminal records, voter
registrations, marriage or divorce papers, fishing or hunt-
ing licenses, dog permits, public library records, Social
Security, last city of residence—archaeological evidence,
the fossils of our existence.

Not one of them turns up for Andrew Brezsky. My
search for his personal history leads me to nowhere but
dead ends. Finally one agency, Ameri-Find, tells me what
I've always suspected. Andrew Brezsky doesn't exist.
That is, he must have been using a pseudonym. This isn't
surprising, given my real dad was basically a stud-for-
hire, and Mother, in the state she's in, has only revealed
conflicting details in sporadic installments, which I am
only able to jigsaw together, haphazardly, over time. To
make matters more complicated, Manila is notorious for

not keeping records. If any are stored at all, they will have been lost by now through force majeure—the perpetual cycles of fire, flood, and negligence that plague that country where lives mean little, and the memory of lives, therefore, is utterly insignificant.

But still one question bothers me: why sign his bequest with a pseudonym? I feel if I revealed the circumstances in which I was conceived, Ameri-Find would know what to do. Their response, not surprisingly, is swift and straightforward. They suggest, no doubt to get me off their back, that I direct my search elsewhere: it is just possible that my alleged brother may have some leads. And perhaps the best way to find him is to first find the notary public who executed the bequest, if that person still exists.

I call Yuki up to tell her what I'm going to do.

"No," she says, flustered, unable to hide her exasperation. I can hear her boyfriend asking who it is. "You have the wrong number."

Their voices are muffled and unclear. Occasionally I can hear something, but it is unrecognizable, some kind of disembodied sound, nonhuman, a nonsensical monotone, her boyfriend asking her the same thing over and over, *You like that? Like that? That?* I lie flat on the floor. My bare chest presses hard against the wood, which is cold against my skin. I imagine I am down below myself, my body smashed tight against hers. They are moaning heavily, they don't care if everyone in the building hears them. I slip my hand inside my sweatpants, press my lips against the floor, and taste dust. I shoot my come on the floor and remain lying there until the voices stop, and all I hear is the whir of the ceiling fan above her bed.

In the next room Mother is breathing heavily. She is fast asleep. I roll on my back. I want so much to sleep. I feel a constriction in my chest, a tightening in my throat. I am surprised by the sheer physicality of it, how it overwhelms my entire body. It bothers me that this is all I feel when I think about Yuki, this physical pain. But no emotions. No tenderness, jealousy, obsession, sadness, or even hate. They are just words. They mean nothing. She can offer me nothing, because I need nothing from her. Or I have convinced myself that I have no such needs. Same thing. The sounds from her apartment fade as I sink to sleep. I wake an hour later. I have had a vague dream of being alone in the wide-open sea. In the dream there was absolutely no sound. Just water. Just vastness. Just me, adrift in an endless calm.

Dear Mr. Brezsky,

You stuck your dick in the cunts of a couple of native women and now it's up to me to clean up the mess you made. I've posted an appeal on the message board of Ameri-Find. But if you think somebody's actually going to find it in that morass of junk on the Internet, you're probably still stuck somewhere in 1972. If you do find my brother, tell him to contact me immediately. Maybe we could piece together the enigma that was you, the guy who sold us for a measly fifteen thousand bucks. Thanks a lot, asshole.

It's just past happy hour at the Pit, happy hour lasting way past ten to accommodate young kids who don't have much money to spend. Yuki mentioned that her boyfriend likes to go to the Pit and has taken her there a couple of times, though it is really more his scene, not hers. All she ever does there is watch him and his friends smoke crack. I don't like the idea of going to places that her boy-friend thinks are cool, but it can't be that bad—Rudolph Giuliani had it closed down twice, at the height of his Disneyfication campaign to purge the city of drugs, pros-titutes, and the homeless. One reason had to do with a young student passing out and dying on the dance floor. It can't be that bad.

I strike up a conversation with a group of students from NYU who are more than willing to show me how cool they are. One of them, a senior, appears to be the coolest of the gang, and keeps yelling in my ear.

"It's those of us who can't afford the city's diversions who soon realize we're all living in a vacuum, a fucking dead-end street. We're trapped in this labyrinth, we've been seduced by it, we live in a fucking dream, and there's no fucking way out. All we can do is watch ourselves sink deeper and deeper into doom."

They introduce me to Ugo, a bouncer who resembles Mr. Clean. Ugo looks me over suspiciously. "He's one of us," the senior tells him, and fifty dollars later Ugo doesn't really care. He tells me to meet him in one of the bathrooms upstairs in the back, and as he walks me over he explains why I am wise to get my drugs from the right source.

"Anyone can tell you it's fucking easier to find your drug of choice nowadays than to find a fucking decent job. The trick is finding out how fucking easy it is. Only unqualified stupidity will get you some fucked-up cock-tail of additives. Lidocaine. Strychnine. Powdered milk. Ajax fucking cleaner. Injected into the bloodstream, that shit will shrivel your brain in seven fucking seconds."

In the bathroom there are two guys inside one of the stalls. They have left the door unlocked, and it's open just enough for me to glimpse what is going on. The white guy, his jeans dropped to his ankles, is bent over, his legs spread apart, his elbows propped against the water tank. There is a persistent thud coming from the dance floor, the sound of a racing heartbeat. The place smells of antiseptic, like a hospital. The white guy's partner, who is black, sticks his fingers inside the white guy's ass, like a doctor feeling someone's prostate. I pretend to look away. I take a piss and then linger at the basins, washing my hands. When the white guy starts moaning louder, I glance in the mirror. The door of the stall has been nudged wide open. The black guy is shoving his fist inside the white guy's ass. When he hears me turn the faucet off, he stops and pulls his fist out and catches me looking. He grunts angrily and mutters something, *Fucking asshole*. There is a crack in the mirror that is hardly noticeable in the dim light of the toilet. It runs diagonally across the surface, like a vein of lightning, and when I keep staring at it, it seems to distort the room in split-screen, myself in one part and the two guys, who have started doing it again, in the other. The white guy's rectum puckers around the fist. I punch the hand dryer, its whirring hardly audible above the steady thud coming from outside. My hands feel warm under the nozzle, the hot gusts strangely comforting, like when you breathe into your fists in winter. I check my watch. The black guy has pushed his fist further in until it disappears completely inside the white guy's ass. Ugo is taking a long time to get here. I punch the hand dryer again but it seems silly to place my hands under the nozzle now, so I just keep punching it over and over. Now the two guys have stopped fisting and are facing each other and jacking each other off. The incessant thud is starting to sound like it's coming from inside my head. I don't realize I still have my hands under the dryer and that it has stopped whirring, it has completely run out of breath, until the men zip up and walk to the basins and I have to move a little so they can wash and dry their hands.

The black guy asks, "You waiting for Ugo, right?"

I say I am.

The other guy laughs. I realize Ugo isn't coming back.

I walk out and stand by a railing peering out over the dance floor. The lights throw fractured images of the dancers at me. Each flash is a frozen moment of body parts, upraised arms, hands, mouths, eyes. I can't help thinking of Madrid—bodies blown up and littered all over Atocha station a couple of springs ago. In a terrorist attack, bodies themselves become part of the ammunition: they break off and fly in all directions, hitting other bodies, breaking windows, and smashing walls. It's pretty stupid to think about it. The music is making me sick. It's a remix of yet another hit from Madonna, one of the surest signs that Western civilization is in decline.

I decide to call it a night. Just then Ugo comes by. "Told you to wait in the bathroom," he says. "You paying attention, or what?" He slaps the packet angrily on my palm and walks away.

I stuff the packet in my jeans and head out. It's half past one in the morning. The music is louder, the club more packed. A long queue has formed outside the door, snaking around the block. Everybody's trying to look bored and blasé. As I am walking out, an amazing thing happens: I have a sense, just at that moment, that I understand what Mother is going through. It doesn't matter to me that the young overdose on the dance floor. I don't care if those two guys in the bathroom shove broomsticks up their asses. I don't care whether Ugo has family or friends, or whether he lives alone and does nothing but shoot junk up his dick. I am, in short, so worn out that all I can think of, seriously, is maybe stopping for a Gray's Papaya recession special on the way home. It's an incredible feeling, or, more precisely, an acute awareness of the absence of feeling. A flash of satori, sudden and Zenlike and inexplicable, an emptiness that has been quietly carving a space inside me for weeks. I once feared it would cause me anguish, this void I have been staring into, down which I know I will someday fall. Yuki was right. Indifference is her drug of choice, and now I realize it is something we have in common. I catch myself smiling as I hold my arm out to hail a cab.

WSOWOB

The good news is Janya's director is pleased with her report. The director is a high-strung wealthy liberal from Massachusetts who talks like the world is always about to end, so her approval is welcome news indeed. In fact, the director likes Janya's report so much she's assigning Janya to monitor a Banana Republic sweatshop that's just opened up at the export-processing zone in Subic. We have to stay in Manila for a few more weeks, and there may be more assignments in the offing.

The bad news is that Phil is very angry. He's on the phone, yelling. It appears that without my realizing it, all I've sent him are videos of the ocean around San Crisostomo, the ones I shot while Janya and I were there.

I tell him I've been feeling a little addled lately, and have to confess that Janya and I went there on a sort of minihoneymoon. We weren't going to tell anybody, but there's no point in keeping our relationship a secret any longer.

Phil warns me, half-seriously, that this has put my journalistic integrity in question. I argue that a documentary is never fully objective anyway. I know Phil. He's not getting into any philosophical argument with me. He finally hangs up after I reassure him that my interviews, due for broadcast in a month, will soon be on their way.

I haven't told Phil about what's really happened to me.

I don't think it's necessary. But the truth is that ever since I followed the doctor's advice, I've been more engrossed in trying to edit Sylvain and Annette's films, and I've lost interest in my documentary.

These are the remnants of the project they were filming for close to a decade, a collection of incidents of religious hysteria, from Madeleine Aumont in Normandy to faith healers in the Philippines, a documentary that for some reason they decided to drop shortly after I came into their lives. I know I can do something with it, but I'm not sure exactly what or how.

They saved me. The least I can do now is to save their film. My sense of compassion astonishes even me. I may have become a bodhisattva.

Or maybe I'm just in a kind of block. I'm not complaining. Nights, I just review Sylvain and Annette's films. Days, I watch Dreyer's *Ordet* over and over, the one other film Sylvain and Annette had been restoring before their car plunged into the Massif de l'Estérel.

There's a perfectly good reason for my doing so, though Phil isn't the type to try to understand. After all, you can't make a film of something you can't see.

In Dreyer's *Ordet*, the country doctor has just saved Farmer Borgen's daughter-in-law, Inger, from a miscarriage, and considers it a miracle. But the pastor insists that healing is an act of nature, not of God.

"Naturally miracles are possible, since God is the creator of everything, and everything is possible to him," says the pastor. "But even though God can perform miracles, he does not. Because miracles break the laws of nature, and God does not break His laws."

"But what about the miracles of Jesus Christ?" asks the doctor.

The pastor replies: "Those were special circumstances."

"Oh, I see," says the doctor. "Your otherwise so reliable God can throw a hitch into the works."

In eight-point type, so minuscule you can hardly read it, there's a one-line acknowledgment of Sylvain and Annette's contribution in restoring Dreyer's films. Janya thinks this is why, whenever I'm not reviewing my parents' old movies, all I do is watch films by Dreyer. I tell her my attachment may have once been sentimental, but it's purely technical now: I think anyone who takes film seriously should dissect Dreyer and analyze each scene, each frame, and learn from it.

I don't really think about Janya's statement until one occasion when she leaves for Cebu. The last time she sees me, I'm watching *Ordet*. I do know I did many other things after that, ordinary things I don't exactly take notice of. I went out. Twice I went to the supermarket. I worked out and bench-pressed a hundred and forty-five pounds. I called Phil and made another excuse about the tapes missing in transit.

But when she comes back several days later, she finds me watching the same film, at the exact scene she had last seen me watching. This distortion of time and space creates for her an illusion of my immobility, something that on a deep level I find disturbing, because I refuse to let her believe I just sat there, motionless, the whole time she was away. But how am I to change that perception, when that is what *she has seen*?

* * *

It's the end of the film. Inger has died delivering a child. The second of the farmer's three sons, Johannes, has lost his mind and believes he is Jesus Christ. He wants to raise Inger from the dead. Everyone tries to stop him, except for Inger's young daughter, who believes he can do it.

"The others won't allow me," Johannes tells her. But the child's faith is enough. He tells Inger to rise. There's a brief pause, infinitesimal, unbearably silent. Inger stirs, her eyelids flutter: she has woken from the dead.

This is possibly one of the most difficult scenes ever portrayed in the history of film. In Dreyer's hands, the effect is shattering. What could have happened after that? The viewer is left to presume that from here on every character's faith has been restored.

But it's too simple to believe the effect will be the same for everybody. God's violation of His own logic will be so devastating the world won't make sense anymore.

Some will turn to faith, which is the easy path.

Others will take the more difficult road, which is to go mad.

Carl Theodor Dreyer was orphaned shortly after birth. His Danish foster parents set him to work at an early age, often reminding him that life was no free ride, and he had to earn his own meals.

He wound up working in a film studio, fell in love with the medium, and decided he was going to devote all his life to it. This devotion was going to be total and consuming. The cruelty of the world, dealt to this lost creature at a very young age, turned providential, even Dickensian: in fact, in a different age, in a different place, one could say Dreyer was among those for whom life bestowed great expectations, one among the chosen, perhaps a prophet, perhaps even a saint.

I've been trying to explain this to Janya, but all she's worried about is that I haven't explained what's going on to Phil.

"What *is* going on?"

"That you haven't been well, and that you need more time to work on the documentary."

"I'm perfectly okay, Janya. I'm not an invalid."

"That's not what I meant. He just has to be in the loop."

"I'll get working on the documentary again soon. There's no need to tell Phil my entire life story. He doesn't need to know anything. And there's a perfectly good reason why I've been scrutinizing *Ordet*. It's not for lack of anything else to do. People used to consult Virgil to answer life's most puzzling questions. Today they turn to the scriptures. I guess I belong to the future, when film will have surpassed, or replaced, our reverence for text. I choose to consult Dreyer. Through Dreyer, I can explain how one fatal prayer that I so casually uttered, half-jokingly, never intending it to be taken seriously, led to my parent's accident. I can eliminate coincidences."

"Mathieu, you're not making any sense."

"I know it sounds weird. But film communicates to me, in a very literal sense. That's just the way I am. Nothing else talks to me more than film. Nothing else explains the world more clearly."

"But to use it as scripture? You don't think that's daffy?"

"No, listen. This is how it goes. I used to think Sylvain and Annette gave me up because I was defective. Now I realize they did all they could, even compromised everything they believed in, just to make me better. They chose to believe, against their good sense, that something in the abbey, maybe God, helped me heal."

"Jesus, Mathieu."

"And because they believed it, because they made that *effort*, I believed it myself. I believed it because of one thing. I wanted to ask God, whatever he was, to remove the reason they left me there. But God couldn't break His own logic—He couldn't come down Himself and fix my brain, for that would be a medical impossibility. So He chose to solve the problem as best He could. He made their car skid off into the gorge."

"Mathieu, that's shot through with so much fallacy."

"God hears people's prayers, Inger tells Farmer Borgen, but He does it kind of secretly, so as not to have too much fuss made about it. That is what Dreyer tells me. God and I have a score to settle, and I've got it all worked out. In order to live with myself, I have to prove that no transaction ever happened. Either God never broke His laws, or God doesn't exist."

"I have one word for you," she says. "*Dostoevsky.* Case closed."

"And then there's the matter of little Mathieu."

"That story's a total dead end. You were right all along. There was nothing there. I should have listened to you. I'm sorry. It was pretty stupid to go to San Crisostomo. Let's forget about it and move on."

"Maybe we left too soon. Just like Sylvain and Annette."

"You said you didn't like the place."

"Maybe I should go back."

"To find what? What are the possible scenarios? That

the boy had been found, and was raised by one of the natives? That they were hiding him from us?"

"The Cathars believed that—"

"Oh, Jesus."

"—if you don't get your shit together the first time, you get a second chance. You get reincarnated. But reincarnation is a punishment. You get punished for not getting it, the way kids are punished in school."

"Christ, Mathieu. I don't know what you're trying to say. Are you saying the boy's been reborn? I mean, fuck. Think about that for a moment."

"There are two steps to solving this mystery. First, Sylvain and Annette, and why they gave up on me. Second, what happened to little Mathieu."

"You left out the third."

"What?"

"Your father. Brezsky."

"I don't care about him. He's not part of the equation."

"He may hold the key."

"I don't think so."

"Well, the first two steps are impossible. One defies logic, *pace* Dostoevsky, and the other just has no facts, as we've found out. End of story."

"Well, yeah, I guess you're right. Pretty stupid, huh?"

"Call Phil. The guy is going to have a heart attack."

I promise to, but don't. How do I explain to Janya that when it comes down to it, nothing that's been said before can help, and unless you reach a point of personal crisis, everything is just wordplay? Didn't Dostoevsky himself say that?

Farmer Borgen's son Johannes disappears, leaving only this note quoting his namesake John, chapter thirteen, verse thirty-three: *Yet a little while I am with you. You shall seek me. Where I go, you cannot come.*

He comes back at the end of the film healed and sane. Dreyer doesn't show us the agony involved in the process of redemption. He didn't need to. Hell is a place you suffer alone.

She's weaving through Manila traffic like it's her own private slalom. Trucks, cars, motorcycles, and pedicabs zip past us, practically scraping the sides of the car. People slither straight into our path, and she swerves deftly, cursing under her breath.

We finally turn toward a wider, empty avenue leading to the university campus. All that green is shocking, like the first time one enters Granada from the arid desert. I tell Janya that's how it feels.

"Yeah," she says. "Funny how these guys are always the ones talking about the real world."

"It's not real."

"Yeah."

We turn left toward a wooded area dotted with bungalows. The campus is a bucolic respite, light-years apart from the lunacy of the urban sprawl. The house we park at has a small garden full of hibiscus bushes. The yawning flowers are in full bloom, sticking out their tongues dusted with pollen.

A man walks out of the bungalow to greet us. He's in khakis and a plaid shirt, titanium-frame spectacles, longish, thinning hair, a preppie in a sixty-year-old's body. He gives Janya a tight hug.

"I feel like I've known you forever," he tells her. "Like my own daughter."

"I love the way Filipinos get so personal, professor," she tells him.

The man laughs. "People call me *professor*, but I'm not. I'm just a social worker. Just one of the people."

"Spoken like a true Marxist."

"I'm not even Marxist anymore. But that's a long story. Is this Mathieu?"

"Yes."

"Hello, Mathieu."

I shake his hand. "So what is it exactly that you do around here?" I ask him.

"Mathematics, occasionally. Social work. Organizing. Rabble-rousing. Rocking the boat."

"Okay." I'm still a little puzzled. "Janya told me you might be good for our documentary."

"I lied," Janya says. "Sort of."

"Okay. Why are we here, Janya?"

"He'll help you with your other film."

"What other film?"

"The other film. Mathieu, he knew your dad. He knew Brezsky."

He lifts his shirt up to show the scar.

"They shot right at us, straight at the crowd. Just to disperse us. We all ran, then I felt something brush against me. I didn't know what it was at first. Then I fell on my knees. Blood was gushing out of my ribs."

"What were you guys out there for?" Janya asks him. "Sorry, stupid question."

"No, not at all. We were out almost every day then. I never got my degree, because I spent all my time out in the streets. But it was a better education. And I was good at what I was doing. I knew how to lead the kids, how to get them fired up about what really mattered. We wanted to put pressure on Marcos. He wasn't dictator back then, just the president. Dictator-to-be. We all knew he was manipulating Congress to anoint him as president-for-life. We decided if the kids were no longer going to classrooms and things were so desperate that we had to spend every minute on the streets, we were going to do it, and the government would listen. The dictator didn't like it."

He smiles at her. His smile is broad and makes him look much younger. His eyes sparkle. He has not spoken to me all this time. Janya reaches a hand out toward him, then pulls back.

"Sorry," she says. "I wanted to touch it. Your scar."

"Oh," he says, laughing. "A lot of people used to do that. I was in a coma for weeks, and all our comrades and friends came to wish me well. They all thought I was going to die. Someone did a shaman ceremony to help me survive. And lo and behold, the next day I was awake. People still think it was a miracle. I was a walking miracle. Some came to touch my scar, the way they touch the feet of the saints. The statues, I mean. Funny how people think like that."

Janya lightly touches the scar. "There. I just touched a saint."

I cough into my fist.

"Sorry," he says. "You are here to talk about your father."

"I don't even know if he's my father, or who my father is."

"Except that there's an interesting connection we've found here."

"So what exactly have we found?"

"A couple of years after I got shot, Marcos did finally declare martial law and threw us all in jail. I was in a provincial jail for a while, down south. They captured me right when I was out on an education mission among fishermen there. And one day the soldiers brought in a young American guy."

"Brezsky?" Janya asks.

"I think that's what he said his name was. He was only there for a while. I wondered why they even brought him in there. It wasn't legal. He could have called the US embassy. But he chose to stay. I thought he was maybe CIA. I thought he was there to, you know, weed out information from me."

"Great," I say. "My dad, who may not even be my dad, was a spook."

"Just listen to his story, Mathieu. Was there anything else?"

"He was very . . . secretive. We only got to talk a bit right before he was released. But when you mentioned the name, it sort of rang a bell."

"Sort of," I say.

"I wouldn't presume anything I tell you should be taken as fact."

"Sorry, man, but you don't even remember what this guy's name was. Or what he did. Or whatever. Janya, can we go now?"

"Oh, Mathieu."

"I haven't really been much help," he says.

"Not really," I tell him. I haven't touched the green tea he's served at all.

"Sorry, it was a long time ago. The only thing I remember is he wasn't the type to be in jail."

"What do you mean?" Janya asks.

"He was, you know, too uninvolved. He wasn't the type to die for his country. Or for anyone. But that's my subjective observation. Not a fact."

"Thanks for your time anyway."

She gets up, but he's still sitting down, as if reluctant to see her leave. "Listen, there's a fact-finding mission coming up in a few days. Up north, among indigenous mountain people. They used to be a very traditional tribe, preserving their own culture, their language and rituals, even their food and ways of dress. Now they're all working for the multinational companies, assembling shoe parts in their backyards. It's the story that's never told when people talk about globalization. The small households who supply unfinished parts for sweatshops to assemble. It'll be good for you to meet them."

"I would love to," she says. "Thank you."

"You drove all the way here to see me. The least I can do is offer you something useful."

"Christ, Janya, let's go."

I walk out. Janya stays with him for a bit, apologizing for my rudeness. I head straight to the car. The light is directly overhead, brilliant and blinding. Through the screen doors I can see them hugging again, and I press the car horn so loud a flock of sparrows skitter out of the hibiscus bushes, sending a dark cloud passing over the windshield as I see Janya hurrying out.

"How long have you known him?"

"A few weeks."

We are driving back to the apartment, past the old part of the city, past the red-light district and the crowded warrens and the slums. There's a new Manila and the old Manila. The new Manila is where our apartment is, next to high-rises and malls, a sort of tropical LA. The old Manila is more rundown and decrepit, the city's old shell that it hasn't been able to discard. The buildings are dilapidated, concrete and wood burnt a deep dark brown and covered with a thick layer of soot.

"How did you get to know him?"

"Job connections. The left-wing liberal community here is very small, and incestuous."

"I bet."

"What's that supposed to mean?"

The streets are a bedlam of cars, motorcycles, pedicabs, jeeps, street hawkers, and pedestrians. Now we're going under through the Quiapo underpass, in the center of the city. The walls of the underpass are encrusted with what looks like dried mud. I can barely see the dome of the church as we drive past, the church of the downtrodden which is said to be the very nexus of the city, the navel of this chaotic, sprawling deformity. It's dwarfed by billboards and electric poles, and surrounded by beggars, pickpockets, prostitutes, and all the quacks and fortune tellers hoping to cash in on their need for reassurance and hope. No matter how fiercely the devotees of that church pray, God in His luxurious heaven must find this too hard to bear, and probably looks away.

"What's that supposed to mean?" she repeats.

"Touching his scar, for Christ's sake. Could you be more indiscreet?"

"The man is more than twice my age!"

"Why did we even have to go there?"

"I mentioned to some people in the university what we were doing here, how there was this story we wanted to investigate. They knew the professor and his story. It's become some kind of urban legend around there."

"That isn't the story. Brezsky isn't my story. Mathieu is. The lost boy. Brezsky is all yours. That's the problem. We are pursuing two different stories. Structural problem, Janya. Logistical problem."

"Okay, you know what, we can't talk about this when you're being so sarcastic."

"Why did we go there?"

"Because I want you to take your mind off the lost boy. That's a dead end. We won't ever know what happened to him. But we can find out what happened to your father."

"He's not even my freaking father, Janya. We have not even established that."

"But that guy from New York said—"

"We're going in circles. You're probably dealing with some psycho from New York."

"Okay. Just thought it was worth a shot. But you can come and shoot those tribes with me. It's an interesting aspect of the story."

"Your story. And his cause."

"He was trying to help."

"Okay. Thank you. I appreciate it. Let's stop talking about it."

"Fine."

A man suddenly steps in front of the car, gazing blankly ahead at us. Janya has to swerve deftly to avoid hitting him. The man doesn't seem aware of our presence at all, or the danger he has posed to us or to himself, but Janya seems to take this near-accident as a matter of course. Her mind is somewhere else. I want to ask her what's going on, because I know something's going on, deep in my guts

I know there's something, and I am frustrated that she has become so closed, so not-transparent to me. Yet by the time we reach our neighborhood, and she drops me off and drives to another interview, I'm all drained out, and only want to crawl back to the apartment.

And all I remember from that arduous trip is the man who stepped in front of the car, doped and desperate and suicidal. I've been wondering if he is symbolic of my visit here. But what would he symbolize? Total obliviousness or indifference to danger? A desperation so deep he doesn't care about his life anymore? A passive-aggressiveness (run me over, if you dare, and I will give you hell)? This country's sense of frustration embodied in his emaciated body, his drugged-out stare, his seething silence?

And again, that sense of horror: I could have been one of them. Someone else could have been saved, not me. It was either Mathieu or Mathieu. The law of equations is simple but hardly comforting.

I come back to the apartment with great relief. The new Manila is a different country, a different planet, and I'm glad I live in it. I turn the video on, thankful for all the gadgets I own, thankful that I am, fortunately, in this bizarre, dysfunctional world, an *alien*.

Janya has to go off on another site visit, and I have to schedule another checkup. I pay a visit to another specialist to get a second opinion, and he tells me I'm okay to go back to my normal work routine. Nothing's shown up in the scans. This is no surprise. Nothing ever did. By all respects, I am adequately healthy, and passably sane.

I'm back in the apartment, watching *Ordet* again. On the leather ottoman, there's some kind of native fetish.

Janya must have gotten it on one of her previous trips.

It's a miniature replica of one of the rice gods of the Ifugao, a fiercely proud tribe up in the northern mountain region of the country, one of the few who had constantly fought a losing battle against the oblivion imposed by Western colonization. It's a figure of a man about five inches tall, in a squatting position, his elbows on his knees, a bright red G-string knotted around his loins. He's wearing a necklace and shell earrings. Chicken feathers sprout on top of his head. It's carved crudely out of what appears to be balsa wood, stained charcoal black, one of those emblems of an ancient culture that tourism, in all its kitsch, has fully embraced. The Ifugao set the fetish at the doorstep of their homes so the dead can find a place to rest in, and from there they look after the living. The dead themselves, on the other hand, appear to have been helpless against the living—the burial caves of the region have all been looted and ransacked in recent years, and mummies buried there for centuries have been stolen and sold to foreign and local collectors.

In the flickering light of the monitor, the carved features seem to become animated. The eyes, two gouged-out holes, seem to follow where I go, and the mouth, a single gash, quivers mutely, incapable of words.

I transfer it to a shelf and position a track light above it, bathing it in a soft, amber halo. Then I put my feet up on the ottoman, aim the remote, and press play.

Janya comes back a couple of days later. She asks me how I've been. She starts to unpack. On the way to the kitchen to get a drink of water, she notices the fetish.

"Nice," she says. "Where did you get it?"

* * *

I find things in the apartment that weren't there before. In the bottom drawer of an armoire, underneath my underwear, there's a worn-out kid's T-shirt, a souvenir from Normandy.

I lie awake at night while she's fast asleep beside me. I hear the patter of feet in the corridor. I get up quietly. I'm drawn out of the room by nothing more than a feeling. Something's leading me in the dark. I follow it downstairs. There's no one there.

I sit alone in total darkness, staring at the video monitor. And suddenly images flicker on the screen. A paper hat, a plastic gun. And then the close-up of the boy stops in the middle of the frame, faces the camera, and speaks directly to me.

"She's trying to get rid of me, you know," he says.

"Who?"

"That little bitch. Your girlfriend."

"I don't think so."

"You'll see. Then it'll be too late."

"Get the fuck out of my brain."

And just like that, he turns away, and I'm looking at the normal footage again. Blinding light. *Shoot him while he blows the candles out. Stop.*

I'm chopping onions for soup. I'm trying to focus on the act, and nothing else. I hear Janya coming in. The knife slips in my hand. I can almost hear it cutting through my flesh, slicing into my finger. The cut is deep. Blood oozes onto the chopping board. I can't feel a thing.

As soon as she walks in, I ask her, "So you spoke to Phil?"

"Yeah."

"When did you talk to Phil?"

"Days ago. Anything new?"

"They got someone else to finish the documentary. I just fucking lost my job. Thanks a lot, Janya."

"What? They can't do that. That's work discrimination. You can sue."

"Yeah, sue a nonprofit. That would be nice."

"I'm going to call him. He can't fucking do this. Jesus, you gotta put something on that finger. You're bleeding like crazy."

"Where did that letter come from?" I point to the stack of mail that has piled up since she's been away.

"What letter?"

"This one," I say, holding up the top one.

"You've already opened it. What does it say?"

"*It is imperative that you come and see me again.* What the fuck does that mean?" I wait for her reaction, but all she does is look at me quizzically, waiting for me to continue.

"Who could it be from?"

"You know who it's from."

"That man doesn't even know where we live."

"Who?"

"The professor."

"How do you know it's from the professor?"

"I don't. I just presumed you're still . . ."

"What?"

"Jealous."

"Of what?"

"Of nothing. Just like you were with Gino."

"Who the fuck is Gino?"

"The guy at San Crisostomo."

"So you think much about that guy from San Crisostomo?"

"Fuck you, Mathieu. He has no reason to send me a letter."

I read the letter again: *It is imperative that you come and see me again.* "Has this something to do with Brezsky?"

"I don't know, Mathieu. I don't know what that letter's about." She snatches it from me. "You got blood all over it. Look, it's addressed to both of us. Not just me."

I take a look at the envelope. She's right. "I need to know what's going on."

She tears off a paper towel and wraps it around my hand. "I need to know what's going on." A bloom of red spreads out as the towel soaks up the blood. "I would never do anything to hurt you," she says.

"Wait. Hurt me? What does that mean?"

"Stop, Mathieu. Just please fucking stop."

the little toil of love:
the missing pages

She picks me up at Manila International Airport & drives me straight to some mansion in the richest part of the city. A guy she knows lives there. Son of a landowner from somewhere, family owns a sugar plantation, buddies with the president, has his own private army. Security people everywhere. Goons with guns. Even her friend carries a gun. Pompous effeminate ass with some phony English accent & an air like some overpampered don.

She knows I don't like this kind of people. She doesn't remember why. We've only been apart six months & she's a totally different person now. One of her people. On the way to my apartment (which her friend has found for me—connections & all that) I tell her she's become bourgeois. She's become the people she hates.

It's a different world here, she tells me. You have to get used to it to endure it. The classes are more permeable, you know people from all walks of life & it doesn't mean a thing. It's not America.

She starts seeing her friend more often. She even talks openly about him. His inner circle, his friends who are the sons or daughters of this or that senator, the sprawling plantations dotted with mansions & surrounded by the most destitute laborers on the planet, the all-night parties at the palace, the private jets. Once he filled his swimming pool with Evian water. Flown in straight from God knows where. Because the president's daughter was coming over & felt like having a pool party. She is awed by the lavishness of it, the Fellini of it, the absurdity. Life, she says, this is real life staring you in the face.

I tell her that's great, it's amazing she's so fascinated by all these people who've fucked the whole place up, yet talk like they're the only ones who can save the country. The arrogance & the blindness, the imperiousness & the stupidity.

I can go on & on. There's nothing I can do. He can help you someday, she tells me. He's a very giving kind of person.

The very adjective makes me want to puke. The hypocrisy of it. The phoniness. I can go on.

Now that she has changed to someone else, someone who baffles me but who I still desire, the only way I can endure a relationship with Liana is to learn to transcend all emotions. Not to stifle or annihilate them. But to be able to feel & stand apart from the feeling. To be Zen, an observer of my own heart. It's the most beautiful & most difficult thing I can ever do.

I've been spending all my time learning this skill. It's an almost physical sensation, like squeezing myself out of a cocoon. Something like this is bound to become useful someday. I can watch her walk, eat, sleep, fuck, get angry, get happy, be lost in thought. Everything she does has become more fascinating. To observe her as she is, with no desire & therefore no anxiety.

Something like this can never be explained. It can only be lived. No matter how I try to explain, it doesn't make sense to her.

She sees it as numbness, ruthlessness, my heart gone cold. I am too dense, I don't understand, I am stuck up & stuck where I am. She can be harsh if she wants to.

I need to find a way to make her realize how I hurt. I need to find a way to convince myself that I no longer care. But that is not what I want to say. We hurt each other by our awareness that nothing essential can truly be expressed.

I walk past Liana's door & catch myself slowing down. My ears pick up the faintest sound, & every sound, no matter what it is—the din of passing traffic, the TV in another apartment, someone on the phone—makes my body ache with an overwhelming exhaustion.

When I see her later, somewhere else, I can act diffidently. I can pretend I'm all right, I can talk about anything, & what has filled me with anxiety is completely invisible except to myself.

Rely on no one. Depend on no one for your happiness. I am declaring my independence. I am establishing a republic unto myself. I am seceding from the human race.

He's been there since 8:30. It's not even 10 yet. They'll be lying in bed, whispering all the shit lovers say after a fuck. Maybe he'll stay over for the night. That means I may bump into him tomorrow. I may have to acknowledge his presence. I may have to say hello.

Nick's apartment is a 1-bedroom. I sleep on the couch. He knows the drill. Every time I stay over, he knows there's that asshole up at Liana's & I have to get away, to be as far away from them as possible. Nick says I should just move to another building, to another part of the city.

He says I can't & I won't. Nick knows me too well. He gets me drunk & stoned & touches my knee. He rests his hand lightly but he knows never to go any further. I know what it feels like. Some things can never happen. Nick downs a shot & says the same thing every time I stay over: We love whom we may, we break when we must.

Nick's never had a lover that stayed for longer than 2 weeks. He says he likes the boy prostitutes best. They're charmingly stupid. They can hardly speak English. They don't even try to act American. They're likely just straight guys with no money. For Nick, desperate poverty is an aphrodisiac.

He came here thinking he'd find someone to love. Now he knows better. Now he's just another foul-mouthed bitch paying to get laid. I got it all figured out, he says every time I stay over. The rent boys are the best, they're less complicated to deal with & you know exactly what they're after.

I've learned a few lessons from Nick. In order to get back at Liana, I take a girl home to fuck all night. I want to make sure Liana hears every minute of it. I enjoy every moment, my pleasure heightened by the fact that I'm doing this for her benefit. Tomorrow she'll hardly be able to look at me. She won't speak to me out of spite. Her heart will burn with rage.

I should have known this was going to happen. What starts as an act of revenge becomes an addiction. Pretty soon I'm like Nick, I have to stick my dick somewhere or else I'll go nuts. Nick & I go out every night, like a pair of bloodsuckers. Nick knows where the best & youngest prostitutes are. His boys are friends with these girls, & some of the boys even fuck them or become their boyfriends. Can't share your body, Nick tells me, but at least we can share the same disease.

It's only her third night in Manila. We're just talking, but the putas cast angry looks at her. They tell her to see the manager about work. I ask her out. I take her back to my apartment. She has two dark moles right under her left breast. Her name is Anna.

She left her town after some jerk raped her, some older guy who's a friend of her father's. It's a story you hear everywhere & it's probably true. She came to the city thinking she'd get rid of the baby somehow. It turned out she wasn't pregnant at all. She doesn't want to go back & face her family just yet. In a town as small as that, if a girl gets raped, people say she probably did her best to deserve it.

In bed with her, I can almost forget about Liana. I can imagine this is the body that I love. I can tell her I love her & imagine I mean it. I can almost taste the sweet syllables in my mouth.

She asks me why I've lived in Manila for such a long time. People come & go, she says. Nobody stays but you. I tell her I like it here. I truly do, most of the time. I have an escape hatch, I can always leave if things get really fucked up.

It's a strange distinction to have. It's something that really doesn't matter to you until you realize other people don't have the same privilege. I can imagine no greater horror than that, to be stuck where you are, in your own inescapable circle of hell.

* * *

Liana says, You think they adore you, but there's an entirely different value system at work here. Around here, any white guy will do. If you're young & responsible, you're a catch. If you're young & penniless, that's fine too. & if you're old & stinking like death, well, a girl gets what she can. Things are so fucked in this country any bitch will open her legs & let the sunshine in. Just to get out. Just to look for a way out.

I tell her the girl loves me & she's going to have my baby. That's 2 stabs straight at her heart. I hope she hurts.

Grow up, she says. You don't even know her name.

She writes to me 2x a week. The letters are postmarked from some barrio that's not even on my map. They're written on cheap paper lined in red & blue, the kind kids use in school. She thanks me for taking her in, for letting her stay with me, for feeding her, for loving her, for loving her body. Her English is simple, childlike, written in a fine, beautiful scrawl.

What do you feel now? Liana asks me, watching me read the letters. Tell me if there's anything happening in that heart of yours.

This place is too close to Vietnam. Everyone's being drafted, even those of us out here. No escape. Everyone I know has already left. Too close. Go home, or better yet, head straight to fucking Canada. Get out.

Not Nick. Nick is staying. He's expecting a green card soon. I'm seeking asylum in the home of the brave, he says. I'm going to be a fucking American. I'll be so fucking American that America won't know what hit it.

I warn him: As soon as you become American, you'll be sent straight to Vietnam.

Not me, he says. I'm too old. I have a fucking heart condition. & I'm a cocksucker.

He doesn't care. He just wants to be fucking American. He's done everything to become American. He's even fucked a couple of American girls in the city. He will use his dick for what it's worth. They don't offer to marry him. But they like his accent, they like his pretensions, they like him even while they suspect that he'd rather fuck a boy.

Nick's got a couple of boys to regularly supply him with weed. It's so cheap he doesn't even make me pay for it. He just stuffs a couple of dime bags in my pocket every time I stay over. One of the boys got busted last week. Then narcs raided Nick's apartment & turned everything upside down. They found nothing. Nick's not stupid. When the boy got busted Nick transferred all his stash to my place. The narcs got tired of watching him after a while. They know they're never getting any money from him.

The boy's body was dumped in a back alley days later. It had ice-pick holes punctured all over its back & all the fingernails had been pulled out. The papers said he was some kind of Communist spy. Nick says they're probably right. Weed grows in the north, where the Communists harvest it in rice paddies. It's cheaper than a meal & so potent it makes you fucked for hours. This is how the Communists are going to bring down the Almighty, says Nick. We will all surrender to the bliss.

I'm walking along España Avenue. About a hundred demonstrators emerge from the side streets, rushing toward me. I duck into a small restaurant. The owner hurriedly closes the place. Through the slats of the accordion metal gate I see a troop of police pursuing the students, armed with AK-47s, truncheons, rattan shields. Molotov cocktail bombs fly in their direction. The bombs shatter on the pavement, scattering in a burst of fire. An officer's shield catches fire. The flames spread to his arms, all over his body, & now he's squirming on the pavement, rolling to put the fire out. Teargas chokes the air. Everything is swathed in a cloud of swirling gray smoke. The scene turns dreamlike, & through the churning smoke there are only parts of bodies, arms, heads, a helmet, a truncheon wielded swiftly down, landing with a crash on nothing I can see.

Draft notice. Fuck. You are hereby ordered for induction into the Armed Forces. Can't focus. To report at. For forwarding to an Armed Forces Induction Station. Can't. If you are far from your local board, go immediately to. Where? Willful failure to report at the place & hour subjects the Violator to fines & imprisonment. If you are far. Violator. You are hereby ordered. Imprisonment. Fuck.

Draft notice won't go away. Staring at my face. On my desk. In my mind. Every day. Mocking me. Can't take my eyes off it. Taunting me in my sleep. Can't sleep. Am going to Nam. Kill those gooks. Get killed. Mother America. My country 'tis of thee. Fuck.

I'm running out of money & so is everyone else & Nick is sick of lending me more. I've just sold the stash he asked me to hide & used the money to pay my back rent. I told him I'd repay him but he told me to go to hell.

Can't focus. Can't do anything. Fear of running out of money is as great as fear of abandonment or death. The prospect of having <u>absolutely nothing</u> makes me physically ill. I'm ashamed to show myself anywhere. I don't go out anymore. The world scares me. Is hostile to me. I meander down backstreets to avoid all the people I know.

I am writing to Anna more often. No one else pays so much attention to me. I tell her I need to get out. My escape hatch has collapsed. I'm like everybody now. I have no way out. I need a ticket & I need a fake passport, anything that will get me out, no matter where, even just as close as Taiwan or Malaysia.

She tells me there's someone there who can get me a new passport. He's been doing it for all the girls. He knows all the right people. He will find me a way. He knows people who can lend me money.

I head south by ferry. I spend 24 hours with hundreds of commuters, our sleeping quarters are vinyl cots laid side by side on the deck, jute blankets barely shielding us from the spray. We're like refugees. For most of the voyage I'm just wide awake, standing on the side of the deck, staring at nothing, the black wide endless sea.

I'm going to make Nick sorry he ever said that. I'm going to go away & Nick is going to miss me so much it'll make him sick.

I find Anna's barrio on the northern tip of the island. She lives alone here, but everyone knows everyone else, and this is her family now. Everyone welcomes me like I'm her next of kin.

She came here with another girl who worked with her one summer near the military base. She came here because she had lost her family in a Communist ambush 3 years ago & the girl was her only friend, but the girl found out she was pregnant & her brothers threatened to kill her if she arrived all knocked up in their barrio. The girl found someone to look after her baby & now she's back as a dancer & hostess in Japan.

Anna looks pretty much the same, but younger. Being home makes anyone look younger. She asks me if I've come here for her.

I tell her I didn't. It's the truth & she looks disappointed. She doesn't ask any more questions. She understands. Or if she doesn't understand, she pretends she does, because that's how she was raised.

She says there's a group of people who've arranged everything.

Define everything, I tell her.

Everything, she says. They can get me out. They can get me a passport. She shows me hers. It's tattered & practically falling apart. It's been pretty useful & efficient.

& you've never been caught? I ask her.

The passport's real, she says. The visa's not. She got busted.

So how is that going to help me?

She says she took too many risks. Went in & out of Tokyo too many times. I was stupid, she says. But you're going away, you're using yours just once.

I tell her it doesn't sound convincing. She says it's my only chance.

She says, I wish they'd issue you a bad passport. But

that's very selfish of me. I wish you weren't going.

I tell her if I stayed, if I got caught, it would be worse. They'll send me to Nam. Either way, I won't be here for you.

Bahala na, she says.

Okay, I agree. Bahala na.

The guy who's talking to me looks like he's a cartoon character from the '50s. He has a razor-thin mustache. Everybody calls him <u>lieutenant</u>. I hear he was actually in the army, an ex-lieutenant, & now he's working for one of the "sugar barons," one of the overlords of the industry & therefore the entire island. Round here, he's as powerful as Jesus Christ.

He's looking at my US passport with a jealous gleam in his eye. This is like gold around here, he says. He wants to keep it for a while.

What for? I ask.

So I can make the best copy you can find, he says. It will be perfect. It will be a work of art. It will be the da Vinci of passports. The Lamborghini of passports.

Okay, I tell him, I get it. When can I have it?

Soon, he says.

How soon?

Relax, Yankee boy. I'll take care of it. He pulls out a pipe, a Popeye corncob pipe, & strikes a match over it. You ever had this shit, Yankee boy? It's the best shit on the planet. Try it. It'll make you a real man.

The guys who control all the businesses in this barrio don't live around here. They come from the island's capital & they don't like to visit here too often. Some of them come from Manila. They're dressed like city people, in smart city clothes. They don't like getting sand in their shoes, mud on their shirts. They wear Ray-Bans, because the sun here is too bright, too hot & oppressive. They don't smell like chicken shit like everyone else does. I've seen one of them, a Chinese mestizo guy, wearing two-toned patent-leather shoes. They dress up like dandies, so everyone gets it. This is what power looks like. Money makes you look better.

The lieutenant does all the business for them, like some kind of middleman. He grew up here & used to be nobody & then he got hooked with these guys & became a big shot & now everyone respects &/or fears him. He comes in a sedan with government stickers sometimes, or an army jeep. He doesn't talk much, doesn't make a show of their operations. He simply drives into town & stops at a hut & talks to the family for an hour or so. But the residents can't help crowding around the hut, eavesdropping while the mother of the house shoos them away.

In this barrio, so remote from the city & therefore from what I'm accustomed to believe as reality, there are 2 things you need to watch out for: natural forces & the armed forces.

Two 10-year-old boys in Anna's barrio are suffering for different reasons. One has been paralyzed for a year by some worm that I thought lives only in Africa. It's a parasite that bores through the skin & burrows slowly through the victim's body. The other boy had his hands cut off by soldiers who raided the barrio looking for Communist guerrillas.

The Communist guerrillas come in now & then &

they're friends with everyone & try to help & they bring food & medicine but sometimes they need food & medicine & everybody has to give what he has.

When the soldiers come everyone has to pretend they hate the Commies. Everyone here is "under protection," meaning they rely on the sugar barons around the village & their own armies to hide them from the war. Or at least spare them from a raid, from burning the barrio down.

But the lines are not clearly drawn. The Commies & the soldiers know what's going on. They even know who's on the other side. They may even have family on the other side. There are so many pieces in this chess game. It's a small, incestuous country. It's hard to tell who's on whose side.

I write to Liana about it. I tell her I've found a temporary home. But no place is really home. Home is where everything is fucked up. That's about every damn place on earth.

I've asked myself this question: which is the greater evil, the one caused by nature or the one caused by humans? I've found no reason to consider the question of any relevance to human existence.

Liana writes back: Congratulations. You now officially don't give a fuck what happens to the world.

It's the men who fuck up & the women who are expected to find a way out, to lift their family from this mess. They're sent around Asia, mostly to Hong Kong. Hong Kong used to send its women here to work. Now they've got their comeuppance, the tables have turned, they're getting so wealthy they can hire other Asians to clean up their shit. There's talk of jobs opening in Japan, in the Middle East,

& there's always Europe & the USA. Any place will do. Salvation is anywhere but here.

Regardless of evidence to the contrary, I stand out like some marvelous harbinger of good fortune. I represent everything they dream about. I am the walking embodiment of my country. Everything I do is important & momentous. Everything I say sounds like the word of God.

But not everyone is impressed. Some girl comes back from Hong Kong or Japan or some other shitty place. She's full of stories of the dazzling cities she's seen. She's full of bruises, has had a few teeth knocked out. She's tried some new drug they're crazy about in Japan. Better than acid, fuck you up like death. She's fucked every trick in sight & she's no longer ashamed to talk about it. Her family sends her away to Manila. She works her ass off but she keeps coming back, harder, more fucked, with as little money as before. She looks at me straight in the eye, so unlike the girls who've had no experience like hers.

Men don't know how lucky they are, she says. Her words are hard, bitter, mocking. Men don't know. All they worry about is their dicks.

One guy I know died in a dingy hotel room in Manila's red-light district, a floor above a whorehouse. He'd OD'd on junk he'd got off the street, puked all over the room. He was found still stooped over the sink. The sink was full of vomit. His body was frozen hard. He'd been dead for a day when the hotel's cleaning woman found him.

Liana tells me I'm the kind of person who'll die alone. That's how I'm going to die, she says. Stooped over my own shit. Or in some barrio where nobody knows me. Or on some dark road, & I'm still going nowhere. She tells me this in a letter, the last I'll ever get from her.

She will never forgive me for not being unhappy.

Anna warns me that the shit I'm smoking is going to fuck me up the way it did the girls in Japan. She's acting like a mother to me. That's her role, that's what she's supposed to be. You shouldn't do that anymore, she says. That thing is going to send you to hell.

Anna's found Jesus, & she goes to church every day now, to ask Jesus to find a way to make her life easier. Jesus is too far to hear, but she prays anyway. I don't want her to start talking about Jesus with me. But she prays to Jesus to make me stay.

The lieutenant doesn't show up often, & when he does it's just to give me more shit. He calls it shabu-shabu, like the Japanese dish the girls talk about, which is some kind of meat fondue or something. I don't know what shabu-shabu is but this shit is better than meat & whacks my brain real good. When it takes me into its arms, the world melts to a dream. I can see the edge of the universe with my bare eyes. I can fly to outer space, to the moon. I can walk on the Descartes Highlands, right past the lunar module, & I can see the Stars and Stripes right above me, unfurled straight out like a plank of wood, ghostly still & unmoving in the solid air.

Boys as young as 8 or 10 are taught how to dive deep to the coral beds. They poke a stick into the corals & nudge the fish out to the surface, where their older kin trap them in bamboo nets. The boys dive with primitive equipment & can hold their breath for abnormal lengths of time.

The lieutenant asks me why I don't go in the water

much. California boy, you like to surf, yeah? I can't even hold my breath long enough to do a couple of strokes. I swim out with them but I cling to the inner tube of a rubber tire, like the younger kids. Like a girl, he tells me. It's a wonder you can fuck at all.

You always have to prove that you're some kind of big-shot dick. Even in a barrio as small as this, the rules of hierarchy are fundamental. The older men who've proven their mettle drink some kind of palm wine all day & night. It looks like vomit & smells like horse piss. They may have been the local Romeos once but now they're ugly & disgusting. It doesn't matter. They stagger home after a night of drinking & fuck their wives, who must submit to them because it's their duty. They have babies everywhere. They can't ever stop having babies. The babies are raised to swim deep into the coral beds. Everyone is useful.

No one's supposed to fuck with someone else's girl or daughter or wife, but it's all talk. If a girl gets pregnant, she's sent away to bear the child alone. She comes back a different animal, without value, a nonbeing. She grows as hard as anyone. She drinks, spits, curses. She's learned to live in the world of men.

He pulls out a long list & studies it intently. I've seen him do it with nearly everyone in the barrio. A list of debts. A kilometric list. Utang, they call it. Everyone has one. It's an essential part of one's vocabulary. It's an unavoidable part of life, like baptism or death.

Your passport was a little harder to create, he tells me. You Americans put so many things in your passports to make life harder for people like me.

So when do I get it? I ask him.

It's going to cost you more, he says.

How much more?

A lot more. & you owe me for the shabu-shabu.

I tell him I'll pay for the passport now & deal with the shabu-shabu later.

He doesn't buy it. You get your passport now, you're out of here, he says. I'm not stupid.

I tell him I'll pay him. I can get him the money. I know I can. I just don't know how. This is something I don't tell him.

You want to get out, right? he asks me.

He knows damn well I have no way out. He's my fucking way out.

Why do you want to get out? he asks. What are you running away from?

I don't respond. He knows.

You'll have to pay me back. I went through a lot of work trying to get your passport. You know how dangerous that is?

I'll pay you back, I tell him. On my word. I won't run away.

I'm going to make you useful, he says. More useful than those deep-diving boys. Those boys, they're going to dive for coral for the rest of their lives, until they get the bends & die. But you're different, Yankee boy. You're blessed by God, all of you. Americans are the best. I know what you can do. You're going to like it. You're a very lucky man. Sometimes I really envy you.

I've seen her around the barrio, jasmine strands in her hand, a young girl of about 15. She's been selling flowers to the occasional passing tourist ever since she got rejected for a stint in Japan because she's underage. But she's been menstruating for months now, & her father's decided it's time to put that to good use. Girls are useless, because you can't make them work the earth.

Watching her with eagle eyes, he decides where I take her, & before we enter the room he offers me a shot of palm wine, which he lugs around in a plastic demijohn. He warns me not to drink too much, because too much makes the dick go limp.

Firewater, he says. Makes you too happy even to fuck.

He says she resisted coming along but learned to obey after a little hard lesson. Some girls just don't know they like it until they do it.

She lies naked on the bed, her arms stretched out. There's a cut on her lip, still raw. She doesn't look at me at all. She spreads her legs. There's a fresh purple bruise on her right thigh. When I enter her, she lets out a gasp of pain, but she keeps her eyes fixed on me & we stare eye to eye. I try to kiss her mouth. She turns her head away.

Anna's waiting for me by the shore. She's been asking to see me all week. I ask her why. She tells me she thinks she's pregnant again. She's been getting weird cravings for guava, jackfruit, durian. That's how you can tell, she says. When your body wants what your tongue hates. She starts to cry.

I ask her if she thinks it's mine. She says she hasn't been seeing anyone since I arrived. She says she should have been more careful. But she thinks, or hopes, it's mine. The night I was with the other girl, she felt something stab deep in her belly. A gut-wrenching feeling, but not pain. Deeper & harder to understand. Like her body was turning inside out. That was when she knew.

She tells me not to worry. She says the lieutenant will find a way.

I ask her what that means.

Just like the girl you loved last week, she says. She uses that word & it hurts her to say it. She says the lieutenant will find someone who will take the baby.

Was that what your friend did, the one who went back to Japan?

Yes, she says. I'll do the same thing. Unless you want it. Unless you really will stay.

I tell her I don't know. All I know is the lieutenant is helping me find a way out, just like she said he would. I promise to stay with her, to wait until the baby's born. I promise, I promise. But I will have to leave at some point. I will have to find some money to leave. But until the baby's born, I will stay. I promise. She knows I can promise anything, but she's used to a world in which promises mean nothing.

That girlfriend of yours, she wants money too, the lieutenant tells me.

I tell him Anna & I have talked about it.

If it's yours, it's going to be a lot of money, he says. White babies, they're top of the line. If she screwed with some black & the baby comes out black, forget it. She's fucked. So if you really care about your girlfriend, pray that it's yours.

It's an entire system run by landowners & politicians. This whole barrio is one big labor pool, & everyone's useful. The system is pretty efficient & covers everybody from life to death.

Labor recruitment, that's a big racket. Everybody wants to get out & work somewhere. Anywhere but here. Everyone knows what the game is but desperation just makes you say yes. Get people to pay up front to work overseas, get them all their papers, get them in so much debt they'll have to work years to pay it off. But off they go anyway, the girls to Hong Kong & Japan, the guys to the Middle East. The guys are luckier. As long as they don't mess up with the law & don't drink or stare at women or fuck boys, they can save up & come home with some pocket money in about 3 years. The girls are not as fortunate. They get raped, beaten up, or killed, or if they're lucky they just become prostitutes. But that's the good part. Sometimes they get to be couriers, spiriting the best shit from Japan & into the country, where demand is always high. Even the faggot boys in those mansions, the sons & daughters of the superrich, are getting all fucked up. Everybody loves to get fucked. My kind of town. But the girls, if they get pregnant, they're fucked, or they can always run back home & get these goons to sell their babies.

That's the entire life cycle—labor, passport, visa, prostitution, drugs, babies. Everything & everyone in the system feeds off one another, like a bunch of lampreys.

Everything in this country is useful, Anna tells me. Look at what we eat. Fish head, innards, duck fetus, blood. Nothing is wasted. If you look hard enough, life is good.

Anna thought she lost her baby, 3 nights ago when she took a bath under a full moon. Any God-fearing woman knows you can't take a bath under a full moon. She was standing in the bathroom for a long time, watching blood streak down her legs.

But today she can feel it inside her. I touch her belly. The little fucker gives a little push. He wants to meet you, Anna says. He wants to take your hand.

She says the lieutenant's already found a buyer in Manila, a woman from New York. She's waiting for the baby to be born. The lieutenant's going to find the baby a good home. She talks of him like a godsend, like a guardian angel. Maybe it's not yours, she says. I was hoping it would be yours. But maybe it's not. Now she says I have no reason to stay.

Maybe you'll just keep the baby, I tell her. Maybe you'll change your mind.

She says that's never going to happen. The barrio's just being nice to her because I'm around, because I'm acting like I'm really looking after her. That makes her baby almost not illegitimate. Not shameful. If I weren't around, she'd be somewhere else herself, somewhere not here.

She says the other girl's doing okay too. Maybe you can be the father of both our babies, she says. Maybe you can stay & be the father of 2, mine & hers.

It breaks Anna's heart to share me like that, but she says she has to understand that there are things in life she can't control, things she cannot have. She talks like she's learned everything from the romantic comics everyone in this barrio loves to read. The stories are always the same. Some guy loves some girl like crazy. The odds are stacked against them—family, community, church. They commit irrational & illicit acts of love. They die lonely, castigated, cleansed of sin.

Everyone lives the same basic story. It's like they're all instinctively living out some perverse narrative. Life is meaningless without suffering. No dreams are ever fulfilled. It all ends in tears.

The midwife comes in the dead of night. She's been brought in from the next town, where she just delivered another baby. People keep getting born, she complains. My work will never stop.

She's a frayed, stooped hag who's been around for a hundred years. She smokes a cigar. She gets everyone to prepare the basin of hot water, the rags. She shoos me away. Men are bad luck during delivery, she says. The angels look away when men are around.

Anna's delirious, in so much pain. She wants me to stay. She thinks she's going to die. When the baby comes, she passes out. I see the women passing by with the blood-stained bundle in their hands. I see a small creature waiting to be loved. I want to reach out & touch it, but I am afraid.

Then there's another commotion going on in the next hut, & the midwife knows it's time to move on. You people never stop! she barks at everyone. They lead her out & now she's delivering the other girl's baby.

It's nearly dawn when it's all over. She waddles out of the hut smoking a cigar. She sees me sitting outside, waiting. I've been up all night. She says she knows who I am. She knows I'm the father of both those boys.

You have a lot on your hands, she tells me. You are now responsible for these 2 lives.

I don't know what to say. Tomorrow the lieutenant's coming to give me my passport. Tomorrow this place is over. Tomorrow I'll be gone.

The midwife is sucking on her cigar & complains that no one's offering her any coffee. She will have to travel all day to another town. Another birth, another life. She will need a lot of coffee.

She says, I am an old thing, but I am fortunate, because so many people depend on me. You are very fortunate yourself. And soon you will find out.

Nothing but dead air. Then a Chinese pusher is executed at dawn. The wretched image of the blindfolded & bullet-riddled corpse is broadcast by government TV. That's the guy with the two-toned shoes, somebody says. No, that's the guy with the Ray-Bans. Everybody thinks they know him. The body's tied to a lamppost, stooping like it just fell asleep. It looks like a ragged scarecrow.

There's just one family that owns a TV here. We're all gathered inside their hut to watch the news. The president has promised to start cleaning the country up. There's a nationwide crackdown on crime. Even the lieutenant is nowhere around. No one, it seems, will be spared.

I'm watching the blue light of the screen flickering on all these faces. All through the rest of the broadcast nobody says a word. Then someone, an elderly resident who'd been sitting in the back, coughs & breaks the silence.

About time, he says. Maybe things will start getting better around here for a change.

The girl's father is freaking out. The lieutenant promised them they would get paid for the boy. Now they're stuck with it. One more mouth to feed, he complains. He's been drinking palm wine all day. He doesn't know how else to deal with the problem. What good is one more mouth to feed? he asks.

The girl's crying. She doesn't even want to look at the baby. You have to take it, she finally says. It's yours. It's your responsibility.

The father's holding onto a piece of paper & then he hands it to me. Those are the people who want to buy it, he tells me. The lieutenant made them a promise. There were people coming to get the merchandise. Life would be good.

There are 2 names here, I tell him.

One's for this boy, the other's for the other boy.

What other boy?

Anna's, he says. She's going to go crazy too.

Anna wants to go out for a while & asks me to look after the boy. I've never been this close to it before. I am afraid I will break it, I am afraid to touch its fragile body.

I ask her how long she's going to be out. Not too long, she says. She needs more milk. There's someone in the barrio who owns a small store with lots of infant formula milk. She wants to get more before the supply runs out. The island's gone crazy. No food's been coming in.

I tell her that kind of milk isn't good for babies. She tells me she has no choice. Her milk has all dried up. Her body won't feed him anymore. She's getting frail & weak herself. She thinks she's going to die.

I wait for her for an hour, then two hours pass & I make up my mind. The baby cries all the time. It stops when I stick a bottle in its mouth. I wrap it in a blanket & then I walk back to the other girl's hut.

Give me some money for the ferry, I tell her father.

He looks at me like I've just come down from heaven.

I'll take them, I tell him. I'll get you the money.

The girl cries even louder, unable to control herself. She comes over to me & takes my hand & for a moment I think she's going to kiss it but she pulls me over to the cot & brings it close to touch the boy.

You will save them, she says. You will save me.

The American woman who's come to take one of the boys asked me if I'm the father of the child. I don't remember what I told her. Things are spinning so fast.

I have just handed the other one to another guy at another hotel, just 2 blocks down. He looks worn out & forlorn. I thought a boy would lift his life a little. He is leaving in 2 days, the sooner the better. You know what's happening here, right? he says. The president has just declared martial law.

I ask him when that happened. Last night, he answers. That's right when I was halfway to Manila on the ferry. He has a thick French accent & his hands are shaking. Everything is screwed, he says. The president is installing himself as dictator-for-life. Soldiers have arrested all members of the opposition, including students, senators, labor leaders, everybody who's in his way. Get out while you can.

Are you the father of this child?

The American woman is standing at the door, waiting for my reply. Things zip through my mind. For a second I want to take the boy back. I don't know why I should, but for the first time I feel truly afraid.

I tell her what the French guy told me. Get out with your son as fast as you can. This country is going to blow up.

Then she asks something strange. She asks me if I have a place to stay. I don't. But I have her money, and the French guy's, & I can get a room of my own.

She's already getting ready to go. She tells me to get a ticket quick & fly out with her. Come with me, she says. Save yourself.

I spend the night on the couch, unable to sleep. I can hear the baby crying. On the ferry over here, people were coming by to look at them. Two sons, they told me, you are blessed by the gods. Two boys to look after you when the time has come to look after you. Don't laugh, they told me, sooner or later we all get old & need some looking after.

I can hear her crooning softly to it. She's going to be good. I will not need any looking after. I pull the money out of my jeans pocket. I count the bills & halfway through I stop. I have enough to buy a ticket. No passport though. Maybe I can take a boat somewhere close, like Malaysia or Singapore. Bribe someone. It's got to work.

In the middle of the night I doze off & I wake to find her stroking my hair. It's too dark to see, but I know she is staring into my eyes.

What is it like, she asks me, being alone in a world like this?

I tell her everything. I don't know why, but I want to tell someone.

Why don't you just sign up? she asks me.

I tell her I don't want to kill any gooks. Gooks never did anything to me.

They're fighting America, she says.

I don't want to kill someone like that, I tell her, pointing to her bedroom. I don't want to die.

But you will get out, won't you?

I tell her I have no passport. I have nowhere to go.

Fly back with me, she says. If you save me I will save you.

Long silence.

I understand, she says sadly. You will go back to her then.

Who?

The girl you left. The girl who gave birth to my son.

Why?

Because only those who truly love us can understand our necessary betrayals.

I tell her I don't understand.

I don't think I understand either, she says. But I think I am beginning to. You cannot betray someone who loves you. You cannot live with that. You will never be whole. You will never be alive. Fate has decided the matter for you.

I don't know about that, I tell her.

You need to be weak to know you are strong, she says. When you find someone who truly loves you, that is the direction you must follow.

Is that why you came here?

Not all of us are as fortunate, she says. Many are lost.

I want you to do me a favor, I tell her. I explain what I need her to do.

Long silence.

I beg her to do what I need her to do. I tell her that is how she will save me. I tell her I think I know what she means. But her eyes turn sadder when I tell her she's right, I must go back. There is no one else who truly loves me. I will have to learn to return that love.

She stops stroking my hair. You are very beautiful, she says. She kisses my mouth.

You will never be lonely, I tell her. Promise me you won't.

No promises, she says. But I will try.

All through the ferry ride to the island, I wonder if I should even go back. I still have the piece of paper in my pocket, the names of the people who have taken the boys. I crumple it in my fist & am about to throw it in the water & again I change my mind. The ferry plods through the choppy water, straight ahead to that endless nowhere. But it's that nowhere that I need to love, it's where I need to disappear.

I will disappear. I will be fictitious & incommunicado. I will be happy in my invisibility, I will forget all & remember nothing. I will be new. I will be more than human. I will live on the moon.

I've been gone a few days & Anna's just got the telegram I sent her from Manila. She meets me at the pier, her face sick with anxiety. She doesn't say anything. She waits for me to speak.

I tell her what happened. I tell her I got her the money. We can start over. We can have a new beginning.

She is staring at me. Just staring. Her eyes blank. Her face unchanging.

Then something strange happens. She shuts her eyes, her torso bends sideways a little, her knees buckle, & her entire body grows limp, like a flower quickly wilting, as she faints.

* * *

I have given the girl & her father their share of the money. But I can't find Anna anywhere. She left in the middle of the night last night. Everybody says Anna's always been like that. A little crazy. Blame it on the shit she used to do in Japan.

I go searching everywhere. She is nowhere to be found. One night I wake up from a terrible dream. I am doing the same thing again, going from one hotel to the other, handing out the boys. I can't tell one from the other. I don't remember which one is Anna's & which one is the other girl's. But it doesn't matter anymore. I have to do what I have to do.

The next morning I'm thinking maybe I can contact one of those people, either the American woman or the French guy, & ask if I can return the money & have the boy back. But which one? I have woken up inside my dream.

Days later, someone tells me there's a woman who can help me. He can tell me where she is. He leads me to a house. As soon as I walk in I see him scampering away, & then I realize what's happening.

The lieutenant's inside, sitting on a chair, facing the door. He's with a guy with an Uzi pointed straight at me.

I knew I could trust you, he says. Thank you for coming back.

We are held in place by gravitational forces

She is explaining to me that *casa* in Italian is pronounced with a *z*, not with an *s*. It's the smartest thing she must have said all night. We have just seen Gianni Amelio's *Le chiavi di casa*, a film about a young reckless father who finally takes the responsibility of looking after his autistic son. In the middle of the film, when the kid gets lost, she takes my hand and places it under her skirt. She has pulled the front of her panties down. The lost kid hops on a train and is found several scenes later in a police precinct, where his distraught father decides he can't carry this burden after all. Her pubic hair is heavily matted and moist. She keeps her eyes closed for the rest of the film.

Later we are sitting in a garden café, surrounded by painstakingly fashionable and studiedly rebellious East Village types. She chose the place herself. She is some kind of poet, activist, and performance artist, and she "blossoms" (her word) in a place like this.

I met her on the Internet. She likes to send random, scathing reviews of books and music to Amazon.com in order to pull their customer ratings down a star or two. I sent her an e-mail saying I admired her candor. That is the first thing we talk about. She says she feels a sense of triumph when other people read her posts and get righteously upset. She imagines her words spreading like a virus, and the author or artist anguishing over her reviews. I imagine her life must be meaningless outside of this activity, but that she is probably unaware of it. She is much older than I expected, but I go to the movie with her anyway. I am convinced that if I could find someone, be in some kind of a relationship, that would even out what I have going with Yuki. It would be a fair balance. She has a small pixie face but her eyes can't hide a certain hostility (toward injustice, racism, or corrupt politics, perhaps) and make her look older and incredibly tired. Her hair has frizzled dry with constant coloring, a kind of Mercurochrome alizarin that glows like embers under the café's track lights. She is a vegetarian, chewing on her salad greens mincingly, like a rabbit, as though the prospect of nourishment terrifies or repulses her.

A few minutes after we sit down, a gray-haired man comes by and says he just happens to be three tables away. He is wearing a shabby plaid flannel shirt and looks like some adjunct in a university somewhere, or a perpetually struggling artist, one of the city's innumerable below-poverty eggheads. Accepting a kiss on the lips from him, she tells him she's busy right now but will give him a call. She tells me he was last week's date. She says she can tell if people haven't been fucked in a while because they start looking haggard and angry, their loneliness seething inside them and pushing itself out until it takes over their physical countenance, like aliens do in Hollywood movies. I wonder if she is referring to last week's date or to me. Yuki and I haven't fucked since her boyfriend came back. It has probably been more than three weeks. I think I should ask if she wants me to fuck her. That might take the edge off her a bit, or make her leave Amazon.com in peace for a while. But that doesn't seem like the proper thing to do, even though she let me touch her during the movie. I have never been with anyone but Yuki. I don't know the protocol. I start feeling hopeless and am relieved that she can talk endlessly, saving me from the responsibility of proposing anything. Her voice is hoarse, like she has a sore throat. No matter what the subject is, she manages to steer the conversation back to her. What she does, what she likes, what she doesn't like. It's an endless loop and I catch on pretty fast and keep the conversation going by pretending I am a reporter interviewing somebody important. She has dated dozens of losers before. I admire her consistency. Before we part (I tell her the truth, that I have to get back to my mother, who I am looking after) she says she likes me. "You're a nice guy, I like you, I really do." I don't really find her repulsive until she says that, because up till then she sounded candid and sincere. She agrees to meet me again the following week. At the last minute she cancels. She doesn't explain why. I feel no disappointment, only relief. We never keep in touch. Like a clumsy reporter, I've even forgotten her name.

In the stairway I see Yuki's boyfriend getting ready to go out. He is some kind of white Latino, one of those Ricky Martin types. I attempt a smile, which must come out as a wince. I force a tentative hi. He heads down the stairs. I cough, awkwardly, to get his attention. Now that I have made the first move, it is important that he acknowledge it. Following him down the stairs, I become more and more anxious that he responds, that he doesn't subject me to the humiliation of being ignored. He looks up at me fleetingly, with what I imagine is a vaguely concealed expression of annoyance, since I am dawdling right behind and give the impression that I might want to pass, but have not yet made up my mind. He is dressed in a tight-fitting black blazer. His shoulder-length hair is tinted with just the right amount of highlights. I feel so ordinary being in the same stairwell with him, and it feels even more imperative that he at least turn around, say something, or at least give a sign that he knows I am anxiously following him, waiting for him to return my admittedly clumsy greeting, a greeting so maladroit and half-hearted I myself would have paid no attention had it been given to me.

But he offers no such sign. He has the casually studied nonchalance of people who are aware of their good looks, who saunter through life with the self-assurance of those who know they are sought after, are welcome anywhere, and have a place waiting for them at the table. I can smell the deodorant cologne he has just sprayed lavishly all over himself. I keep staring at the top of his head, his thick head of chestnut-brown hair. I could bolt down faster, overtaking him, providing me with the chance to pretend I don't care, to show that I am in a hurry myself and that my attempt at friendliness is nothing more than an exercise in civility, that I would have offered the same greeting to anyone else. But I keep walking behind, slowing my pace so that I won't have to subject myself to the ignominy of asking his pardon and slipping past him. A fucking metrosexual, I tell myself. I know what I'm going to say to Yuki next time we meet: *Scratch a metrosexual and you get a faggot.* I have to keep myself from blurting the words out loud, so fierce is my rage, and finally, as we reach the front door, he does turn around and, almost imperceptibly, deigns to offer me a quick nod of the head. It's too late, my fury is boiling over, my face is flushed, I am trembling with fever, and the smile I am finally able to evince comes out as a grimace, and I must look like I am about to cry. And in my head the words that I try desperately to hold back pound like blood. *I hope you die, you cocksucker. I hope some FedEx truck runs you over as you walk out this door.*

Yuki's right, as usual. Heroin keeps Mother in a transient limbo in which she is temporarily free from suffering. Under the spell of the drug, her body is a vehicle that is so easy to let go. But as she becomes addicted to it, her delusions make more and more sense to her. Her dreams are bizarre, sometimes euphoric. She tells me she has seen Frank many times, and he has left his girlfriend and wants to come back. They visit Asia together, saving a newborn baby from the continent's black hole. No one wants to bomb her out of existence, no one wants to cast her soul in hell, and her past sins have been expiated. Somebody from the Life Crusaders comes crawling to her bed, weeping and asking for her forgiveness. But the dreams, so solid, so convincing while they are being experienced, melt stealthily into her waking hours, when her body asserts its demands, and once again she is wide awake, keenly aware of all the stabs of pain she is going through.

"You know you'll have to be prepared to keep giving it to her, right?" Yuki says. "To stop now is cruel."

I wonder if I have done the right thing. I try to stop giving her the junk for a few days, but she plunges into even more agonizing pain, and I relent and get her more. I am in this shipwreck as much as she is, as equally addicted to the idea of a cure as she is to the idea that there is none.

Yuki assures me my concerns are not singular. "You're talking about contraband here, Jordan. They're illegal for a reason."

I am coming to rely more and more on her experience and common sense. In fact, I am relieved that it is Yuki who, in a way, has made this decision, not I: I am more than happy, on this occasion, to surrender my freedom to her.

And yet, I tell Yuki, when she began to suffer from Cotard's syndrome, Mother and I switched places. Mother lives in a make-believe world, a world I can't understand and makes sense only to her. A nonworld, an afterlife in which there is no life, in which the body refuses to pull back, but instead makes her witness its slow demise, its odoriferous dissolution, its messy farewell. It is she who lives in a world more real than mine, because my world is founded on what is now becoming even less possible to imagine: that she will come back and make it whole again.

"Once you give it, there's no turning back," says Yuki. "These are the facts of life, Jordan. Welcome to the real."

I do try to pull her back, to convince her that she has to see clearly, the way she always did, the way she always wanted me to. And failing that, the only thing I can do is to push her farther into that other world where I am the gatekeeper, but can't get in.

"I wish you could see it the way I do," I tell Yuki. "I wish you could see how much I suffer."

"I do, Jordan. I do care so much about you." She leans over and gives me a kiss. I close my eyes. I can smell her skin, the scent of soap. Then I open my eyes and realize she is not there. I've been talking to myself again, going through this conversation over and over, trying to find a way to convey to Yuki what is going on inside me, trying to lure her to *come in.*

One evening, before picking up Mother's junk at the Pit, I put on a suit coat and sneak out. I have hired a young immigrant from Mali to look after Mother on certain weekdays. Simone is patient, quiet, and uncomplaining. Leaving Mother with her frees me from any guilt. Yuki is fucking her metrosexual again. I can hear her stifled yelps as I pass by their door. I walk aimlessly and take the C train downtown and catch a dance performance at the Joyce. I walk in during the intermission. Nobody stops me—nobody stops a man wearing a suit. I don't really care what is showing. I just need to do something.

Two dancers race round and round the stage, an endless movement that seems hopelessly trapped in its orbit, the instinct and volition of celestial objects which appear to have been designed for some mystical, awe-inspiring purpose, but from which the only escape is not refusal, for no such thing is possible, but to go off-kilter, to collide, to submit to total destruction. The music stops. The dancers fall completely exhausted. That's the way it is with Mother and I, with Yuki and I, the only two constant celestials in my life. We are held in place by gravitational forces. As long as we maintain the right combination of attraction and repulsion, we will manage to keep one another in orbit.

In Aleksandr Sokurov's moody, meditative film *Mother and Son*, a man carries his dying mother through a landscape that seems defiantly fertile, alive, and indifferent to the anguish of separation these two beings are undergoing. He takes her across lush, winding paths, through a sudden squall of rain, and back to their home again, the entire journey lasting more than half of the film, mostly in silence, punctuated only by brief, oblique reminiscences of the mother about her hard life.

In the opening sequence, the son recounts a dream he had the night before. "For a long time, I was walking along a path and someone was following me. Finally I turned around and asked him why he was following me. Guess what he said."

His mother replies, "He asked you to remind him of several lines." And she quotes, "*I am seized by a suffocating nightmare. I awake, terror-stricken, covered in sweat. God, dwelling in my soul, affects only my consciousness. He never extends beyond me to the outer world, to the course of things. My heart is heavy from such imperfection.*" Finally she adds, "I saw and heard all of this."

"In your dream?"

"Yes," she says. "In my dream."

"That means we have the same dreams."

"Yes," she says. "We do."

I can imagine no deeper form of intimacy. Sokurov was able to portray this within these few minutes. But such a profound, spiritual connection also anticipates grief, inescapable and inconsolable. In the end, before she dies, she tells him, "I am afraid for you. For the life I have gone through, and which you are still about to experience."

I watch the film over and over, for months on end. I can bear to watch nothing else. In order to understand what Mother is going through, sometimes I imagine myself as that despondent, dutiful son, whose destiny is linked inextricably with hers, and whose narrative is a continuation of hers. Love and solitude: no other forces can be so gravitational and bring two bodies so close to collision.

The more I watch the film, the more I get in the habit of thinking of myself in the third person, a character in a film, in a narrative that needs only to be spoken. There, I convince myself, in that meshwork of memory, contemplation, emotion, and fact, lies what Mother's doctors once referred to as the *zombie human*, the mind's perception and reconstruction of the body it hasn't seen, but lives in.

Myself in the third person: He's lost all interest in his immediate environment, and even less interest in other people. But he's aware of everything that's happening around the world, watching with his mother, despite his frequent admonitions to avoid the news, the BBC at six and the same rebroadcast at seven. He himself prefers to get the news from the web, sifting through its mines of factoids, biases, inanities, and lies, like the *gam saan haak*, the immigrants who sailed from China to look for the Gold Mountain in California, digging for nuggets not of truth but of the plausible. Occasionally, on impulse, swayed by e-mails soliciting money, he sends small donations to activist Internet organizations like MoveOn.org, but he doesn't feel strongly about issues, and people in general exhaust him. He finds them petty and ridiculous, but as long as he dealt with them at a distance, as he did on the web, they didn't really bother him. He abhors crowds and the subway. He hates being touched by strangers. He brushes his coat clean with a hand towel every time he comes home.

* * *

Yuki tosses a document on the table for me to see. I pick it up.

"A notary public?" I ask her. "The notary public that signed Andrew Brezsky's bequest?"

"The very same one."

Incredulous pause.

"A simple thank you would suffice," she says.

"I've almost given up on it. On the whole thing. My mother's story about Andrew Brezsky. About my adoption. About the money being wired back to her. Even my half-brother in France. It all just seems so . . ."

"Unreal?"

"Yeah."

"Well, this guy's real all right. He even has a name. See? Nick. Nick something. Sounds foreign."

"And he's a real estate broker now? Wow. Hey, Yuki, you know what I do when things start to seem unreal? I think of myself in the third person. Sometimes it's easier to take this all in if I think in the third person. Then I can think of myself as maybe a character in a film, in a story that maybe I can create myself."

"Yeah? I like to do that sometimes too. Pretend I'm someone else. Someone prettier, happier."

"Okay. Jordan can't believe this is happening. He wonders what he should do next."

"Well, Yuki thinks Jordan should try and get in touch with this Nick, just to find out."

"Find out what? Jordan wants to know."

"If everything he's heard about his real father is true."

"How did Yuki find this guy?"

"Yuki likes to use what some people call the Internet.

Makes life easier. You can find anything on the Internet. A pair of shoes. Your long-lost father."

"Okay. Jordan says okay."

"Yuki thinks Jordan's not exactly jumping with joy."

"Jordan's lost all interest in his immediate environment, and even less interest in other people. But he's aware of everything that's happening around the world, because he watches the news all night with his mother, who seems to like to watch nothing else."

"Yuki thinks Jordan's decided not to see this Nick at all. Yuki wonders why. You seeing him or not?"

"Jordan's still thinking about it."

"Okay. I did what I could."

"Jordan thinks—"

"Okay, stop. This is getting a little weird."

"You get tired of anything new after a while."

"Yeah. That's the reason I never got a dog."

"Dogs are no problem. You can always take them to adoption centers when you get tired of them. You can always have them put to sleep. It's the most humane solution we have found for redundant relationships. In fact, human relationships should end the same way."

"But that's kinda like what Andrew Brezsky did to you."

"There you go. He did the logical thing."

"Do you ever wonder if you could have wound up like those babies your mom used to cut up?"

Long silence.

"Kinda gave you pause, didn't it?" Yuki says.

"My mother did what she did, but her intentions were good."

"I know, I'm sorry."

"Mine was a totally different case."

"In what way?"

"I wasn't going to get, you know, cut up."

"Okay, sorry. Forget I even mentioned it."

"I was made to order. Like a Mini Cooper. No one was going to cut me up."

"You're special. I get it."

"Yeah. Just like Mother always said."

"I didn't know you felt that way about relationships."

"What relationships?"

"Redundant relationships. I thought you were more like, you know, romantic."

"You're the one who gets tired of novelties so easily."

"If I recall, we were just talking about dogs."

"Same thing."

"The more I know you, the less I know about you."

"The less a man is compelled to come into contact with others, the better off he is. Jordan has always believed in that."

"Yeah. Well, tell Jordan fuck him too. I really thought I could help you. Great going, Yuki. Great fucking going." She gets up and leaves.

I sit at the table, pick up the document, and stare at it for a long time. It only occurs to me days later to remind her that those words are not mine, but Schopenhauer's. Great going, Jordan. Great fucking going.

I keep returning to the Pit until Bloomberg has it shut down and the owner gets hauled to Rikers Island. But by then, thanks to my casual chitchat with Ugo, I've come to know more about the wonderful conveniences of this city of ours.

There is, for instance, a car service number that you

can call on Seventy-Third. If you drop a name they know, it's easy as ordering Szechuan takeout, but it's important to speak the jargon. If you ask for, say, a Mercedes, you just ordered marijuana (hydroponic, excellent stuff, and not cheap). I'm looking for a Hummer, hard to find in the city lately, but not impossible. After all, the Afghan poppy business is back in full swing since Bush chased the Taliban out of Kabul. And if worse comes to worst, our borders are porous, homeland security is a joke, and there is always cheaper junk from south of the border.

I pick up my orders regularly, every Tuesday, on my way to collect the laundry. The guy who sells them, a certain "Bob," initially cautious, understandably suspicious, eventually warms up to me and considers me a regular, if not a friend. His apartment reeks of cannabis. There are vials, canisters, sachets, pillboxes—a cornucopia of everything anyone needs to get by. Bob likes me. He likes it that I am there punctually, and that I have nothing much to say to him. The first time I meet him, he gives what I soon learn is his obligatory first-timers-only spiel:

"What's the purpose of self-narcotization? To get over emptiness by intoxication. You know who said that? Music is intoxication. Cruelty, sadism, these are forms of intoxication. Deep feelings for a single human being, love or hatred, that's intoxication. Science, the quest for knowledge: intoxication. Self-pity, mysticism. Art for art's sake, pure knowledge, these are narcotic states of self-loathing. Continuously working on something, fanaticism. Debauchery. You got it, all forms of self-narcotization. The closest we can get to belief in the fucking soul." A pause. "So how many Hummers do you want?"

"Just one for now," I say. Bob holds on to the dime

bag. He seems like he still wants to talk to me, and I feel I have to say something. "Buddhists don't believe we have a soul."

"What's that?" he responds.

"They don't believe there's a permanent soul. There is no god. There is no one who rewards or punishes us. We are merely the result of all past action, ours and others'. But it's unbearable not to believe in a soul, or a fatherly god, or an afterlife. So the idea is necessary, just like morphine is necessary for someone in pain."

Bob stands up and, like a demagogue at a pogrom of one, he declares, "My friends, it sucks to be young. We suffer youth like a serious illness. That's because of the times we live in. A time of inner decay and disintegration and uncertainty. We live for tomorrow, because who knows what comes the day after tomorrow? Everything on our way is slippery and dangerous. The ice that supports us has become thin. We all feel the warm, uncanny breath of the thawing wind. Where we walk, soon no one will be able to walk . . . You know who said that?" He hands me the dime bag. "You sure that's all you need?"

"Nietzsche," I say.

"Yeah. Everybody in this fucking city reads Nietzsche."

I sneak out whenever I can, but especially when I know Yuki's boyfriend is around. I can hear them practicing together, he on the violin, and I am shocked and dismayed that someone I detest so fiercely can play so well. Then I hear dishes being washed, conversation, the TV. That's it. I can't stand that everything they do sounds so *domestic.* I have to get out.

At Hernshead in Central Park there is no one else but

a couple of kids, maybe about senior high school age, sitting in the gazebo. I climb up the schist rock protruding out to the lake. The sun has just set. In the blue light I can see and hear what the kids in the gazebo are doing. They are speaking softly in Spanglish. The girl has pulled the boy's cock out of his pants and is rubbing it and making it hard. He has his hand up her blouse and is kneading her breasts. He lifts her blouse high enough to expose her nipples. They are large and dark like Oreos. She hitches her skirt up and pulls her panties down to her knees. She turns around and sits on his cock, doggy-style. The boy is going, *Yeah baby yeah baby,* and something else in Spanish, and the girl bounces up and down on his lap. The girl's skirt is hitched high enough to show the dark thatch of her pubic hair. I slip my hand inside my jeans and rub my dick.

Then the boy sees me. He says, *What the fuck?* and pushes the girl off and stands up. I scramble down the rock. There is no way out of the area except past the gazebo. The boy steps right in front of me. His pants are still unzipped and his hard dick is bulging inside his boxers. He says something like, *What the fuck, you pervert?* and the girl says something like, *Fuck off, faggot.* The boy spits as I hurry by. I walk away as fast as I can. My heart is pounding. When I reach Central Park West, in the midst of rush-hour traffic, an electric current of pleasure is still buzzing in my head.

"Okay, here's the deal," he says. He likes using expressions like that, thinking it makes his accent less obvious. He's Greek and speaks as though he is always mad at you. "There's this two-bedroom, really fabulous, south-facing windows and all that shit. It's rent-controlled. How much money do you think a fucker like that would cost you?"

We are at La Boite en Bois, a couple of blocks from his office at Torres Realty on Seventy-Second. The café is empty. A waitress is idling by at the bar, eavesdropping out of boredom. I think about his question. "A couple thousand. Maybe more."

"Where the hell will you find a fabulous two-bedroom, hardwood floors, in a beautiful prewar building, in that neighborhood, for the price I'm going to give you? Where? You tell me, my friend."

"Nowhere," I say. "It's a steal."

"It's a fucking steal. Now how much are you willing to pay for it?"

"Whatever it's going for. I mean, if it's rent-controlled—"

"Listen. People will suck my cock to get this apartment. I'm not saying I want you to suck my cock. What I'm saying is—you know what I'm saying."

"People will kill to get that apartment."

"At any fucking cost."

"But you guys can't raise it over the rent allowed, right? I read it on the Housing Board website. You can only raise the rent, what, like three percent or something, right? So it doesn't really matter who gets it. You get the same max rent no matter what."

He opens his briefcase and takes out a sheaf of papers. "You're wasting my time," he says, shaking his head. "I have an appointment in an hour. I'm auditioning for a part. I told you I'm an actor, right?"

"Yeah, I know."

"I hate doing this to you, you know that, right? But what am I going to do? Starve my fucking ass like everyone out there? No way. I'm very good at what I do. Look at this script. Damn fucking hard to memorize. But I can do it. I'll get the part. You should watch me. I'm damn fucking good."

He drinks his espresso in one gulp, tilting his head back. The waitress leans over the bar and asks if he wants another one. "No, dear," he says. "She's an actress too. But you see what I mean? I'm not going to serve damn espresso to anyone."

"What I really wanted to talk to you about—"

"Listen. People would give anything to live in that neighborhood. Look around. Banana Republic. Starbucks. Gap. Swatch. Even fucking Kangol just opened a shop. Anyone would easily give me fifteen fucking thousand just to get that apartment."

I lean back. "That's a lot."

"Fucking Kangol. You know where they opened the only other shop like that? Fucking Tokyo. Anyone else would give ten thousand up front just to move into that neighborhood."

"Yeah, I bet. If I had that much money I'd do the same thing."

"How much do you think people would give me just to move in? I can easily make five thousand, right here and now. There are hundreds out there hoping they're at the same table that you are right now. Think about that."

He begins reading his script, mumbling the lines to himself. He is wearing a gray blazer and a turtleneck sweater with yellow stripes. He is clean-shaven, but the skin around his jowl sags a bit. His nails are meticulously trimmed and gleam with some kind of polish. He is wearing a baseball cap that says, *Nick*. I figure he must be maybe fifty-five, sixty years old, which is just right. I say, "Nice cap. Nick, that's a typical *Greek* name, right?"

"My real name is Nikolai Kostakopoulos, but I changed it to Nick Costas. I'm part Italian, French, Greek, Spanish, and I speak all those languages. I'm an extraordinary man. This apartment, you planning to get one so you can fuck your girlfriend in peace, right?"

"No."

"So how come you're moving out of the one you have? What's wrong with that?"

"Nothing's wrong with it. That's what I wanted to talk to you about."

"I don't give a fuck who fucks who around here. I only do my job. I only want to make people happy. She's gonna love this apartment, the girl you're fucking. Have her talk to me. I can't talk to you. I can't figure you out. I'm speaking very frankly with you, but you keep making me guess. It's the Asian in you. I like your people, but you're so fucking inscrutable. The owner will like you living there. He likes Asians, the Japanese especially. You're lucky you're not black. He doesn't want black people in the neighborhood. I want to do you a favor. I like you. Think about it. Here. You're Therese." He hands me the script.

"Therese?"

"I've got the lines all in my head. Go ahead. Read."

I scan Therese's lines. "What's it going to take, Jim, for you to realize this is over?"

"It's not over. You know that as much as I do."

"I can't live like this anymore. And Brenda."

"Brenda's going to be fine. She needs to be away for a while."

"Away from whom? From you and me? What are we doing, Jim? What the fuck are we doing?"

"We're doing the right thing. I've given it . . . Fuck.

I missed a line, didn't I? She's in good hands. What did you think I was going to do? I've given it a lot of thought."

I put the script down. "I'm looking for Andrew Brezsky, Nick. That's what I wanted to talk to you about. The only way you'd see me was if I were looking for an apartment."

Nick glances at his watch. "What the fuck," he says. He slips the script back in his briefcase. "You're fucking wasting my time."

"He knew you in Manila or something. You were a notary public there. You processed his bequest to his two sons. I'm one of them. I'm one of Andrew Brezsky's sons."

"He said *what* to you?" Yuki asks me. "He said, *Suck my dick, asshole?*"

"Yeah. *I don't know what you're talking about, you fucking piece of shit.* It sounded like he was reading from the script. Pretty cool guy."

We are lying in bed. I have just seen Nick that afternoon.

"What if I gave him a call?" she says.

"What would that do?"

"I have strong powers of persuasion, if you know what I mean."

"Forget it. I don't want him anywhere near you. Fucking sleazebag."

"Well, we tried."

"Mother wouldn't have believed him for one minute."

"So what are you going to do about your mother?"

"Nothing. I'm going to do what I've been doing the last six months. Mother's going to be all right."

"Don't you ever try the junk you get for your Mom?"

"I don't like to get myself fucked up."

"So you like getting her fucked up?"

"I like seeing her not being unhappy."

"You're a kind man. Maybe you should get her to go out. She's okay to go out, right?"

"She doesn't want to. She's scared."

"You guys are in there all the time. It's like living at the Bates Motel. Good thing your name isn't Norman Yeats."

"That's not funny, Yuki. In fact it's fucking tasteless."

"That was a joke. If only your sense of humor was as active as your cock. You should feel lucky I'm showing some interest in your life. You come to see me only for a fuck. You haven't even asked me what I do exactly, aside from the cello. If I'm in some orchestra or something. If I'm in some fucking *band*. You never ask me anything about my *life*."

"Yes I do."

"What have you asked me?"

"I asked you if you ever felt concerned that your boyfriend is away so often."

Long silence.

"Are you ever concerned that he's away so often?" I repeat.

"You son of a bitch."

"Are you? I want to know."

"When he's away I feel incredibly *volatile*. Next question."

"There's no next question."

"Why?"

"I'm afraid of what I might hear."

"See, you can't even be *attentive*. You can't even reciprocate my *concern*."

"Yeah. You know so much about me. I don't like it. I

feel invaded. You can see me plainly, and you've already made up your mind what to think about me. There is nothing I can hide. I don't want to talk anymore. Can we just not talk so much anymore?"

She's deep in thought. Then she says, "Lorenzo wants to go away for a while."

"Who the fuck is Lorenzo?"

"My boyfriend."

"Where's he going?"

"I don't know. He doesn't know. Buenos Aires. Shanghai. Or something. He wants to try his luck somewhere else. He says he's freaking had it with New York. I don't know."

"What did you tell him?"

"What the fuck could I tell him? Go where your dick wants to go. I don't care."

"When is he leaving?"

"I don't know. He doesn't know what he wants. I bet you he's not even leaving at all. I bet—"

I kiss her on the mouth to make her stop. I want her to stop feeling what I know she's feeling, I want her to stop the loneliness that I know is forcing its way out of her skin, that slow, quiet explosion I know so well.

"I'm sorry I was such an asshole," I tell her. "Thank you for finding Nick. Thank you for trying."

She has her eyes closed, and for some reason I want to see her cry. For her boyfriend, for anyone. But she's lying still, unmoving, unmoved. I kiss her nipples and run my tongue down her torso, down to the line of her pubic hair. She hardly stirs.

Dear Mr. Brezsky,

   There's this guy who's possibly the only one who can tell

me your story. He's the guy who did all the legal shit for your
bequest. So kindly tell this cocksucker friend of yours to pick
up the phone or shove it up his Greek ass. Only say it nicely,
if you can.

I tell Yuki I was staring at my inbox, unbelieving, for a
long time.

"Let me guess," she says. "Mr. Brezsky finally wrote
you back."

"Even better. There was a brief message from someone who claims to be writing from Manila. He's using the
alias *masque de fer*."

Yuki and I are at Les Deux Gamins in the Village. It's
a small bistro with lots of lesbians, a place she frequents,
she clarifies, for the dinner fare not the crowd. It's the
first time she and I have gone out together. I suggested it,
but wasn't expecting her to say yes. Her boyfriend's been
away for a while. I have been spending a lot of time at her
apartment. I thought it was time for the two of us to act
like a real couple, though I never said it that way. I'm hoping to show that I am interested in her beyond our furtive
assignations while her boyfriend is away.

"What's *masque de fer*?" she asks.

"Iron mask. I did ask him why he chose that particular net ID. The legendary *masque de fer*, the man in the
iron mask, was incarcerated in Fort Royal on Île Sainte-
Marguerite in 1687. The island is one of two called the Îles
de Lérins. The other is Île Saint-Honorat. They're both off
the coast of Cannes in Southern France."

"I'm not sure I get it, Jordan."

"He wants to know if I've found out anything about
Andrew Brezsky. He says if I can give him any leads, he

may be of some help gathering information. He has been spending a bit of time in the Philippines. I wrote back to ask him why he's interested in Mr. Brezsky. And this morning he replied that he knows for a fact that Mathieu Aubert spent one summer recuperating in the monastery at Îles de Lérin."

"Wait. Matthew *who?*"

"The other guy, Mr. Brezsky's other son, aside from me."

"Okay, getting more and more suspicious."

"And, if all goes according to plan, Mathieu will get in touch with me soon."

"Jordan, let's keep focused here. You have a mom who needs a lot of help. What are you going to do about her? What do you really want to do with your life?"

"I'm going to find my brother, Yuki. Then everything in my life is going to change."

"Okay," she says. "Good luck."

Two women at the next table have been staring at her all evening. They must have been eavesdropping, and one of them flashes Yuki a broad, inviting smile. I know Yuki's aware of the attention she's getting. I touch her hand. She pulls it casually away.

"Get real, Jordan. Please."

I look out. There are red lights strung in front of a bar across the street. "That's nice," I tell her. "That string of lights out there at that bar. It's like Christmas."

"It's a Portuguese restaurant. Not a bar."

"Your plate looks good. What is it again?"

"A crêpe with mushrooms and goat cheese."

"I'm having sausage and ham."

"Sounds delish. Enjoy."

* * *

Myself in the third person: Jordan Yeats is moving furniture. He's thinking of getting a couple of AeroBeds: there's reason to believe he'll contact his brother soon, and he's cleaning the place up in preparation for his arrival. He's washing the windows, mopping the floor, checking to see that everything is working all right. He remembers how van Gogh in Arles painted his entire apartment yellow in honor of the arrival of his best friend Cézanne. Yellow, the color of happiness. Sitting before his computer screen, he can feel his words burn through the cables, staring back at *masque de fer*. Weird, yes, but as long as no one can see, weirdness doesn't exist.

Happiness comes with trepidation, because we are aware, deep down, that happiness is fragile, ephemeral, constantly endangered by its opposite, or its absence. Like the human body, which carries the chemicals and bacteria that will devour it after death, happiness contains within it the very forces that will initiate its disintegration. What we seek is not immortality, but immortal happiness. Jordan Yeats has found an alien presence in him, an emotion so big it just might burst out of him. He lives with it as with a stranger, a guest grudgingly accommodated, and with whom he maintains a polite, uneasy distance. Its presence gives him a mix of discomfort and fascination. Its habits are bizarre and erratic, its history and future unknown, its itinerary a complete mystery. He immerses himself in ordinary chores, hoping exhaustion will distract him from this unfamiliar creature, but try as he might, he finds it hard to make sense of this visitor, and futile to calm it down, to make it settle and be still.

Somebody stop him: he wants to paint the apartment yellow.

Nick finally calls back. "I'm going to give you one hour. Just one hour. Because I'm through with that lawyer shit. I'm a broker, okay? A damn good one. I did Brezsky a favor. That's all it was. Who you are or where you came from is not important to me."

It starts to rain. It has been raining almost every day, the rainiest spring I've seen in years.

I keep my umbrella low, just enough for me to see where she has turned, and who she is talking to. She's talking to Nick. A thin waterfall of rain drips between their umbrellas. He hands her a manila envelope. A corner of it gets wet in the rain. She pulls it from him quickly and tucks it under her coat.

She lights a cigarette and offers him one, which he declines. She smokes absently, a mechanical impulse, devoid of attention or pleasure.

They talk a little longer, and he points out that water is seeping down the collar of her raincoat. The manila envelope is soaked. I can almost hear her say, *Fuck*, I can see her lips spit the word out, and a short, embarrassed laugh.

She walks away. Nick heads back in the other direction.

I walk toward where they've been standing. It's the kind of day when all color seems to have washed away. It's a black-and-white kind of day. I can still smell the cigarette smoke lingering in the thick, rain-choked air.

Half an hour later, as I expected, Yuki is walking up Columbus Avenue. The rain is pouring steadily now. I listen, my heart pounding, as the front door opens with its usual clangor, a metallic clatter that echoes through the stairwell. I move away from the window and look around for something to do. I wish I had a book to read. It's important not to look like I've been waiting.

She must be walking up the four flights now, pausing briefly on the third floor, as she always does, to catch her breath. On the kitchen table a two-week-old copy of *West Side Spirit* is spread out on the horoscope section. My horoscope says I am drawn to people like her, a partner who will either nurture me or whom I will nurture. That's what she once said herself. I circle the statement with a marker pen to make it look like I've been busy. Her exact words were, I'd end up in a kind of *astrologically dictated codependency*, which is how she says the universe is strung together, a web both cosmic and karmic. I don't even know what that means, but I scribble it inside the margin anyway. My shirt is still damp. The newsprint leaves a black smear on the cuff of my sleeve.

I can hear her fumbling with her keys. I look at what I've scribbled and realize my script is indecipherable, a tangle of squiggles. I can't keep my hand still.

She takes a couple of steps in, one hand helplessly glued to the door as she struggles to pull the stubborn key out of the lock. Her nylon coat, bought at a Benetton winter sale, drips pearls of water on the hardwood floor. The key finally released, she chucks it on the table, right smack on my horoscope, and touches my shoulder lightly without saying a word.

I follow her into the bedroom. We lie in bed, listening to the rumble of thunder, muffled and far away.

"I saw you," I say. "I saw you talking to him."

She doesn't respond. The wind drives the rain against the windowpane in a steady pizzicato. I think I am going to doze off until she brushes her hand against my jeans, resting it where she feels her boyfriend's keys snug in my pocket. The sound of the rain drumming above us makes me think that something massive, a freak medusa, has crawled over the city and is drilling its thousand tentacles through the tar on the roof.

She turns over and unzips me. I raise my arms and tuck them under my head and feel the stretch coursing through my torso. She sucks me slowly, running her tongue along the length of my cock. There is a stain on the ceiling where the rain has started to soak the plaster. It looks like an island on an ancient map, intricately detailed but inaccurate, out of scale. *I saw you*, I say, but this time in a whisper, lost and feeble in the surrounding wall of rain. A web of dust has gathered in a corner of the ceiling, a small, black wisp, a diaphanous nebula seemingly suspended of its own will, barely clinging to the surface, defying gravity, perhaps teeming with brief, invisible life forms, quivering almost imperceptibly as a fatal draft seeps through the shut window. *I saw you talking to him.* I prop myself up on my elbows to watch her, holding back from coming for as long as I can. She makes me think she wants to merge with me, like cannibals do, like Holy Communion. *You need me as much as I need you.* I want her to hear me say it, truthful and obscene. *We hold on to each other not out of love but fear.* I can tell she is feeling very lonely, because of the rain, because of me. Because there is nobody else around but me. When she lets me come in her mouth all I feel is gratefulness, a grateful relief. I've already forgotten what I've seen, the bitterness of the afternoon as I stood in the rain.

"You never told me you knew him."

"I didn't. I do now." She hands me the couple of pages Nick photocopied for her. The edges are stained wet with rain. "I did it for you. Consider it a favor."

"It's so convenient that the notary public who allegedly executed my supposedly biological father's bequest should just happen to be working in the same neighborhood I live in, isn't it?"

"It's fucking eerie. What can I say?"

"It's funny how he should suddenly be so, well, solicitous. So willing to help. After he blew me off. Did you do him a favor too?"

"Fuck off, Jordan. Just fucking read the fucking thing."

I skim through the papers. They are written in a tiny scrawl, on a lined notebook, but the photocopy is so bad the words are almost illegible, if not ghostly. "Brezsky's journal? Written when he was in the Philippines? You really believe this shit?"

"You believe those e-mails from your so-called brother. Why not take a chance on this one?"

"Because it's so fucking blatantly a scam."

"You wanted to know so bad. I tried to help. I wanted you to get over it. Get over Mr. Brezsky, Jordan. Now you know, now you got what you've been looking for. Start living your own life."

"So you and Nick just made this up? What about those e-mails I got? Are you *masque de fer*?"

"Jesus, Jordan."

"Or maybe Nick's been sending those e-mails. Nice try."

"Okay, you know what, maybe I'm not good at this. Maybe Nick's a fraud, maybe I got sucked into a scam. I thought this would give you closure. Isn't this enough?"

"I need to write to Brezsky. He would know what to do."

"Forget Brezsky and move on. I wanted to find a way to help you do that."

"People look for your weakest point, then they strike."

"You're so fucked up, Jordan. I wish you weren't so fucked up."

I can hear her playing her cello. I have never heard her play like this before. It is moving, and, though hard for me to admit, achingly beautiful. She once said that whenever she plays, her mind is nowhere else but on the music. The sound comes up through the windows, through the floor between us, filling the apartment with Janácek. I imagine her lost in it, in a world made purely of sound. I have always envied musicians that ability, to be able to interpret their bodies through music, a mysterious transcendence.

Then she is joined by a violin. I listen closely, stupefied, unwilling to realize there's someone else with her. It takes me a long time to accept that her boyfriend is in town and they're back together again. Something in me switches gears. Everything she has said to me is counterfeit. Even the idea that she can block out everything while she plays, to live in a world of pure sound, fills me with repulsion. I slip a CD in my boom box. I feel like listening to Fugazi, something mournful but not self-pitying, furious but not out of control, the perfect balance of anger and pain. Guy Picciotto's lacerated yowling conveys exactly how I feel.

Warning
the threat of morning
that just extends you another day
some lights were shining
not much for seeing
but you'll be leaving the way you came . . .

They play on, oblivious to the ruckus I am making. Maybe they can hear it. Maybe they're just ignoring it. I dial her number. She doesn't pick up. I wait just long enough to hear her voice message on the machine. Then I hang up.

I tell Mother I have found pages from Mr. Breszky's journal. I tell her I am going to send copies to Mathieu Aubert. He might or might not agree that it's all bullshit, but it will be a good excuse to break the ice. Of course, I am presuming he's real and willing to come and meet me. The more I tell her about it, the more I realize I am working purely on assumptions, and I regret ever having mentioned it—I regret the act of sharing, which chips away at what I have so firmly believed in.

She hasn't heard me at all. Or so I think. She talks randomly, absently, to herself, to no one. In her world I have already begun to disappear.

"Have you written to your father lately?" she asks.

"Frank? No, I don't have anything to say."

"I meant the other one. The one who lives on the moon."

"No, not in a while."

"He would know."

"Know what?"

"Where your brother is, if you have one."

"You believe me then." I lean closer, eager to hear what she has to say.

"He told me to get out quick. The country was going to explode."

"Yes, you told me."

"I asked him to stay with me."

I wait for her to continue. "Did he?"

"What?"

"Did he stay?"

"He was such a beautiful boy. You could tell he was going to die young."

The Abbaye de Lérins, a monastery located in Saint-Honorat, is run by a congregation of contemplative monks of the Cistercian Congregation of Senanque. It seems that Mathieu Aubert stayed briefly at the abbey, sometime in the late 1980s. I imagine how he must have found it comforting, the perfect antidote to whatever it was he must have been suffering from (*masque de fer* didn't really elaborate). According to their website, the island is also some kind of bird sanctuary; the words glow on the screen, foreign and exotic, soothing as music, which Mother's caregiver, Simone, reads back to me: *corneille noire, faucon crécerelle, rossignol philomèle* . . .

In a later e-mail, *masque de fer* finally signs his message with a real name. He turns out to be a she. She signs it in lower case letters simply as *janya*. She doesn't explain why she wants information about Brezsky, only that it is important for her to know. In a final e-mail she says it is a matter of life and death. I begin to wonder if there has been a mistake in Brezsky's bequest, if perhaps one of his children was a girl. I ask *janya* if this could be so.

I wait days, then weeks, for a reply. Nothing comes back. Just as quickly as she appeared, she drops out of sight, and though I send one e-mail after another, eventually dashing off several a day, my messages bounce back, as her ID can no longer be located.

Dear Mr. Brezsky,
"Masque de fer" has disappeared, and my hopes of finding Mathieu Aubert with her. So do me a favor and tell her it's all right. It was just an elaborate joke. Tell her this: Jordan Yeats is looking for his brother, Mathieu Aubert. He knows where Mathieu lives. He lives with you, in the Descartes Highlands, on the Moon.

WSOWOB

Janya's director is having a breakdown. She's hyperventilating, talking at a hundred words a minute, calling to tell me it's "absolutely imperative" that Janya contact them soon. Janya's been missing her appointments, she hasn't shown up anywhere, and hasn't even returned "the hundred messages" the director has left her.

The last time I spoke to Janya, she was telling me what she had learned from the professor: the new middle classes of Asia have their own private backyard sweatshops, with often a handful of young girls—daughters and cousins and neighbors—working three or four shifts. They're sprouting everywhere, and now that she's pursuing that lead, Janya is overwhelmed by the work, traveling around the region more frequently. One person alone can't keep up with the seemingly effortless proliferation of outsourcing minifactories. When she's not auditing sweatshops, she's training new hires or attending conferences and meetings. China wants to demonstrate it can play fair, or make a show of it, and pretty soon she'll have to inspect factories in their industrial cities as well. We might even have to move to Shanghai.

She comes home days later, breathlessly talking about work. "Cheap labor is available in over half the surface of the globe. The global market, a world divided between billionaires and slaves, is the unavoidable future of the human race."

I tell her about the director's call. She stops in mid-sentence, realizing she's been caught off guard. "She knows exactly where to reach me," she says. "She's under a lot of pressure, the organization's falling apart, and she's just passing on the pressure to me. Typical of her. Stupid bleeding-heart left-wing bitch."

There are letters from people I don't know that she refuses to talk about. Meetings that are unexplained and unnecessary. Bills and receipts, some items blacked out with a marker pen.

Every time she goes away, I inspect her things. I look for signs. I find nothing, but that doesn't mean she's done nothing.

I call her director to tell her that I feel something's wrong. The minute I say so I realize I shouldn't even have considered confiding in her.

She replies enigmatically, "We are very concerned about her." It's one of those American expressions that merely fill up space, and don't really mean a thing. "Please keep me posted."

I tell her I will. I know I won't, but from then on every word Janya says is suspect, every single object is damning evidence: I have already betrayed her.

Once, she leaves her laptop logged on to her e-mail server. I find the address of the guy she's been e-mailing in New York. I read his e-mails, bizarre, outlandish vignettes about his life in New York, his mother, his paranoia, his everything. I hit *Reply* and type, *hello.* I stare at my message for a long time before deciding to delete it, but somehow I press the wrong key and the message is sent. I see it being sent in the viewer, the blue bar inching its way through cyberspace, and nothing I do can stop it.

I devise a better tactic to deal with the situation. From now on I say nothing either. Everything must be as covert. I don't want to drive her away with my suspicions. When she comes home, I inspect her luggage and her clothes as she takes a bath. I look for unusual smells, telltale stains. I check her tickets. There are stopovers, detours, side trips that she never mentions. There are changes in her that are imperceptible to others but me. Sometimes she's happier, more tranquil. Or sometimes things bother her that I don't understand, that she doesn't want to talk about.

My inability to probe the mystery, her refusal to let me take part, makes me more anxious, even more doubtful. I follow her around the city to see who she meets with, where she goes.

One night she takes a taxi to the business district, to a condominium apartment in Makati. I stand outside the building, staring at the lights of the apartment. She's there for a very long time. It starts to drizzle. I smoke one cigarette after another, each tasting more and more bitter on my tongue and drying my mouth until I'm sick of smoking, but can't stop. I keep standing there, waiting for her to come out. She never does. My entire body feels drained out. I'm getting sick.

I come back and find that she's already been home for the last two hours, wondering where I was. I should be relieved that she's home. But the emotion I felt, standing in the rain, waiting for her, refuses to let me go. It's a sickness that's already contaminated my blood, that's filled my heart with poisons. I am incurable.

* * *

It costs about forty-five thousand pesos—under five hundred euros, just barely nudging eight hundred dollars—to hire a private detective in Manila. You probably get your money's worth. But they're hardworking and they have no scruples. They can weave their way through layers of bureaucracy and corruption. They're sneaky as weasels.

Early evening at a café in Remedios Circle. The rotunda is the city's hot spot for trendies, trannies, hookers, and pushers. It's a bit ramshackle now, tourist traps crammed around a sorry excuse for a park where homeless children sleep off tonight's dose of glue and cough syrup. I'm looking at them, lying side by side on a pile of flattened cardboard boxes, from a window partly covered by an Italian lace curtain. In a while they will wake up and accost the tourists, holding their palms out to the promise of the world.

There's a blackout in the city, one of many sporadic power outages that people take for granted now. He has a funny way of describing it—it's God taking His time to blink. A generator is whirring in the back like a chainsaw. Candles have been lit around, and the place has a funereal air. The kitchen staff looks lazily at the bruise-colored light on the street outside, nothing much to do, just waiting for people to come in. Around here, come blackout or floodwater, as long as the foreigners are around, it's business as usual.

He's a middle-aged man with a fatherly air of both distance and solicitude. He's seen it all. He has a full head of thick black hair, matted down by sweat. His dark complexion makes him seem to fade into the backdrop. I can't help staring at his hands—large and chunky, a boxer's hands—to anchor his presence here. I feel like I'm talking to no one, to myself. He's asking me about my film. It's an odd thing to talk about. I've told him what I did, mainly to impress upon him that I don't have much to pay him; I am not the loaded tourist they all think we are. That hasn't sunk in. The flickering candle casts quivering shadows on the table and makes me imagine that my hands are shaking. I grasp my left hand in my right.

"She disappears for long stretches of time but refuses to tell me why. She wasn't always like that. She says she doesn't need to explain it to anybody. Not even to me. She goes on these periodic bouts of—I don't know what it is—solitude, I guess that's what it is."

"But you suspect there's more to it than that." His voice is dispassionate, an even monotone.

"She travels a lot, you know. She has to. It's her job."

"And that's something to be concerned about?"

"No. I don't know."

"You think it's an excuse."

"No. She says she needs to be alone once in while, which is okay. I need a little space myself. Once in a while. But I don't, you know, keep things from her. So how can I get rid of what's nagging inside me, unless I know for sure? The problem, you see, is not her but me . . ."

He's staring at me. I can tell he is. I can sense his eyes, cold and calculating.

"Maybe I should talk to a therapist, not a detective," I tell him.

"There are no therapists in Manila. Only detectives."

The power comes back now. It's a blinding burst of light, like a flash. The café is garishly lit all of a sudden. I can see his face clearly. He's getting thick around the middle, his face has the tiredness of one who's been making ends meet to support a family with four children. He needs me, I can tell.

"You can think about this for a while, and get back to me," he says. "But I suggest we start immediately."

I stop him even before he finishes. "I want to know everything."

One day I suddenly come up with the idea of doing something new. I am going out to shoot my own response to Sylvain and Annette's unfinished film. It will be a dialogue of generations, their skepticism juxtaposed against the twenty-first century's need—*my* need—for something to believe in.

The concept strikes me as brilliant. Immediately my spirits are renewed. I feel buoyant, and even though I know that in a few days I will abandon the idea, at this moment I am motivated simply by the awareness that I have managed to eject myself out of the cycle, that I am acting *out of my own insistence.*

No matter what I do, ultimately I always cave in. One night, I sneak out to the red-light district. The girl I choose is an old hand, to use a clever pun. I am in good spirits, and when she asks me to buy her shot after shot of rum, I do so generously, though I know it's actually just tea. We all lie when we must. I try to taste it, the putrid brown liquid half full in a Nescafé glass, which she pulls away from me.

"No, no," she says. "That is lady's drink." She jerks me off under the table. Her hand is large and clammy, genetically predestined, I realize, for the work she does. She keeps looking around the place, smiling at the other girls who are doing the same thing to their clients.

"Keep your eyes on me," I tell her. "Don't look anywhere else, or I don't pay."

"Jealous man," she says. "I like jealous man, make me think you love me."

Her smile is saccharine and phony, the way I like it. I tell her to get down on me.

"Under table?" she asks, as though this is something no one has asked before.

"Yeah, under table."

"Pay extra."

"I'll pay whatever you want."

She slides daintily from the seat and kneels between my legs. I look at my watch. I don't want to pay for an extra hour. I grip her head with both my hands as I come in her mouth. She gags and tries not to swallow, though she knows she's already taken a great risk. She spits my come in the Nescafé glass. A ribbon of white ooze sinks lazily to the bottom. She wants another glass of rum. "Look what you make me do, now I got nothing to drink." All I want is to get out of there and go back home, back to Janya. I've done what I wanted to do. It's knowing that I've betrayed her that gives me a sense of power.

Back at the apartment, I sit with Janya and have mint tea, converse, even read a book beside her. My body's still burning, my cock stinging with pleasure.

"You're flushed," she says. "And short of breath. You smell different."

I tell her I ran up the apartment stairs instead of taking the elevator. Lying about it makes it even more exciting. It's the lying that I've been looking forward to.

In a way maybe I want her to find out. Soon I'm going out with women that we both know. Some of them work in the same field as her, some are artists, others are just wealthy bitches with nothing to do but hang out in bars. Nights with them are long, tedious, and exhausting. I get tired of them pretty fast. I'm sick of these bored, sheltered, lonely women who aren't Janya, who never can be. All I want is to expend this fury inside me, all this pent-up energy that finds its release only in seeing Janya again, in choosing her *as its object*.

And when she does find out, it's so easy for me to say it's nothing, it means shit, it's just a fuck. Because that's the truth.

"You're going to be all right," he tells me.

"Sure. Sorry." I can't stop shaking. I feel like I have a fever. The rains have come again. The city is blurred by a cheerless sheet of gray. I rub my eyes. I haven't been sleeping well. My eyes sting all the time. He's waiting for me to say something. "She's seeing someone, right?"

"We're not sure yet."

"I think I know who it is."

"Okay," he says. "I can always use another lead."

I hand him the letter.

"Is this blood?" he asks.

"Mine. Accident. Long story."

He tucks it inside his shirt pocket. He's wearing a plaid cotton shirt that looks too young for him. I wonder if he's cheating on his wife himself. Everybody here does. I am staring at the coffee stain on the front of his shirt, wondering how the end of the world could be so banal, that this is what I see before my world falls apart. He notices me staring.

"We're going to get you everything you need," he says.

She has this power over me: she knows my need is stronger than hers.

In bed, she holds me so tightly it feels it's not out of affection, but desperation or fear. She knows how I love the smoothness and color of her skin, her scent of orange blossoms. She's a small creature, her breasts are small, her arms are skinny and frail.

"When I hold you," I tell her, "it's like holding a fifteen-year-old girl."

"But you like that, don't you?"

"Uh-huh."

"One of these days you're going to turn into a pedophile. But that will be our little secret." She puts her lips against my ear and says, "Call me Vasin."

"No. Not anymore."

I can feel her body stiffening underneath me. I roll off and listen to the hum of vehicles snarled below. A sudden downpour always tangles up traffic. Everybody's got his hand pressed on the horn, and there's one long, angry dissonance of horns blowing. The rain pours steadily, but there is no relief to the humidity, and we're sweating profusely, the heat bearing down on our bodies, solid and sticky.

"He was my uncle," she whispers, almost inaudibly. "I was very young."

"You freaking fucked your uncle?"

"Just a fuck," she says. "Like any other fuck. There are worse things on this planet."

"Yeah? What could be worse than incest?"

"He'd never had anyone. Only prostitutes, not a real

woman. I felt sorry for him. So I let him fuck me."

"A *mercy* fuck?"

"We didn't even get it on. We were, like, just fooling around. Now you know my dirty little secret. I have nothing to hide from you."

"Do you still think of him?"

"He taught me something important."

"Which is?"

"I have to stop looking for somebody perfect. No one is. No one can be."

Silence.

"Vasin," I say. "You like to hear his name."

Silence.

"You like older men. Is that where you're looking for perfection? Maturity, confidence, security—"

"Fuck you, Mathieu. Age has nothing—I like you."

"Not mature, not confident, not secure. Utterly damaged. But I *am* older than you. Goal."

"Yeah, well."

"So is Gino."

"Oh, Jesus."

"So is the professor. I can see a trend now."

"You wanted me to share a secret. That was the best I could come up with."

"I'll say."

"I thought it would be the bombshell to end all bombshells. I wanted to make you happy. Okay?" She's staring at me. "Tell me something."

"What?"

"Have you been fucking someone else?"

"No."

"No one?"

"I would never do that to you."

She turns her back to me. "Liar."

She whispers something strange in my ear: "*Fa-rung-sayt.*"

The heat sticks to our skin like sheets of plastic. We are lying in bed, watching the ceiling fan idly spinning, barely stirring the air, two sweltering bodies dumbstruck by its uselessness.

"That's what the Patpong hookers call their boy-friends," she says.

"I'm not one of those."

"But you like them. The mountain girls from the Karens or the Hmong. Phil said so. He said he watched you do it with one of them."

"Phil's an asshole."

"It wouldn't be a surprise, your leaving me."

"I'm not leaving you."

"But it wouldn't be a surprise. Nothing's ever going to change between East and West. The West is always going to fuck the East, the Old World is always going to screw the Third. The two of us alone aren't going to change anything."

"That sounds like the professor speaking. Are you picking up ideas from him now?"

"Oh, Mathieu. How can you be so blind?"

"About what?"

"We agreed, when we first started seeing each other, that words are ultimately meaningless. Language is a manner of distancing. Only our bodies can meet. Fucking makes people say things they don't really mean. My desire makes me commit acts of irrational devotion. My madness is an act of love."

"I don't like it when we talk like this. I find it hard to bear."

"Only our bodies can meet. In everything else, we're all alone."

She likes to say things like that. She wants people to see she's not your typical Thai girlfriend. There's a certain aggressiveness that you find in people who believe they're oppressed, a kind of defensive pride. I always thought I knew her so well.

"When did you start feeling this way about it?"

"I've always said exactly the same thing. You just weren't paying attention."

When I first met her, I found it exciting, this second-guessing, this looking for subtexts, this Asian inscrutability. A game, a ruse, a kind of foreplay. Now that we know so much about each other, or rather, now that I know there are things I will never know about her, it's become a malfunction, a fatal flaw.

"Paying attention to what?"

"My point exactly."

In time, of course, I catch on. We must speak only with our bodies, not in words but in acts. Then I can play along. This is important to me.

"I know who it is," he tells me.

It's taken several weeks for him to find out. He's followed her everywhere, intercepted letters through connections at the post office, bugged her phone, taken pictures— lots of pictures.

We're back in the same café. There's no one else on this lazy late afternoon except for a group of young people at the next table, three girls and two boys, one of whom is telling them a story in exaggerated, almost clownish gestures, to the amusement of his companions who are all listening intently, waiting to see how his elaborate, theatrical anecdote will turn out.

"I don't think I want to know," I tell him. "Now that I've thought about it. You know, maybe it's over. Maybe it didn't happen at all."

At the bar counter, the coffee machine sputters, the sound filling the café. One girl has both her hands over her mouth, unable to endure the suspense, but at the same time casting quick, annoyed glances in the noise's direction. Leaning closer to the storyteller, she claps her hands over her mouth even tighter, as though she ultimately intends to suffocate herself.

"It's not over until you know," he tells me. "And you have to know."

"All right."

"You know she's been e-mailing someone in New York City, right?"

"That's a dead end. You don't have to follow that."

He shows me a printout. He traces his finger under a line. *You can never save someone who refuses to be saved.*

"She wrote that?"

"No, he did."

"Who's he?"

"The one she's been in touch with." He shows me another printout. *If I cannot save Mathieu I will save you.* "This one she wrote herself," he says.

"This doesn't mean anything. She doesn't even know the guy."

"They're all connected."

"Who?"

"This guy, the professor, the one in San Crisostomo."

"What do you mean, they're all connected? You mean a conspiracy? Give me a break."

He hands me the photographs. She's with the professor, sitting close together, holding his hand. They're in places I've never been to, mountain towns, picturesque, heartbreakingly beautiful, surrounded by natives who look straight out of a Native American reservation camp. The pictures could just as well have been taken in the 1930s, back when white tourists loved to show off the Indians. I can't focus. I feel like I'm in a time warp all over again. I feel like I've already been here, I've already seen these pictures, I've already lived the end of this story. One photo shows them leaning so close they look like they're about to kiss. I can't stop looking at it.

"She's expecting something from the so-called professor," he interrupts my thoughts. "She is sending it to the guy in New York. She is getting something in return. I still have to figure out what it is. But I will find out."

"And the guy in San Crisostomo?"

He shows me a letter addressed to her. *You must be very careful. You must not let him know.*

"What does that mean?"

"I'll find out and let you know."

"You have nothing. These pictures don't mean a thing. This was a bad idea. I need a drink."

"She knows you've hired a detective."

There's a burst of laughter from the next table. The girl who had her hands over her mouth is now pounding them raucously on the table, like a drum, unable to withhold her glee.

"Be prepared," he tells me. "She knows."

* * *

I stand outside the café for a while. I'm not sure where I want to go. Through the window, I can see the group inside, still laughing at the joke. Their mouths are wide open, their eyes brim with tears. I can hear no sound. Just the rumble of taxis passing by. But even that fades away, a sound effect displaced and edited out. I look at the group inside again. No sound, how can so much laughter have no sound?

My heart is filled with poisons. I can hear my heart pounding inside me, I can feel it pumping its lethal corpuscles through my body. I am incurable. Night comes quickly here. A curtain falls, and then it is dark. I have never gotten used to the suddenness of it, the immediate turn from light to dark. No transitions, nothing in between.

I can see myself out on the sidewalk, one arm raised, a taxi slowing down to pick me up, its headlights beaming toward me. My eyes flash in the dark, like a cat's. The taxi swerves to a stop. I get in. We weave out of darkness into deeper darkness. The driver asks me where I want to go. I have no idea. He keeps driving, deep into the labyrinth of nowhere, the warren of Korean bars, the soot-covered apartments, the mass of bodies milling along the street, nonbodies, bodies with no lives and no names.

"Where to go, sir?"

"Straight ahead. I'll tell you when we get there."

"You all right, sir?"

"Yes. No."

And once again, against my better judgment, I find myself asking for the impossible—that the source of my suffering be taken away.

*　*　*

And then she springs it on me.

"Maybe it's time we did the tourist thing, like everyone else."

The tourist thing is the row of clubs and bars in the red-light district, where backpackers get doped up and fuck the local boys and girls for the same amount of money they pay back home for a CD. When we first came to Manila, Janya and I promised ourselves never to go that way. It's what people without imagination do around here, tourist-industry scum, Japs and Eurotrash and American pedophiles.

This has got to be the weirdest thing she's ever said to me. "Why the tourist thing?" I ask. "And why now?"

"I want you to go out. Stop editing those films for a while. Give Dreyer a rest."

"That's not the reason."

"Okay, how about this: it's conceited to think you and I can ever help a country as messed up as this."

At Octopussy, underage girls newly plucked from the provinces parade naked across the bar counter. Janya rolls up peso notes like cigarillos and inserts them into their smooth-shaven vaginas. One girl gets on her knees to plant a long wet kiss between her breasts, leaving a fierce red smear.

At Apollo, she sits close to the platform, the better to see geriatric American men drip hot candle wax on the nipples of adolescent boys. The boys sit on a bench facing the audience and masturbate. There's a round of cheers and applause as their sperm spurts and lands on the dirty floor, forming specks of dust-coated pearls.

At Circus, she insists that we stay for the night's main event, when a man and a woman both insert fresh eggs into their anuses, perform some kind of mock tango, and expel the eggs into each other's hands, while the audience, prodded by an emcee, coaxes them with clucking sounds. At the end of the act, the man raises his arms and crushes both eggs in his fists. Streaks of thick yolk drip down his glistening biceps.

Watching Janya enjoy the spectacles, I feel a pang of jealousy shooting through me, a sensation so physical I must wrap my arms around myself, as though I'm freezing in the club's relentless heat. They're giving her a certain thrill that I can never offer again, the thrill of the illicit. Everything between us is above ground. This, I recall, averting my gaze from her, from the sight of her pleasure, is why we'd decided never to do the tourist thing in the first place: it's pointless to think in moral terms when everything is permissible. We have become the people we detest. We have lost the capacity to imagine what is forbidden. We have been freed, in other words, from our own hypocrisy.

We are walking away from Circus when the guy who had performed onstage, who smashed the eggs in his fists and let the yolk dribble down his arms, stops us and asks if we'd like a private show with him and the girl. We tell him we're calling it a night. He won't let us go. He says we can whip him with a belt, he knows that's what tourists like. He drops his pants to show the welts on his butt.

"Five pesos for every time you whip," he says. "Just five, really cheap."

We move off, trying not to laugh too loud, but he remains standing in the dark alley and calls out, "Fuck you tourists, fuck you people from Japan and America."

By the time we reach the apartment, I'm grabbing Janya, teasing her about holding a private performance of our own.

But she pushes me gently away. The buzz in my head, the fierce and desperate words of the man as we took off, the din of traffic as we maneuvered our way back to the hotel, reverberate in my head.

I follow her into the bedroom. She lies on the bed with one arm over her eyes. I lie by her side. The air conditioner is humming and the room is cool, a universe away from the oppressive heat outside. I ask her what's wrong.

"Tired," she says. "Dead fucking tired."

"Why did you want to go there?"

"So I can see why I hate this place so much. And I do."

We stay that way for a long time, side by side, not speaking.

"I have to go away for a while," she says.

"Where?"

"Somewhere. Away from you."

"What the fuck does that mean?" I say it in a low voice, without meaning to sound angry.

"I just have to. One of these days I'll explain."

"One of these days? What the fuck, Janya."

She rolls on her side and reaches out to pull the lamp switch on. Suddenly the room is filled with glaring, blinding light. I notice for the first time, in this light, how she seems to have aged since we took that trip to San Crisostomo. The shadows under her eyes make her look as though she's just come out of a season of grief. "I'm going back to Thailand. I'm taking the earliest flight available."

"Are you going with the professor? With Gino?"

"Jesus, Mathieu."

"I'm going with you."

"We'll be quarreling about it all the way to Bangkok."

"Okay then. I just want you to say something. Be straight with me. Tell me what this is really all about."

She gets up and pulls her luggage out of the closet. She's already packed.

"Just fucking say it's over," I tell her. "If that's what this is about. Just fucking say you've changed your mind. I shouldn't have let you know all that shit about me. I shouldn't have been so open. That's what this is all about, isn't it? Just fucking say it."

She sits on the bed, looking very exhausted. "Fucking pollution," she says. "This banana republic will never get its act together. It will always be fucked."

"Just fucking get the nerve to say it, Janya."

She walks to the window, peering out at the snarled traffic below. Two bands of light, one red, one amber, snake through the entire length of the boulevard. No one's getting anywhere for hours.

With her back to me, she says, "Everyone in your life keeps making sacrifices for you. Even the boy who got lost at sea. Even he disappeared so you could have a life. And none of that makes any sense to you."

We check in at a cheap hotel in Patpong. It's the kind of place European backpackers and neohippies go to. She doesn't want to stay anywhere fancy. She says she's sick of everything and everyone, and the stupid foreigners who come to Bangkok, who think of Asia as their own private playground, make her sick the most. Tomorrow she's leaving in a futile attempt to search for a place where she won't run into them.

We spend an uneasy night together. She takes a pill to cancel out the unbearable carousing of drunken Germans in the bar below. I drink myself blind and go to bed. Sometime in the night I wake up to find her sucking me off. I try to push her away but she clings to me hungrily, and I don't want to resist. She keeps sucking even after I come. The sensation of tender pain sends a chill throughout my body.

I wake up early the next morning, my head throbbing with a hangover. The light hurts my head. The scent of orange blossoms fills the room. Through the window facing east I see the silhouette of a woman on a porch among the cluster of tin roofs and wooden shanties. She's washing her hair, a long, shimmering cascade of black over a tin basin. She and I are the only ones awake at this hour. Watching her, distant and unreachable, I feel a loneliness that's intensely physical, choking the air out of me.

Janya is stretched out flat on the bed. She's totally naked. She's so skinny I can see the outline of her bones. She's breathing softly, though her rib cage is rising so slowly it appears she's not breathing at all. The heat's already starting to rise. The room is stifling. I can peel the heat right off my own skin. I get dressed quietly, catching my image suddenly in the tin-framed mirror hanging on the wall. I don't recognize myself. My hair is gray. My eyes are sunken. The stubble around my jaw makes me look primitive and haunted.

Downstairs, out on the street, vendors are setting up their kiosks, pirated CDs and DVDs nestled between hills of gaudy batik T-shirts. Even their singsong chatter sounds like a jackhammer pounding mercilessly in my head. In a few minutes Bangkok is going to be all heat and noise, one massive sticky hell. I walk around aimlessly. I eat a bowl of tom yum at a kiosk, hoping the chili will help get rid of my hangover.

A stream of monks passes me by. It's the hour when they come out to beg for alms. I follow them back to a temple. I sit in a hall that reeks of jasmine. A young monk, about nineteen or twenty, is watching me. He follows me out and asks me a strange question: "Have you been inside a monastery before?" He says he'll show me their dormitories, if I want to see them. I don't really want to, but I follow him anyway. I figure he'll ask for money after the tour.

The dormitories are in the back of the temple. The rooms have about a dozen beds each, folding metal cots like those in army barracks. There are posters of deities on the walls, like rock stars. The residents are young men who are following the custom, devoting a year of their lives in a monastery before they join the real world.

"What's bothering you?" he asks me.

"Why do you think something's bothering me?"

"I'm going to kill Janya."

I stare at him in disbelief. "What did you say?"

"I will have to, or else she'll kill me. One life will replace the other. That is the law of equations, so simple yet so astonishing."

I stagger and fall backward. The monk reaches out to help me, but I brush his hand away.

"What's bothering you?" he asks again.

"Nothing . . . I'm not feeling . . . anything. Why do you think something's bothering me?"

"Something's always bothering somebody. That's why they come to the temple so early."

Later that afternoon, I go back to the hotel. Janya's already left. All her things are gone. The maid came in earlier and cleaned and aired the room. It smells of Lysol and Clorox bleach.

Through the thin plywood walls, I hear a couple arguing in German. I look out the window. There are neon ads and billboards lit with glaring fluorescent lights. Smog shrouds the city in a thick gray pall. People are flowing in and out of wooden shanties. Fragments of people. There was a girl washing her hair at her sunlit porch this morning. I'm never going to see her again.

A narrow canal runs through the back alley. It's an open sewer, a streak of black water clogged with toothpaste tubes, plastic cups, condoms, and clumps of human feces.

The sun has never been so golden, sinking into a net of TV antennas and telephone wires.

the little toil of love

I got them, says Nick. I got the missing pages back.

How'd you do that?

I told the lieutenant I'm your lawyer. Oh, & by the way, the name's Franklin Downey the Third from now on.

Do you have everything? All the missing pages?

Every fucking one. As far as I can tell. You said a lot of ugly things about me. Why'd you do it?

Do what?

Bring the babies to their foster parents. You could have just walked away.

Everyone was gone. I went to one of the businessmen's houses. It was all boarded up. They'd all been busted. I wrote about it. If you'd read everything, you'd know.

I haven't read the entire thing. Your handwriting's pretty illegible sometimes. Fuck, Andy. Those guys in the business, they're fucking military people. The whole business goes all the way to the top. The fucking president's probably getting a cut from it. They were probably just lying low until things settled. Just to show people the president means business. You should have known that. You should have done the same thing.

I tell him I was well aware they were military people. But I wasn't going to leave those kids on somebody's doorstep. Nobody in the village wanted those kids. They weren't meant to be there & everyone needed the money. Their life depended on the money.

You're not like that, Nick tells me. You're not telling the truth. I know you.

I explain how I wanted to give them their share of the money. I'm not an asshole.

But you didn't, he says. And you are. Why didn't you call me when you were back in the city?

I figured you were still mad at me. I don't blame you.

You were going to take the money & run, he says. You son of a bitch.

Hell no, Nick. The country was getting really fucked. I knew it was time to get out. I was going to find a way to fly straight to Canada. A bunch of guys I knew are already there. They won't touch you in Canada.

How do I explain that to Nick? I went to Manila & I met this woman, one of the foster parents. I stayed with her for a while. She didn't want me to leave. But I asked her to do something for me instead. I asked her to deposit everything in my account.

Why did you even go back? Nick asks.

I found out something. About myself.

Give me a fucking break, Nick says. This time he's really pissed off. He's shaking his head. I can't defend you if you don't tell me the truth.

Hey, Nick, I tell him, I'm sorry I sold your stash.

Fuck that, he says.

You got to believe me, man.

I don't know what to believe, says Nick. Not anymore. I'm tired of trying to save you all the time. Even a fool like me gets tired.

Remember. Remember. That evening Anna & I are walking along the shore & it's a full moon night. She's leaning her head on my shoulder & I recite to her this poem from memory:

> since some industry must be,
> the little toil of love
> is large enough for me.

She listens intently & when I'm done she says, If you & I ever get married, I want you to say those words at the ceremony.

Do you understand the poem?

No, but the words are beautiful & that's all that matters.

So I say let's get married now, with the moon as our witness.

Why the moon? she asks.

Because whatever imprint you leave there will live a million years. Like the moon rover's tracks. Up there, on the Descartes Highlands. I point it out to her. I tell her that's how people a million years from now will remember our age, how they will remember us. We remember the Aztecs by their temples & the Egyptians by their pyramids. We wonder who they were. We imagine what their lives could have been, & they live forever in our imagining. Up there, on the Descartes Highlands, is the monument that people will remember us by. You & me & this evening & this time. Can you see? Can you see the tracks?

Yes, she says, I can see.

So I begin the ceremony: I, Andrew, take you, Anna, as my lunar wedded wife . . .

After the ceremony we go back to her hut & fuck all night & all the next day. Then she has this wild idea, we exchange clothes, she wears mine & I wear hers, & then we undress each other so we can feel what the other feels, see what the other sees. We merge identities, we become mirror images of the other, not man, not woman, not brown, not white. We have become twins. Out of my shirt her breast appears, smooth & ripe like a mango. Under her skirt she finds my penis & when I unzip my jeans I find her open & yielding, her soft reassuring darkness.

Remember, remember. Only by remembering will you be saved.

The guy with the Uzi flicks the light on & kicks us out of our cots. It's four in the morning. He drags the student out back somewhere. I hear an ear-splitting howl. I hear the lieutenant barking orders, then laughing that insane laugh that sounds like he's choking on a bone.

Eddie's down on his knees, mumbling to Jesus into his tightly clasped hands. Every time the howling gets louder he curses along with his prayers, <u>Jesus, puta, Jesus, puta</u>.

The guy with the Uzi comes back & yanks me up by the arm. I hear someone yelling something incoherent, a strangely bestial howl, & I realize it's coming from me. It makes him panic, the lieutenant's voice booms from another room, <u>Don't let him scream</u>, & he rams the butt of the Uzi against my head. I feel it slam against my left temple, something like a car crash inside my skull, I hear it & taste it, iron on my tongue & all inside my head, all sound & taste, bitter & deafening. But I feel no pain.

The student & I have been transferred to a smaller cell.

There's a lightbulb hung from a wire that's been tacked to the ceiling. The wire snakes under the door & is connected to a plug outside the cell. It glares all day & night. There's no window. There's not much room to move.

We sit on our cots all day. One shift in position & the other has to move as well. Our uneasy politeness quickly turns to annoyance & then to downright gruffness. We communicate in grunts & loaded silences.

Nothing much happens after we're transferred. There's an unnerving stillness, an absence of anything that makes the waiting even more unbearable. We can't tell if it's day or night. We count the hours at first, but after a while we lose track.

What do you think is going on? I ask the student.

You know damn well what's going on, he says.

I stand by the door & yell until my voice gets hoarse. I slump on the floor. The student's looking at me like I've gone mad. At least they let you keep your notebook, he says.

Yeah, right, I respond. I should consider myself lucky.

He smiles painfully, bitterly. He says, The history that you write is not the history of the country that you plunder, but the history of your own nation & all that it skims off, all that it violates & starves. You know who wrote that? Why don't you write that down?

I don't give a fuck, I tell him.

Write while you can, he says. It doesn't mean much to me, Yankee.

We're 2 people on opposite sides of a war that will take some time for either of us to make sense of. Our confine-

ment together will never be anything but combative &
uneasy.

He tells me Filipinos are in jail because we Americans
want a better world for ourselves. It's America that gives
ammunitions to the dictator. He says, Your corporations
can do whatever they want here as long as our government protects them from our discontents. It's you who
will benefit from a Philippine dictatorship.

Always it's <u>you, you, you</u>. As though I'm personally
responsible for the shit these people are in. Their poverty,
the exploitation of their women, their tortures, their de-
spair. & I find it impossible to disagree.

America: the name itself is synonymous with impe-
rialism—you've taken the name of two entire continents
& claimed it as your own, & shut out anyone else from
using it.

He must have said this to me 10x today. We have very
little else to say to each other. We sit in silence for hours,
each staring at his own side of the wall. Every so often the
power fluctuates & the lightbulb hisses & sputters. Then
finally it goes out. Neither of us moves.

If the students & workers take over, the first thing they'll
do is throw people like me in jail. Yankees, the bourgeois,
the professionals, people with property, intellectuals, po-
ets, artists, all the detritus of colonial society.

<u>What the people demand is not the settler's position
of status, but the settler's place</u>.

I know that shit too. You're not the only one who's
read that shit. Whoever wins a revolution like this will
consider me the enemy. In this drama, there's no world
I'm welcome to.

* * *

I know why you came here, he says.

Everybody knows, right? There are no secrets in this goddamn hellhole.

A lot of you are here to avoid the draft.

Yeah, fucking big deal, right?

This is not the right place to avoid the draft.

Well yeah, so maybe I'm here for something else, ever think about that?

I know the young people of America are taking to the streets & speaking out against the war. I know many of your young men are in jail simply because they oppose the war. You believe you're fighting a losing war, a war against a people who don't want America to tell them what to do.

Yeah, all right, so you know. Shut the fuck up, man. You don't know fuck. You don't know what we really feel. You haven't seen what we've been through. You're so caught up in your hatred for America, nothing will convince you that as individuals, we are lost. We feel shame for a country that's gone the opposite of everything we believe in. How can you even understand that? For you we're all just the same bunch of people. What I believe in doesn't mean fuck to you, right? So let's just shut the fuck up.

You came all the way here to stand by your principles, he says. You risk your life to oppose your government's policy of war. Yet you feel no shame about using our women for your own self-interest.

What the fuck does that mean?

Everybody knows why you're really here. Everybody knows what you did.

You don't know crap, man.

Standing by your principles. That's nice. That makes you some kind of a hypocrite, doesn't it?

A dream.

I am in Manila again, shuttling from 1 hotel to the other. But I have nothing in my hands. I knock on a door & there's a guy there. Not the American woman, not the French guy. It's the boy I was carrying, nineteen years later. We're the same age & for some reason I know it's him. We stare at each other. & I can see the hate & the sadness burning in his eyes. & I cannot form the words to say sorry, & the door closes slowly, & I am spinning away, out of the city, out of my body, out of his life forever.

The guy with the Uzi comes & grabs the student out of the cell. I pace back & forth in the space between the cots, a small space that doesn't let me do much pacing. I mark time by the number of times I go back & forth, like a pendulum. When I reach a couple hundred I feel seasick & nauseous. He's gone for much longer. Then the guy with the Uzi brings him back. He's half naked, dripping wet. He dumps him on the cot. The student curls up like a fetus, shielding his head with his arms even after the guy with the Uzi goes away. The skin on his back is raw. It looks like it's been peeled.

What did they do to you? I ask.

His jaws are locked in pain. His lips are all cracked. He spits blood. He keeps his face hidden in his arms. He doesn't want to look at me. He doesn't want me to look at him.

Talk to me, man, I tell him. What do they want from you?

I don't know, he answers. They didn't say.

The lieutenant's sitting at his desk, face-to-face with the student. It looks out of whack & surreal, like they're just drinking & playing cards. Winged termites buzz around the bulb over their heads. They smash against the hot bulb & burn. Their wings, like small sheets of glass, flutter down & glisten on the surface of the desk.

Now we're really going to have a good time, the lieutenant says. He doesn't say it directly to me but to the student. The student keeps his head down. He doesn't even look at me. The guy with the Uzi sits next to him & starts dealing the cards. The lieutenant fills a shot glass with rum. I don't think I want to offer you a drink, he tells me.

I didn't want one, I say.

The guy with the Uzi's dealing the cards without looking up. He mumbles something in Tagalog. The lieutenant laughs. That weird laugh again, like he's about to choke. He's wearing my T-shirt & my jeans. He shows them off to me.

What do you think? he says. God bless America. You make the best jeans in the world.

He pours the rum into the same glass. He passes it to the guy with the Uzi, who downs the shot. Then the lieutenant refills the glass & hands it to me. I say no thanks.

The lieutenant swipes the glass away. It hits the far end of the room. The guy with the Uzi stops dealing. The lieutenant starts cursing me: <u>Puta, puta</u>. The guy with the Uzi tells him to cool it, snickering like he's enjoying it. He stands & picks up the glass. He fills it & hands it again to me.

Okay, one shot, I say. Just to show you we're okay. I drink the rum. It burns my throat.

The lieutenant is happy. Are you going to write about me? he asks.

No, I'm not.

You going to write about this place? About the president? You going to talk to foreign media? Get us in the news?

No, it takes a lot more for something to become news.

This isn't interesting, is that it? I'm not interesting?

I'm not a reporter, okay? I'm nobody. I'm not getting anybody in the news. That's not what I do.

But you're always writing.

Just for myself. Just to remember.

You want to remember this?

No. Not this.

You don't want to remember it? You don't find it an interesting story?

Not you personally, but if I had a choice I'd rather write about less unpleasant things.

You talk like a writer. You learn to talk like that in school? Maybe you went to a nice school in America. You went to Berkeley, maybe? All the Communists in America go to Berkeley, right? You see, I'm not dumb. I know a few things about America. & I didn't even go to school. I hate school. School is for sissies. You want a story, right? Something you can tell back home. To your nice sissy friends. I can give you a story.

Not really, no, I don't want anything right now. I just want to know why you're keeping me here.

Suddenly he grabs me by the arm & pushes me out of the room. On instinct the student makes a move to protect me. The guy with the Uzi shoves him back to his chair. He says, snidely, & loud enough for me to hear: Don't piss him off. Your American friend will be okay.

The lieutenant forces me out through another room & then another. I go through some kind of dreamlike warp & imagine this place is endless & I'm being forced through an infinite number of empty rooms. Finally we reach a cell with no windows. There's a strong smell of dung. There's no light. In the shadows there's someone lying on the bare cement floor.

It's Eddie. He's been trussed up, his wrists & ankles bound behind him, like a pig. He looks up & tries to say something I can't understand. His lips are battered shut. One side of his face is grotesquely swollen.

He didn't like to drink either, says the lieutenant. A classy bitch just like you.

I can't say anything but finally I choke up a few words. What's he done to you, man? You can't do this.

No? the lieutenant replies. He kicks Eddie in the ribs. I hear something crack. Eddie groans & squirms in pain. I can do anything I want, the lieutenant says. This is my country. He kicks Eddie in the head. This time I hear nothing because blood's rushing to my ears.

You & your friend, the lieutenant says, you talk a lot about Mao? About revolution? About drugs? Americans come here for the drugs, right? & the chicks. You like to fuck our chicks? You like our drugs?

No, I don't.

You don't like to fuck our chicks? You <u>bakla</u>? You a faggot?

I don't like the drugs.

We found lots of drugs in your apartment. You know what that means?

Is that what you're keeping me here for? You a narc too?

The lieutenant pulls a .45 from under his belt. Do narcs carry these?

I don't know. I've never met any of you before.

Narcs don't carry these. Do I look like a narc?

No.

But you said you never saw a narc before.

No, I haven't.

So how can you say—

I don't know. I really don't know.

Don't cut me short. It makes me mad.

Okay.

Okay what?

Okay, man, I won't cut you short.

I'm still mad, he says. I'm still raving mad.

He points the pistol at me, nudging the muzzle against my ribs.

Ever shot a man before?

No, I say. I don't think I'd like to.

I don't think I'd like to. You talk sissy. You a sissy? The guy who comes & visits you, he's a cocksucker, right? Your friend back there, the Communist, he a sissy too?

Not that I know of.

Four hundred thousand pesos is a lot of money around here, you know that?

I don't respond.

That's a lot of money to steal, he says.

Is that what this is all about? You want the money back?

I don't care about the money. You Americans, you don't care. What's it to you? In America, money grows on trees, no? Here, trees don't even grow shit. But we're okay. You think that's all we care about. You think we have no pride. You got us all wrong.

He cocks the pistol & points it at me.

<u>Sa ikauunlad ng bayan, disiplina ang kailangan</u>, he says. Nice, ha? I can be a poet too. You know what that means?

I don't respond.

So the country will prosper, is we need some discipline, he says. You like that? You like my English?

Tell me what you want, man. Is it the money?

Ever shot a man? he asks again.

No.

He points the gun at Eddie. Don't blink.

He fires a shot into Eddie's head. It bursts open like a fruit. Blood spurts in jets across the room.

The lieutenant sticks the pistol back in his belt. You think I like my job?

There's a stench like sour milk inside the room. It's coming from Eddie. The lieutenant turns to face the wall, holding an arm against it to keep himself steady. Thick, sticky vomit spatters to his feet. He turns around to face me. His face is ashen, like someone who's just come out of a long & terrible illness.

I like it a lot, he says. I like it a whole fucking lot. He spits & staggers out of the room.

I'm trying not to look at Eddie. I pull my T-shirt over my mouth & nose. I'm watching a black streak oozing out from under the body. It's inching its way to me, just one thin greasy line. It creeps forward then pauses then crawls forward again. It seems like a thing alive in itself, coming closer & closer to the edge of my feet, driven by a need to make contact with anything. Even when the door opens & the guy with the Uzi tells me to get going, I'm still watching it. I can't make my body move.

Let's just give them the fucking money, Nick says.

It's been weeks since I last saw him. He's raised hell to find me. It usually doesn't work around here, but Nick's one guy who knows how to raise hell. Just let it go, Andy. We'll make up for it somehow.

I'm not giving them anything. I made a promise, I'm going to keep it. Nobody's going to fuck with me. They fuck with me, I know how to fuck them back. That money belongs to Anna, Nick. She's been waiting for it.

Nick isn't saying anything. I tell him to speak up.

Anna's dead, man.

Fuck, Nick. Don't you fuck with me too.

They found the body. She was hanging from a tree or something. Killed herself, or got killed. Hard to tell. I talked to so many people, they all had so many different stories. Sorry, Andy.

I can't talk for a bit. I can feel something inside me, like my entire skeleton is melting. My hands & feet are cold. I tell Nick my hands & feet are fucking cold. Then I hear something strange, coming out from somewhere close to me. It sounds like something howling, but there's no sound, only something internal, & I'm only hearing it in my head.

I'm not giving him the fucking money, I say.

So tell me what to do, Andy. I don't fucking know what you fucking want anymore. He calms down a bit

& says, Liana's going to call the embassy. She'll get you out.

Fuck, Nick. I told you not to tell her anything.

There's no other way, man.

I don't want her help. I don't want anyone's help. I'm not going to fucking Nam. I know what to do.

Yeah, what?

If there's a problem, eliminate the source of the problem.

What the hell does that mean?

It's Buddhist, Nick.

It's crap. It doesn't mean shit. You got fucking useless crap all inside your fucking head. It's not going to help you.

I'm not fucking giving him the fucking money. It's not his, it's Anna's. Maybe he's already gotten his share of the other girl's. I don't give a fuck. But this was Anna's. If she's not getting it, I know who should get it.

She was right, Nick says, shaking his head. Liana was right.

About what?

About you. You're too full of your own shit to accept kindness. Even when you so fucking need it.

Talk mojo, Nick. I got it all figured out.

All right, I'm not listening.

I'm not going to tell you some numbers. They're not my bank account.

Okay, not getting it. Why not?

Don't send the money to the kids.

Not getting it. What?

Don't send the money in the bank to the foster parents. The kids' foster parents. The ones I didn't take them to. Just split the money fifty-fifty. Don't split the money. You get it.

Fuck, that's what I thought. What the fuck are you doing?

Listen, man, just pay attention. Just tell them I'm sorry, but it's all that's left. I'm going to tell you their names. Remember them & walk away. You got it?

I can't do this, man. I'm not like you. I can't remember anything.

If they want to know where it came from, tell them it's from Andrew Brezsky & he lives in the Descartes Highlands, on the moon.

What the fuck, Andy? What does that mean?

That way they'll know where not to look for me.

You're nuts, you know that, right? You got me really fucking worried, you know? You've just gone totally wacko.

I know that. You be not okay, all right?

Yeah, I won't try. I don't love you, man.

I know, man. I know.

A story: Two spaceships depart from two distant civilizations on opposite ends of the universe. Using technology that warps & compresses time, they reach the other's planet, but it's eons later, & all they find is a burnt-out, uninhabited wasteland.

They fly back to their home planets & confirm to their populations what they've always suspected: that they are indeed alone in all of creation.

This, as far as I can recall, is the entire poem. I've posted a copy of it over Eddie's cot.

I had no time to hate, because
the grave would hinder me,
and life was not so ample I
could finish enmity.

Nor had I time to love; but since
some industry must be,
the little toil of love, I thought,
was large enough for me.

Eddie once told me that some days the sun doesn't rise. He knew this for a fact. Today I understand what he meant. Ragged finches, perched on barbed wire, chatter ominously in the dark. Day & night no longer exist. My body doesn't know when to sleep, wake, eat, or shit. I'm totally out of sync.

Eddie, hope you like the story I wrote for you. It's a little late, but I did it anyway. I made a promise, & I never break a promise.

Strange as it may sound, everything is still. Maybe that's how death is supposed to feel. Not private, individual, lonely. But collective, one big bang, the entire universe imploding with you. Because, after all, who gives a shit after you're gone? It's the living who have to mop up. We're hurtling toward nowhere, toward infinite space.

The greatest gift nature has given man is the promise of oblivion. Although I resist it, I know this now for a fact.

Although I resist it.

I resist it.

We are held in place by gravitational forces

An Oz Moving truck is parked in front of the building. A bunch of Israelis are hauling furniture into it. A sense of foreboding comes over me, a feeling that someone in the building has just died. I bolt up the stairs and find Yuki's apartment almost empty. She is standing by the door, talking to her boyfriend on her cell phone. When she sees me, she turns away and continues talking. Then she flips the phone closed and turns back around and says hi.

"*Hi*? What's with the fucking *hi*?"

"Okay, I'm not in the mood for any of this."

"You're fucking leaving, and you didn't fucking tell me?"

"I didn't have to tell you. I don't have to tell anybody anything. Least of all you."

"*Least of all you*, that's very nice, you fucking bitch."

"Jesus fuck, Jordan. Let's just say goodbye. Let's be friends. Let's keep in touch."

"You're going away with him, aren't you?"

She doesn't respond.

"He's just using you," I tell her.

"Yeah, well, story of my life."

I close the door and wrap my arms around her. My lips brush against hers. She doesn't turn her face away. I slip my hand inside her sweater. I touch her breasts and then I pull the sweater up and lean down to suck her tits. She pushes me gently away.

"Why are you doing this?" I ask her.

"You gave me no choice. I had to look for a way out."

At Westside Market, a late-middle-aged man is following a Chinese guy and exclaiming some kind of nonsense word: "Ching-gato!" The man is dressed in a three-piece brown wool suit, the kind that's in vogue this season. He's obviously some well-to-do show off, probably some theater fop who lives in an overpriced condo nearby. Whenever he bumps into the Chinese guy, he booms, "Ching-gato!" in a stage voice that sends the Haitian cashiers and Dominican deli butchers tittering. The Chinese guy is no dumb immigrant either. He knows what's going on. He tries to avoid the man as best he can, but the supermarket only has two aisles and everywhere he ducks the asshole is there, shouting "Ching-gato!" at him.

Observing this scene, I feel a rage so powerful it constricts my chest. I feel almost paralyzed, unable to walk away. I don't know why it should concern me so much, but I want to break that asshole's skull. I want to see it crack open, I want gratuitous, graphic violence, special-effects violence, Hong Kong–wuxia violence.

I have not felt so strong an emotion in a long time. It comes as a shock to me, like a bolt of adrenaline. It has no purpose, no object meaningful to me. But it lingers, an alien in my system, a virus spreading through my body, ever so strong that it obliterates everything else, and I see and hear nothing but the pounding in my head as I walk home.

* * *

That evening I come back and find Mother in a pool of blood.

She had been dreaming. She was back at a farm where she had taken me, up in Keane, when I was five. We were watching a farmer slaughter a young goat. The goat was squirming to loosen the tethers knotted at its feet. The farmer was whispering, *Easy, easy*, like a father soothing his son. *Easy, easy*: and then the blade slid across the young goat's throat, and a lip of muscle and blood curled open.

She had cut her own wrists. She thought she was doing so inside the dream. The cuts weren't deep enough to lacerate the veins, but blood so red it looks black drips from her wrists and stains the sheets. Even in her half-sleep the pain was swift and piercing. A jolt shot up the length of her arms and spread through every part of her body.

For several nights after that, she dreams she is caught in a tidal wave, and she cannot escape. There is no end to her drowning. Her body is a weight she is tied to, a slab of concrete. She keeps sinking to a bottomless depth. Her voice, when she wakes up screaming, is a mournful bellow. It comes from a darkness submarine, no longer human, no longer alive. Even the air she breathes feels thick as seawater. She chokes on her own spit.

Awake, plucked from the drowning dream, she finds everything worse. Mirrors reflect not her face, but an impostor's. Rust-colored stains ring the bandages on her wrists. She has been bleeding again. Her body has so much blood she feels her heart is all dammed up and about to burst. And any minute, the shrapnel lodged next to her heart will finally come just this close, pierce the pulsing membrane, and she will explode.

She has already thought it over. As far as she is concerned, it is the logical thing to do. She says she is a soul dangling over her wrecked body.

"I was dreaming," she says. "I dreamt I was drowning. Then I saw you, and I came back."

Her arms and legs are punctured with all the needles I have jabbed in her. She is living in someone else's unspeakably grotesque body. She wants so much to let go. Nothing I say can dissuade her.

"Hold on to me," I tell her. "I'm not letting go of you."

"It is so hard to live. It is even harder to die."

"I love you, Mother, you know that, don't you?"

"This has nothing to do with love. I'm just asking you to kill me."

In the *Bardo Thodol*, the first phases of dying show the basic elements overwhelming each other, causing physical signs of dissolution. When the earth element goes, the body feels an unbearable weight pushing down on it. Then the water element goes, and uncontrollable fluids leak out. The fire element goes next, causing either fevers or chills. Air is the last to go, a final dissolution that disconnects the life force and unhinges consciousness.

I keep an eye on her, waiting for the signs. "Don't let the bastards grind you down," I say.

"Give it to me."

"No."

"You are very cruel."

I walk out of the room and stand by the window. It's shut tight. There are children playing on the street below, they are laughing but I can't hear a thing. Trucks are moving out of the garage, huge brontosauruses that

clog traffic for a few minutes and send the taxis blaring
their horns. I should hear the rumble of the trucks and
the ground shaking, but I can't hear a thing. Right next
to the garage, two homeless people, a scraggly woman with
clumped-up, oily blond hair and a scarecrow of a man in
a frayed tweed jacket, are digging into the trash basins,
plunging their arms in and pulling out plastic boxes of
half-rotten tomatoes and salad greens. They are talking to
each other, they are overjoyed by what they find. I can't
hear a thing.

"You wanted this to happen." Mother's voice is a long,
painful rasp, and every word burns into me. "You asked
them to punish me. You always get what you want."

I feel my knees buckling. I fall down, unable to hold
myself up any longer. I can feel the world closing, my
eyesight grows dim, and something inside me is turning
inside out, and I want to throw up. I realize I have the
syringe in my hand. I have this fleeting image of myself
jabbing the needle in her arm. She is watching closely as
the clear liquid oozes into her body. Her eyes grow heavy.
She smiles at me gratefully. I hold her hand. It is small
and bony. It feels like I am holding air.

"I can hear the waves," she calls from the room. "I
can't breathe."

I struggle to get up and try to yank the window open.
It's stuck. I keep pushing it up, throwing my entire weight
against it, convinced that only by getting it open will I
save this moment from being itself. Salvation, the end of
suffering, this entrapment inside the body, the inescapable, purgatorial necessity of it, depends entirely on this
one act, ordinary and meaningless, that I yank this window open, that I pull her out of the waves.

After a few minutes, my strength is all gone and I finally give up, hitting the pane with my fist. I turn around and walk back into the room. She has closed her eyes. At first I think she seems peaceful, but she is clutching her belly, her withered hands clawing at her clothes as though she wants to rip something out, the pain, the memory, the trapped soul burning inside her, the creature that wants to burst out and be free.

The furnace door has an intaglio design on it, a depiction of an armored angel coming down to raise the dead, whose torsos, half-buried, bone-thin, rise like smoke from the bottom edge, as though they are oozing out of hell. I think of pictures of cathedral doors in Umbria, in towns whose mellifluous names I can't remember anymore; Mother used to show them to me when I was a kid, telling me that one day she and I would go and see the real thing.

Behind the door I can hear mechanical-sounding bumps, like something beating to get out. There's no one else in the crematorium. Outside, Hunters Point is a place that's nowhere to me, a dot on the subway map, forty minutes on the train.

It's over in a few minutes. An attendant comes out. I had expected him to hand me a receipt and a jar of fine gray dust. The jar would feel warm in my hands. Body warmth. But all he does is say, "We will send you the ashes in a few days." Seeing me dawdle, he asks what I am going to do for the rest of the afternoon. He is an immigrant from Bolivia and has buried many bodies where he comes from. He seems concerned that no one has come.

It is a fine spring day. I have a bit of an allergy. My eyes are moist with tears. I tell him I am going to get lunch in the city. It's a lie. I don't know what else to say.

He is surprised that I would do something so banal. He gives me the number of a pastor somewhere in Jackson Heights, if I want a real service. The pastor is Bolivian himself and has already saved many souls. I thank him and slip the paper in my pocket. I shake his hand. His palm feels rough, and his handshake feels like a clench.

As I walk out, someone comes in to pay her respects. It takes me awhile to recognize her. Then I realize it's Simone. Her brother has just arrived from Mali and she needed to help him settle in, get a work permit, find a job. She's upset that she missed the service. She asks if Mother gave up because she had been away so long. It's a strange question to ask. She believes she had been doing a good job, that because of her help Mother had been certain to heal. She is the kind of person who feels the universe is her entire responsibility.

I don't feel like telling her much. She hardly spoke to me all these months, except when I spoke to her first. I wonder if I should tell her that I read Mother the pages I got from Nick, and that, to my mind, kept her going a little longer, like Scheherazade with her fabulous endurance, staving off the death sentence of the brokenhearted Shahryar. I decide that won't be interesting to Simone, if she knows the story at all. So I tell her what she wants to hear.

"It was like she just went to sleep. She's in a better place now."

Painters are all over Yuki's apartment, coating the walls with white primer. I walk in. I tell them I am the one moving in. It's a lie. They move paint cans and brushes to let me through. They're a bunch of Mexican immigrants who probably get paid shit to do this kind of work. I walk along the tarpaulin, inspecting the rooms. There's a scratch on the floor where Yuki's cello used to be. It looks like it's been gouged with a knife. One of the painters tells me not to worry. They are sanding everything down.

Back in my apartment, I look around at the equally empty rooms. I have donated Mother's things to a Housing Works branch on Seventy-Fourth. She didn't have much left to give away. I had everything packed and ready to go in three boxes.

I am moving around the apartment, which looks bigger now. I pull up the window that looks out on the street, surprised that this time it gives in so easily. The sound of children's laughter rises from the street below. I close the window again and turn the lock. Like light fading in a darkened room, the sound slowly disappears.

The phone rings and I pick it up.

"You still want to see me, or what?"

"My Mother died, Nick. I just had her cremated."

"Yeah, I heard. Listen, you got the photocopies, right? You really want to know about this Andrew Brezsky, right?"

"Yeah. Yeah, I do. Let's meet, Nick."

"Okay, tell you what. How important is this information to you? Like are you going to fucking die if you don't get it?"

"No."

"Then what the fuck do you want it for?"

"Just a need to know on my part, you know what I'm saying? Know thy fucking self, Nick."

"So it's all curiosity. So it's not worth like a rat's ass to you."

"It's worth a lot, I just don't know how much."

"It's priceless."

"Yeah, kinda like that. You couldn't put a price on it."

"Okay, come and meet me at the same place tomorrow, at two."

"The Boite en Bois?"

"Yeah, the Boite en Bois. I'll give you the whole shit. You want me to give you the whole shit?"

"Give me the whole shit, Nick."

"How much will you give to get the whole shit?"

"You asking for money, Nick? Jesus fuck, Nick."

"How much, Jordan? I'm being very straight with you."

"What've you got?"

"Every fucking thing the motherfucker wrote, pages from notebooks, the backs of cigarette foil, all kinds of shit."

"How'd you get them?"

"He gave them to me, all right? In secret, page by fucking page. He knew someone was out to get him. The rest of his personal shit the military turned over to me a week after he died."

"Is that right, Nick? Tell me, why'd you keep them all these years? Just because you liked him?"

"He was a friend. You look a little like him."

"Yeah? How did he know my name? Or the other guy? Where'd he get that information?"

"He didn't know, all right? I did. That was my job."

"Where is he now?"

"I just told you. He died."

"Yeah? How?"

"I don't know."

"Of course you don't. Bet you didn't see the body either."

"I don't know, okay? I never heard from him again. I think he, you know, died. You know, maybe in Vietnam. But the body was never found. I can't help you with that, if that's what you're looking for."

Long pause.

"He was a friend, okay? I did what I promised I would. That was all. Listen, gotta take another call. I'm fucking doing you a favor, all right? I just want to make you happy. I know you. I know people like you. I'm very good at what I do. I can see right through every fucking body."

"And what do you see in me?"

"I can see that you need this more than I do. You want this shit or not?"

Sometime later Bob calls up. I can't remember who he is at first. Bob, he says, the car service. He has been wondering why I've stopped coming. He wants to make sure I get what I need. Once you're in the loop, customer service is impeccable.

I tell Bob I no longer need anything. I've decided to go straight.

"Yeah, okay," he says. "Good for you, bad for me. Glad you got your shit together, man."

WSOWOB

I take the next bus to Chiang Mai, where Janya has family. That's the first place I figure she'd go to. The bus is smelly, crowded, and infernal. The air conditioner isn't working. Some idiotic pop song keeps blaring out of the stereo system. By the time I get to her family home, I must have aged ten years.

A growling, mangy mutt with matted fur lurches at me, its mouth thick with yellow foam, its neck twisted by the chain that's holding it to a post by the door. Janya's mother stands inside the door, one hand holding on tight to the knob. She keeps shaking her head when I ask where Janya is. I take one step closer and peek in. Several men are standing behind her. I've never known Janya to have so many male relatives. I ask who among them is Vasin. Her mother tells me more insistently, in English, in words so difficult for her to say they seem like they're the wrong size for her mouth, "Go away now, *fa-rung-sayt*, go away."

I search for days. I ask local people if they know of her. No one wants to help. Everyone looks at me suspiciously. At a bus depot's eatery, the jukebox plays the Doors' "People Are Strange." I don't fail to notice the significance. The guy who picked the song lingers by my table. I've seen him before. He's a little man in a rumpled shirt and soiled khakis, a guide who drives a rundown truck. Suddenly he and the owner get in a heated argument. The man keeps pointing angrily at me, without really looking my way. In fact he seems to be avoiding my gaze entirely. The owner gestures for him to take me outside the depot, and the man responds in a high-pitched, terrified voice that sounds more pleading than angry. Finally he faces me directly and apologizes profusely. He tells me there's someone who's waiting in his truck for me.

I follow him out. A nun gets off the truck. She's almost as small as he is, engulfed in the saffron-colored robe she's wrapped around herself so that only her face shows. She's heard about me. She's heard that I've been bugging everyone in town. She tells me she can take me to Janya, to a place a few kilometers outside of Chiang Mai.

"What is that place?" I ask. "And how do you know her?" She won't tell me anything else. When I ask her if Janya's all right, she shakes her head and says, "Very bad."

We reach a sprawl of bare-bones bungalows inside a gated compound. The driver tells me to leave all my stuff in the truck. No bags are allowed in the buildings. We are at a local sanatorium.

The nun leads me inside to a small room. There's a table where a young woman is lying, covered up to her shoulders with a white sheet. She must be completely na-ked, and her arms, resting above the sheet, are all bones, dark and shriveled. I come closer. The young woman's eyes are wide open. She's breathing hard, but is barely able to open her mouth. She stares at me with a glassy, terrified expression. She must be in a great deal of pain. I realize that the lower half of the sheet is soaked in blood, the hemorrhage creating a dark patch just above her crotch.

I stagger out of the room and run after the nun. She's already walking out of the hall.

"It's not her," I call after her. "It's not who I'm looking for."

The nun gets back on the truck and a heated argument between her and the driver ensues.

"That's not the person I'm looking for," I tell them.

The driver angrily starts the truck, swerves it around, and drives out of the compound. I follow them out, still confused about what's happening, and then I walk faster and faster, not certain if I should run after the fleeing truck, until, on impulse, I break into a sprint. I keep running even when I lose sight of it, I don't know for how long, and then I find myself back in the center of Chiang Mai. Only now do I realize that I've lost my backpack, my wallet, and my passport.

I ask around for the police, but nobody understands what I want. Night has fallen. The night market has already opened, a deafening cacophony of people selling and haggling, their voices meaningless like the chatter of birds they carry for sale in flimsy bamboo cages.

In the park, a performance of a native dance is underway. I wander toward it absently. I feel like I'm inside a dream, unable to resist anything. The dancers, with their long nails of gold, remind me of the shimmer of sunlight on water. It's getting close to Christmas. The park is all lit up with garish lights and plastic images of reindeer and Santa Claus. The sound system is primitive, a tin-can clatter that's grating to the ear.

I stand close to the stage. Under lights as flat and harsh as these, the performance is blinding, a glare of gold. I can't look away from the silk costumes. I can't escape the pentatonic clangor of the music. One of the dancers keeps her eyes on me. It's a blank stare, devoid of meaning. Her mind is on the music, on the undulating movements that have taken over her body. Her lashes are clumped thick, her face whitened with powder. When she turns her face to the lights hanging from scaffolding above the stage, shadows form under her eyes, giving her face an unexpected sadness, no longer just a mask. For a few seconds she seems almost real.

It's a couple of days after Christmas. I've spent the entire holidays alone in Chiang Mai, mostly waiting for police to finish filing my records. I check my e-mail at a cybercafé and discover a message I've missed since my stuff was stolen. It was sent on Christmas Eve.

Janya says she's down south, in Khao Lak, but tells me not to follow her. She won't be there for long. *I need to sort this one out on my own. Then I'll come back and we can talk.*

None of my e-mails gets any further reply. I send a flurry of frantic text messages, *PXT*, please explain that, *WAN2TLK ASAP*, and that most juvenile and saccharine of messages, which now seems most profound and most urgent: *MUSM*, miss you so much.

No reply.

I decide to head down south myself. On the afternoon that I'm scheduled to depart, all flights are cancelled. I'm fuming mad. Yelling at the uncomprehending ticket clerk, I insist that I need to travel south as soon as possible, that it's a matter of life and death. A Dutch tourist tells me that's exactly what it is, not just for me but for everyone stranded at the station.

Earlier that day, a tsunami hit most of the southern coast. Many of the villages have been wiped out.

* * *

In Khao Lak, the earth has dried quickly under the tropical sun, but it still reeks of something waterlogged, a smell that's hard to pin down, like fruit both sweet and rotting. It's taken me days to wangle a train ride south, and only after claiming to have a relative who's possibly been swept away by the waves.

I arrive at a village unrecognizable in its grief, piled with mounds of debris. Lacerated suitcases and children's shoes litter the beach. Bodies still float in the now languid sea, tied together by their limbs to prevent them from being lost. In front of a temple that survived the waves, on top of rubble, hundreds of unclaimed corpses lie piled up on wood, palm, and stone, decomposing in the sun. They rot rapidly in the heat, and whether they are Asians or Europeans no one can tell. In this widespread, leveling presence of death, race no longer exists, the body's identifying markers are erased . . .

In a makeshift mortuary set up in the town center, I add Janya's name to the list of the missing, one name buried under thousands of others. Days go by. Bodies are excavated from the rubble, but Janya's never shows up. I look at one corpse after another, insisting that the next one is her. I hang on to the idea even when it becomes clear to me that I'm wrong, and I let go only when another one shows up, and I realize my mistake. Then I think she must have been somewhere else, she was never here at all, this trip has been a mistake. Not finding her here is all I need to give me hope. Yet that hope is not reassuring. It puts me in an even more unstable limbo between doubt and possibility, and though I dread to think about it, only by finding a body can I put an end to my searching.

No further e-mails reach me, no matter how persis-

tently I send messages to her. The detective superintendent, a man sent from Britain whose few harrowing days
here have given him the look and demeanor of a prophet,
advises me to go back to Bangkok, where they will inform
me as soon as they hear anything.

Weeks pass. Khao Lak is slowly rebuilding itself, clear-
ing the rubble, burying whoever has been found. In a few
months, by the time the peak season begins in October,
tourists will start to trickle back. Forgetting will be as
crucial to survival as remembering.

I don't hear from Janya again. The superintendent tells
me the policy is that if they haven't found her, and she in
fact was there at the time of the tsunami, his crew will
presume that she was lost to the sea.

They send me a telegram a month later, informing me
that for the sake of the disappeared, the surviving residents of Khao Lak have arranged to burn offerings at the
shore, according to custom, as an act of returning to the
gods. They ask me if I want to come. I scribble a note
at the local telegraph office telling them that there's no
point, it won't make sense, and least of all to her. At the
last minute I decide against sending it. No one, except
perhaps Janya, will understand.

I tape the ceremony, a blur of night enclosed in the
frame of the hotel TV screen, a hundred lights lifting in
paper lanterns up to darkness, to nowhere—

I spend a few days back in La Napoule. I find some of
her stuff still there, clothes, books, documents, letters—
lots of letters. I sort them out in boxes, and then realize
I am doing this because I have given up hope, and I stop.
For the next few days I read her letters. I can do nothing

else. And reading one, I suddenly realize I know the key. I know what's been going on.

The next day, I book a flight back to Manila and a connecting flight to San Crisostomo, because (only she would understand) in the mysterious cycles that govern our existence, what was lost at sea is bound to return. We must be ready for such encounters.

the little toil of love

Nick's finally got his green card.

What are you going to do now? I ask him.

What else? I'm going to be so fucking American nobody will recognize me. I'm going to make a lot of money. So much money no one's ever going to fuck with me. This time it's me who'll do all the fucking. I'm going to be the biggest capitalist motherfucker you've ever seen. & I'm going to love every minute of it.

He pauses a minute. I know something's not right. What is it, Nick?

I'm leaving this shithole for good, he says. No more Third World shit for me. No more sucking up to dictators. If you don't watch out, you get sucked in. You get to be like the rest of them. You get contaminated. No one is spared.

Talk mojo, Nick. Talk fucking mojo.

He's fidgeting. He doesn't look me in the eye.

Tell me what the fuck's going on, Nick.

I've transferred the money, but it's still with me. I'm afraid I'm going to keep it for myself. I can't help it, Andy. I need it to get out of here. If you don't want to use the money, then let me use it. I'll pay everything back. Besides, you still owe me.

Hell no, Nick. What the fuck?

Stop acting like you care, Andy. You don't give a shit

who the money goes to. You didn't really give a fuck what happened to those kids. You never gave a fuck about anything or anyone. All you care about is your dick.

I look in his eyes. There's no anger there, just a lot of sadness.

You don't know me, man, I start to tell him. But he's sick of anything I have to say & cuts me short.

I've informed the embassy, Andy. They're going to come & get you out soon.

What the fuck? I told you not to fucking do that.

Better you go to a US jail than spend the rest of your life here. I'm sorry, Andy. I'm getting out of here & no one's going to watch out for you when I'm gone. No one else is fucking strong enough. Or patient enough. Or stupid enough. If you don't want to save yourself, there's only so much I can do. So I'll see you there, man. We'll work things out when we get there.

You're one fucked-up son of a bitch, Nick.

Visiting hours are over. He gets up to leave.

Don't fucking do this, Nick.

He walks away, his head bowed, not even looking back at me.

Poor fucked-up Nick. I think he'll wimp out.

Nick, you don't know fuck about me. I feel like one of those guys who are wrongly accused of a crime. The judgment has been passed. But I plead on & on, still proclaiming my innocence as I step up to the guillotine.

I keep thinking of things to tell Nick. There's still a lot I want to tell him. I'm as stupid as a junkie, looking for someone to plead my case to. I feel sick not having anyone to talk to. That's pretty stupid too.

It's stupid that I actually miss poor fucked-up Nick.

With the money gone, there's no business left for me in the precinct. If there's a problem, eliminate the source of the problem. I always knew that was going to be useful someday.

Nick hasn't shown up again, but I still hope he does so I can say I told you so.

Sure enough, the lieutenant & the guy with the Uzi ease up on the beatings. We've become completely meaningless, just another task, another chore. One evening we even get an extra helping of smoke-dried fish.

Days later, out of the blue, with very little ceremony, I'm told I'm free to go.

I have a feeling I'm watching myself from somewhere else, and I'm not totally inside my body. I mumble my name to myself over & over. I have to remember that it's still me.

My name is Andrew Brezsky. I have to say it over & over until I get used to it again. That's all I need to remember from now on.

No one's ever going to read this. I'm going to leave it here, where no one will remember who I was or why I was here.

Only Anna would understand. Only she would try. Sadly, the people who matter to us most are the ones we drive away. I know that for a fact now. Although I resist it. I resist it.

Before I go, I ask the student his name.

Victor Santiago, he says.

A revolutionary's name, I say.

Yeah, I'm going to be a professor when I get out of here. First I'll teach the kids to overthrow this government. Then we're going to fight you.

All right, I say. I ask him if he would do me a favor.

No. No favors for the enemy.

Okay, I say.

You be careful. Wherever you will be.

You sound like you care about me, man.

We hug awkwardly. We'll never see each other again.

We are held in place by gravitational forces

Homeless panhandlers shuffle in and out between the subway cars, spouting the same rehearsed speech over and over.

"I am not an addict and all I need is some money to buy a decent meal."

"Last week someone raped me."

"If you could find it in your hearts . . ."

One of them passes close to me. His coat, a faded black bag of dust, frayed at the hem, stinking of urine, brushes against the hem of mine. I pull a handkerchief out and frantically wipe the spot. Someone sitting across from me, a middle-aged woman looking up from her book, her glasses perched on her nose, gives a conniving, knowing smirk. If I could only explain to her that I have nothing against these poor souls. It's merely the idea of contagion—that something like this could happen to me—that fills me with terror, *the possibility of the real*. But she has gone back to reading her book, this momentary distraction now the farthest thing from her mind.

On my street, I avoid looking at the scavengers as they stagger away from the mounds of black trash bags piled in front of my building. The sight of them, prowling like alley cats through the discarded sandwiches outside Food Emporium, their heartbreaking camaraderie, their politeness toward each other, and the way they share their find with whoever is scrounging with them—all this makes me nauseous, my bones weak and soft with horror.

A woman is sitting on the stoop, filling a tote bag with the discards. She doesn't move to let me pass. Instead she pulls out an apple from the bag and offers it to me. I thank her and decline.

"It's a perfectly good apple," she says.

"Give it to those who really need it," I tell her.

"We all need it sometime or another." She pushes the apple against my ribs. "Here, take it."

I stand there dumbfounded.

"Take it," she says again. "We all could use some help."

I take the apple hesitantly. She grabs my hand in both of hers and smiles. She has several teeth missing. Her eyes are a blur behind thick lenses. I am almost grateful, almost to the point of tears.

And then I see Simone. When was the last time I saw her? At the apartment, when she was still looking after Mother. No, at the crematorium. She was late and short of breath . . . She stops briefly to say hello, apologizing for having to rush, as she is about to meet some friends, part of a group she's just recently joined. She is staring at the apple in my hand, and keeps furtively glancing at the woman, who has gone back to the trash bins to search for more treasure. I feel only relief when Simone finally walks away.

I have been scanning jobs that sound passably tolerable to me. Every job in the city sounds like a condemnation to a life of extreme agony, eight hours under the gaze of a charlatan who hides her incompetence with duckspeak, like "surface the document" or "process-oriented." I might as well go pick grapes with Mexicans under the blazing sun.

A temp agency finds me a job in a nonprofit. My "supervisor" is a troglodyte who reminds me of Bette Davis in *What Ever Happened to Baby Jane?* Same thick smear of mascara and raccoon eyes, same trailer-trash just-got-out-of-bed hair. She backstabs everyone in the office, and when I am out for lunch she backstabs me. I am always afraid I will find a dead canary on my desk one of these days.

She clawed her way up the ladder and founded this organization a couple of years ago. It's supposed to identify failing colored kids in public schools and force them to paint their school buildings, the experience of which will hypothetically inspire them to be responsible citizens. I asked her, during the interview, if the kids ever felt the program was a form of detention or punishment. Her voice went up a couple of decibels as she proclaimed otherwise, that the kids in fact feel a lot of pride seeing their handiwork every day, forced labor not being the issue. She's an "industrial designer" who's used this organization to hand out "awards" to leaders in the industry, a ploy no doubt that helps her advance her own lackluster career. "Just the fact that you ask that question shows that you've failed," she told me. She hired me on the spot nonetheless, because A, the agency highly recommended me, and B, no one's ever stayed longer than a year with her and she's desperate.

Needless to say, her organization is all fucked up and everything's a mess. She screws up every little thing she's supposed to do, and when the board yells at her she blames it on the fact that her "associate" doesn't have the necessary "skill set." I must say her deviousness is rather breathtaking. We share a small office, painted in bright primary colors courtesy of a paint company she's managed to cajole into supporting her "cause." There's me and her and a couple of administrative assistants who fawn over her because they know that's how you keep your job. Every time I have to pick up a call, she claps her hands over her ears, grimacing as though the mere sound of my voice feels like a stick being plunged into her ear canal. She has no wrists and no ankles and she always puts on a smile so phony it makes her mouth curl down, giving her a tired, sour look that can curdle milk a mile away.

On my second day I rewrite a letter she has written for a fund-raising campaign. She reminds me that she has "trophies" lined against her wall, kudos she had won while operating a similar organization (which promptly went bankrupt) in Michigan. She has covered an entire wall of the office with plaques, given by this council member or that paint company, just to show everyone she is an "award-winning artist" with an altruistic vision to save poor colored kids from Harlem and the Bronx.

"I am an award-winning artist, Jordan," she tells me. "You cannot possibly edit me."

She can't write a simple declarative sentence without misspelling at least two words. She breaks the rules of grammar as though she were breaking the walls of Jericho.

But I apologize, and she spends the rest of the day scanning her copy of the *Chicago Manual of Style*, only to discover that I am right and she is wrong. She stays late through the day figuring out how to justify her mistake, and the following morning, bright and early, she tells me she has "conferred with colleagues" and the "alternative expression" she used was indeed acceptable, if one were writing *informally*.

I don't argue with her further. People like that need to constantly feel they are infallible, like the pope. She has a picture of the pope stuck with a magnet to her filing cabinet. As I walk away from her desk, I hear her mutter, softly to herself, "Wiseass baby killer."

Before sending the letter off, I decide to do just a little further revision. I add:

> We believe that it is the mission of white people today to ensure that colored children find opportunities to practice manual labor, as they have been historically destined to do. In doing so, we create a new generation of subjugated and submissive youth who will thank us for helping them overcome their dark nature. If you are gullible enough to believe in the crap that this organization stands for, by all means please send us a check at your earliest convenience.

Once the letter is sent, I head out during my lunch break and, like a serial killer coolly walking away from the scene of the crime, I head straight to the temp agency to explain why I can't keep the job.

The agent, a sweet old Polish woman named Amy, tells me sweetly that I have no choice, because, "Frankly, Jordan, you're poor."

The next day, Simone pays a visit. She's brought her copy of the keys back. She apologizes for not having returned them sooner. I feel compelled to invite her in. She remarks how different the place is now that I've given away many of Mother's things.

"It looks empty," she says. She has a couple of bags of groceries with her. She asks where she should put them. She hopes I don't mind, but since she's earning more money now, she thinks it's the right thing to do, considering how generous my mother and I were to her, back when she was new in the country and no one would hire her.

I tell her it's totally unnecessary, but she has begun to unpack the bags, placing the goods in the cupboards, the way she used to do when she was caring for Mother. I keep objecting but she only nods her head, saying, *Yes, yes,* while she arranges the goods neatly on the shelves. I have nothing on the shelves except an old canister of salt that's been there for so long the bottom half of it has a moisture stain. She looks around the kitchen, as she used to do, and remarks that the apartment needs a lot of cleaning.

She pulls a mop from the kitchen closet and starts mopping the floor. This time I raise my voice in protest.

"No, you mustn't do that anymore, I can do that myself, if only I had time . . ."

She ignores me and keeps on working.

I find myself getting more and more agitated. Finally, I can't stop myself from bursting out: "Stop doing that, Simone! You don't work for me anymore!"

She stops, apparently shocked by the force with which I blurted the words. I am trembling all over. I reach out for a glass and turn the tap on too abruptly. The water quickly overfills and splashes on my shirt. I put the glass down and lean against the counter, covering my eyes. My head is spinning. I can hardly keep standing. "I don't have the money to pay you," I finally tell her.

Her response is quick and sincere: "But I never asked you to pay me. I just came here to help."

"I don't need your help, Simone, please." I feel I am going to get sick. "Please go away."

And at that moment, something inconceivably kind and gentle comes over me, and pulls me out of this situation. My mind goes blank, like a TV screen: I fall into total darkness.

Simone has become a regular visitor. She stays for just half an hour, with or without food, although she makes it a point to ask beforehand if she can bring me anything, often some dish she cooked herself or takeout from dinner with friends. She has made many friends since coming to the city, some of them, she says proudly, not just from Mali. She has joined a tantric New Age group downtown whose membership is open and democratic, and whose members come from various professions—bankers, lawyers, artists, educators, and even laborers—but who, during the hours they meet and practice the teachings of some expatriate guru (I don't remember who), discard their worldly titles, their illusions of themselves, and just mingle with one another on "a pure and basic level," as the ten-page booklet that Simone encourages me to read says.

She wants to take me there. They meet every Friday, when they chant and meditate and share a potluck dinner. I try to deflect the invitation as much as I can, saying I have things to take care of, a lie which is becoming more and more obvious to her, until finally I have to tell her that it sounds like some Christian renewal thing where people get together and exchange niceties and small talk, something they do in lieu of, say, therapy. No, she insists, it isn't like that at all. Once I met them I would change my mind, I would find these people truly interesting. And besides, she says, it's become a network, people there can help me find a job . . .

Since that day when I passed out, Simone's attentions have begun to wear me down. But soon I get used to her visits, which usually happen around the first couple days of the week. One time, she fails to show up. I get worried, then upset. When she finally arrives, I tell her it is rude to simply drop off like that, there's the telephone, she can always call to say she isn't coming so I won't have to wait to let her in, and besides, it is an imposition to have to plan my life around her. She apologizes, admitting that I am right, that is the proper thing to do, and she will remember next time.

I accept the apology. Exhausted by my tirade, I tell her I am going to do some work on my computer in my mother's room, which I have converted into my study. She follows me, asking what I am working on. I have been obsessively typing Brezsky's handwritten journal. I have discovered several discrepancies in the text, somewhere in the last few pages. I have been wracking my brain about the authenticity of it, and about the trustworthiness of the man who so eagerly entrusted it to me (for a hefty fee). The task has been taking up all of my time. Simone asks if I am going to make money out of it. The question is so stupid I don't even have the heart to respond. I realize I have been toiling away at the journal because it gave me the impression that I am doing something, that I am working. This thought makes me resent Simone all over again.

At that moment the doorbell buzzes. I ignore it, and when it keeps on buzzing, she asks me if I am going to ask who it is. No, I tell her, pranksters are always buzzing people's apartments, and I am getting tired of playing along. The bell keeps on buzzing, short, electronic burps that reverberate throughout the apartment. Finally, she herself gets up and presses the talk button, and asks who it is.

No response.

It happens all the time, I tell her, and in fact, if I had my way, I'd rip the buzzer off altogether, since there is no need for it anyway.

Then someone buzzes again. This time she is clearly incensed. "Why don't you look out and see who it is?" she asks.

I tell her that is impossible, in order to see who's at the door I have to lean out a bit, but the window has been stuck for a while and I can't lift it open. The sound keeps on blaring through the apartment. She presses the talk button again and asks who it is, and finally I lose my patience and press myself close to the glass of the window.

A taxi is parked on the street below. The irate driver is yelling and honking his horn at someone who must have been standing at the building's entrance. I push the window harder. The buzzing is still going on, louder and louder it seems, and Simone keeps asking me, "Who is it? Can you see who it is?"

Finally, I heave the window up with such force that I hear a crack. I have bent my thumb backward, though I feel no pain. I look out and see a man getting back in the cab, and the vehicle speeding away. The passenger turns to look back (I can see this clearly) and for a minute I have a weird sensation—I think it is I in the cab, or someone who looks exactly like me.

Simone lets out a scream and takes my hand in hers. My thumb has bent back grotesquely, and only then do I feel the pain shoot up my arm and all over my body. A cold sweat is trickling down my forehead. I grip my own hand and, with all my strength, I pull the thumb up. It snaps back with a click. The pain quickly subsides, like a sea wave receding, leaving only a lingering discomfort. A sense of exhaustion sweeps all over me. Simone is crying loudly and holding my hand. She wants to take me to ER, and though I protest, saying it's all right and I feel no pain, she will have none of it, and she rushes downstairs to grab a cab.

I stand by the window once more, looking at nothing, just gazing out with a blank stare. I realize Simone is the only person in the world who cares about me, stifling though her caring can be. I see her running up and down the street, her arms stretched out, increasingly furious that no cab will stop. And I find myself wishing she'll get so frustrated that she will simply walk away, and never come back.

Back from the hospital, Simone helps me into bed.

"I'm all right, Simone, you can leave me now."

She's hovering, looking for something to do.

"I want you to leave, Simone. I want you to leave me alone."

"I want to help you."

"I don't need your help. I don't want to see you ever again."

"Why are you so hateful?" She says this under her breath, as though she has been struggling to for a while, and when the words finally come out, she regrets them immediately, and claps her hand over her mouth. "I'm sorry, I didn't mean to—"

"I *am* hateful," I say. "I am despicable and mean. I don't know why you keep coming back here. I don't know what you want. I never asked you to come here. I'd like you to leave me alone."

"You were so kind to your mother. You sacrificed everything to look after her. A man like that cannot be so hateful."

"See, Simone, you're contradicting yourself. Am I or am I not hateful? Make up your mind, and leave."

"I believe you are good," she says. "I believe you are a good person. But you refuse to see it."

"Well, you see, that's all delusional. Is that what that 'temple' teaches you? Nobody's a 'good' person. The world isn't a 'good' place. The most we can do is to be less evil than others. But evil we are, and if you're looking for goodness, you're in the wrong place, Simone. The wrong universe."

"You can't be evil," she says. "Not when you can also be so kind."

"When was I kind, Simone? When I offered you a job? That's the only act of seeming 'kindness' I can think of that I've ever done. That's why you've been looking after me, right? Because you feel obliged to repay my 'kindness.' But do you really believe it was an act of kindness? I hired you because I was sick and tired of looking after my mother. That was all it was. I didn't do it out of kindness. I did it out of selfishness."

"You gave up your life to be your mother's only friend."

"Do you know what I did to my mother, Simone? I wished that those lunatics would blow the clinic up, and make us move on. And they did. Do you see what an evil, hateful man I am now?"

"A wish like that can never come true. It is not possible."

"Well, apparently it is. I don't wish for fucking world peace or love or riches. I wish for death and destruction, and somebody up there, the Lord Fucking Buddha or something, finds that so easy to give. I am an evil man, and I should be punished. Nothing less would satisfy me. If that deed goes unpunished, then I will lose my faith in this imperfect world. I will lose my belief in the logic that sustains it. Evil must not go unpunished. We must meet the fate that we all deserve."

She starts to cry, quietly, turning her head away. I can hear her stifling her sobs, which annoy me even more than if she just burst into tears. Finally she says, "You tell me these things only to drive me away. I'll go away, if that's what you want."

"Yes, that's what I want. I don't need your sympathy or your charity. I never asked for it."

She gets up and heads toward the door. But she stops and turns and, standing straight, defiantly fighting back her tears, she says, "I never came here to repay your kindness. You're mistaken about that. I came here to prove to you that I am no longer needy. I, too, acted out of selfishness."

She bolts down the stairs. I stay next to the sink, gripping the edge of the counter, trying to keep standing. I feel I am inside a loop in which stories get repeated over and over, in an endless and dizzying circle, and I am reliving what others have lived before me. I catch my image on a feng shui mirror hanging on the wall. I don't recognize the old man staring back at me, the sad, cynical eyes, the drooping lips, the rabid stare. I think of that woman at the nonprofit, her porcine face and the acid of bitterness burning through her heart, and I imagine her face melting into mine, her soul eating my soul.

I look out the window. I am hoping I will see Simone down the street below. I want to call her back, but to what purpose I don't know. I am certain that if I did, and she did come back, I wouldn't have the decency to apologize. I want her back only because I realize, at this moment, that she is the only person who understands me.

I spend the next few days alone, recuperating from my exhausting confrontation with Simone. When I finally summon the nerve to go out, it is freezing cold. I take the subway downtown, with the intention of visiting the library. But I stay on the train even as it reaches my stop, and somewhere farther downtown, I get off and cross the platform and take the uptown train back.

Across the seat from me, a homeless person is slouched against the wall, fast asleep. Before him is a cart loaded with all his possessions: a soiled comforter, a battered boom box, trash bags full of junk he probably picked up on the street. In front of the cart he has taped a piece of cardboard with a long, wordy, hand-scrawled message, in letters so tiny all I can make out are phrases about putting your trust in the Savior and the world coming to an end. I can't take my eyes away from the wretched figure asleep before me, that grizzled, scruffy Job, his half-open mouth caked with dried spittle.

I finally reach home just before dark. I boil some tea. Night is falling quickly. It is the hour that I dread the most, that buffer zone of time when forms vanish, and everything seems to float freely in one indistinguishable mass.

I go to my mother's room and turn the computer on. I check my e-mail and find, to my surprise, a message from someone I never expected would get back to me, and whom I had presumed was nonexistent:

Janya wanted you to have this, so here it is. But I have something to tell you myself. You want to know where you came from, how you got where you are now. You told Janya your mother kept all that information from you for a long time, because if you found out, you'd do exactly what you're doing now. You want to know if you have a long-lost brother. But she won't allow that. Because your search for your brother would be the beginning of your freedom. You must learn to live, maybe for the first time. You told Janya, over and over, that all this time, in order to atone for hurting your mother, you've chosen to be dead yourself. But guess what. You are the only one that keeps her alive. She is the only one that keeps you alive. You love one another simply because you need to. Sad to say, love never gets better than that. So I salute you, my maybe brother. Because you come from the wrecks of love. Give my best to your loving, long-suffering mother. Maybe you're right. Maybe we are brothers. I have never been so honest in my entire life.

I open the attachment and stare at the screen for a long time, rereading the document over and over. Someone presses the doorbell. I remain sitting, trying to ignore that insistent buzz as it echoes throughout the hall. I feel light, weightless, gladly exhausted, and grateful to finally get some sleep.

WSOWOB

After the ceremony at Khao Lak, Janya's director invites me to a small memorial at the office in Bangkok. It's an awkward, hastily assembled event, with only a handful of their staff and one other monitor who just happens to be in town. There are drinks and canapés, and a brief, sentimental round of speeches in which everyone is asked to say something they remember about Janya.

When it's my turn, I tell them that I've just bought a ticket back to Manila and San Crisostomo, but as I do so I suddenly break down. Everyone quietly slips out of the office, and finally only the director is left to clear out the canapés and half-consumed plastic cups of wine.

Later that evening, she takes me back to her apartment and we fuck. She's much older than Janya, a recently divorced American with three kids. Afterward, I tell her I didn't mean to bawl like that. It had nothing to do with Janya. I was just exhausted. There's nothing else to talk about; Janya's our only connection. I don't want to stay too long, so I start to get dressed. She says she understands. "We were very concerned about her."

"What about?" I ask.

"We felt she wasn't doing things right. I don't know if I should even talk to you about it."

"What wasn't she doing right?"

"There were rumors that some of our monitors were selling out, you know, like taking bribes. But they were just rumors. And Janya seemed, well, so furtive. Her long absences, her unscheduled meetings and unexplained expenses. We didn't really know what was going on. But I shouldn't even be telling you all this. It's probably not true."

"No, it can't be. I would have found out. We shared everything. We kept no secrets."

"You must miss her a lot."

"It was a kind of pact, to share everything. I know that sounds idealistic, if not impossible. But that's how we were."

"That could backfire on you."

"But we tried our best. And it worked for us."

"Would you have told her about us, if she were still here?"

"This wouldn't have happened if she were here."

"Fair enough," she says. "How I envied her sometimes. How I envied her happiness. At my age, with all the bad decisions I've made, all I do is look back, and all I see is envy. Or regret. I find it unbearable that the young can be so happy. There were times when I really hated her."

Four or five canoes are still out at sea. It's starting to rain. I recognize his station wagon by the pier. I squeeze into the driver's seat. There's an unbearable, deathly stench inside the car. The floor of the hatch is littered with bloody fish, their bodies mangled and ripped, pink, shattered flesh oozing out of lacerated skin.

The rain is getting heavier now. It pelts all around me, looking for a crack to crawl into, smashing itself against the windows, the windshield, the roof of the car. Water leaks through the roof, slowly at first, then becoming a steady trickle. A puddle gathers at my feet.

Someone taps on the window. "Move, move." It's Gino.

I slide to the other end of the vehicle. He sloshes in, his yellow raincoat drenching the seat. He pulls the hood off. His skin's burned dark, darker than I remember. He wipes his face with the front of his wet shirt. Water continues to dribble down his face. The windshield clouds over. He rubs his hand against it, resolutely, as though he's trying to erase the blurred image of us reflected on the glass. For several minutes there's only the sound of his hand squeaking against the glass. He's missing a finger: the ring finger. He notices that I'm staring.

"Dynamite," he explains. "The Taiwanese trawlers catch everything. So sometimes we have to try harder to coax the smaller fish out."

"What do they taste like?"

"What do you think? Like dynamite."

"Sorry," I say. "About your finger."

"I lost not just the finger, but my wedding ring as well. Fourteen-karat gold. But I'm lucky. My older brother, he wasn't very lucky."

"What happened to him?"

"Sometimes you throw too much dynamite, or you don't throw fast enough. He didn't throw fast enough." He stops wiping the windshield. The glass immediately clouds over again. He rolls his window down a bit. The rain pelts his side, making spattering noises on his raincoat. "Is Janya with you?"

"No. I wanted to speak to you alone."

"You came all the way here to speak to me? It must be really important."

I show him the letter the detective found. *Let me know what you decide to do . . . You must be very careful.* "I want to know what was going on with you two."

"You don't beat around the bush, do you?"

"I need to know."

"She said she was looking for a cure."

"For what?"

"For something that happened long ago. She said it wasn't for her. It was for you. What's wrong with you?"

"You a doctor too?"

"I do whatever I can. No one is beyond help."

"Then I need your help."

"Tell me."

"You know something that Janya wanted to keep from me."

"If she wanted to keep it from you, you're not getting it from me."

"Tell me what it is. I have to know."

"I never break a promise."

"Janya's dead." I look for a reaction, but find none. "We were going to talk about it, but we never got to."

"Even worse. One never breaks a promise to the dead." He rolls the window down and looks out. "The rain's stopped."

Fog is lifting off the water. Everything is suddenly very still.

"You shouldn't have come," he says. "Both of you. Then you wouldn't be in this sorry mess."

A liter or so into the demijohn of palm wine, Gino starts

talking. There are no windows inside the house, just square holes bored right below the ceiling through thick limestone walls, like in medieval fortresses, small enough to ward off the constant rain and let a little light in. I can see the sky in small, successive frames, like a strip of film, an intermittent blue in this soot-blackened room. The soot comes from the wood that's constantly smoking underneath fillets of swordfish that have been strung up for curing. I have to crouch low to avoid them. Several lines hang like buntings from every part of the two-room house.

Gino holds his arm out in an arc, mimicking the swell of a wave. "That's what it looks like," he says. "That's the kind of wave that takes anybody, no matter how strong they are. Nobody can survive a wave like that."

"Did anyone ever find the boy? Or a body?"

"The sea never gives back what it takes."

"And what happened to them, to Annette and Sylvain?"

"They left as soon as they could. Just like that. They packed their bags and took the next plane out. There was nothing the police chief could do. They weren't being held for anything, after all. We were going to have a memorial service for the boy. But they just wanted to get out. People started to talk. People asked me a lot of questions, why I rented them a boat. I told them what I tell you now. I just let them use my boat. The sea never gives back what it takes."

"Do you know the professor?"

"Who?"

"Janya's friend, the professor."

"I have never been anywhere but this island. I don't know anybody. Except the ones who live and die here."

I glance around the room. "This is where you bring them in. The ones who are found."

"The ones who die on land. The ones who are not lost."

"I saw Janya coming out of here, the first time she came to see you. She looked terrified."

"She should be."

"Why?"

"Because I told her what I saw."

"What you *saw*?"

"I told her the lost boy was happy that you'd come back."

"You're not making any sense."

"The ones who are lost will always find a way to come back. And you gave him that chance. He was going to come back."

"How did you *see* that?"

"In a dream. A week before you came."

"So you saw the boy himself."

"As though he were right here, in this very room, like the first time I saw him."

I show him a clip on my iPod. "Is that him?"

He tries to avoid it, but finally looks. "Yes."

"You sure?"

"It was he. I know. He knew his time had come."

"That's the superstition around here, right? Janya told me about it. But that's not the only thing you told her."

"She told me you must never find out."

"Find out what? You have to tell me."

"That she was pregnant."

The words leave me dumbfounded.

"That's why she was so sick," Gino says. "But she

made me promise not to tell. She said if you put two and two together—"

"I was so stupid. I had no idea." Then another thought occurs to me. "Did she ask you to abort it?"

"She asked about it. There are some things I cannot do."

"She kept writing to you, didn't she?"

"She wanted more advice."

"On how to get rid of the child?"

"Or how to keep it."

"She was going to keep it?"

"If she was left with no choice."

"And was she ever going to let me know? I mean, how could I not notice sooner or later?"

"That's why she ran away. She didn't want you to know."

"Did you tell her to do that?"

"No, she decided that on her own. Surely you know why."

"No, I don't."

"She was afraid you'd ask her to kill it."

"Why the fuck would I—"

"She said you were acting strange. You were getting sick again. You were saying it was the boy."

"But you said it was."

"I didn't say that."

"You said he knew his time had come . . ."

"That was what I saw in my dream. But whether he was Janya's child, I could not tell. I only know what I know."

"It was you that spooked her. You and your super-stition."

"She said you were going to ask her to abort it. I asked

her what she wanted to do. She said she was either going to keep it, or give it away. That's all I know. I never heard from her since. There, I hope you're satisfied. I just broke my promise to the dead. Now I must ask her forgiveness. Now you must leave me alone."

. . . Then she is leaving the house, holding her hand over her mouth. I see her walking out, resolutely heading toward the sea. Gino runs after her but decides to leave her alone. I can see it clearly. I can see that I am standing some distance from the house. The wind is cold on my skin. The air is filled with the odor of brine. Clouds roil overhead, passing above the island slowly, turning the sky into a luminous gray, like mother of pearl.

Gino's station wagon passes me by. I can tell he's looking at me through the rearview mirror. The vehicle is skidding this way and that, avoiding a group of children who've just streamed out of the schoolhouse and are crossing in front of him.

I can see Janya walking toward the sea. I hurry after her. The faster I run the longer the road stretches ahead of me. I call her name. She stops and turns her head, briefly, in my direction. But all she hears is the roar of the sea. She cannot see me. Yet I know I am there, I am following her, we are in the same space, the same time.

Memory and imagination have become interchangeable. It's residual light, the light that is both clear and deceptive and makes us see what's no longer there. Everything about that afternoon strikes me with such keenness, such lucidity. Her distance, the children crossing, the sound of their laughter, the roar of the sea, and the pallid sky.

And yet, looking back now, I realize I saw nothing, and I must go back to where I began. A story can never be told the same way twice.

I've made up my mind what to do with Sylvain and Annette's films of the lost boy. But before I do so, I take another look. I find a few more clips I haven't seen before. Here's one:

Annette tells Sylvain about an unusual story. "Is that on? Okay, here goes. Out there in Sampetro—that's the island you see behind me—there's a community isolated for centuries by the monsoon. The residents are descendants of Portuguese sailors shipwrecked in the sixteenth century, who were saved by the natives. No one has been able to migrate to that island since, and no one wants to. It's a desolate place, as barren as the moon. The natives aren't hostile, but they're aloof to outsiders and indifferent to the rest of the world. Inbreeding has made them sickly, eccentric, if not totally weird. They're said to be of a pleasant, though sometimes addled, disposition. Their skin is pale, their eyes sometimes green, often blue. They have no electricity, and the constant typhoons make no communication possible. They survived the centuries through sheer persistence, accepting no commercial or medical aid from anyone else. Many of their offspring are born practically blind. A sad thing, isn't it, to be in a place so haunting and beautiful, and to be born blind? . . . Sylvain, that red light's blinking again. Is it time to change the tape? . . . No, I'm all right. This is what's really unusual about those people: they are said to be able to heal themselves through no more than the will alone. They can heal themselves. So blindness is not a problem . . . so Mathieu

. . . so this is why we must go there. Are we all right? Did you get all that, Sylvain?"

In another reel, you can see the boy staggering forward, holding out his arms before him. It's a wide-angle shot, and you recognize Gino's cramped house with the smoked buntings of fish hanging from the ceiling. The boy stumbles and falls on his face. He's trying to explain something to someone (Annette, maybe). The words come out in a drawl. He struggles to get up, turns around, follows the sound of her voice, and finds her outstretched arms. He walks with his eyes half closed, and, as the camera zooms in to an extreme close-up, he reaches out to touch Annette's face: only his small hands show in the frame.

"We'd like to rent a boat," she says.

You can hear Gino's voice off-camera: "It's dangerous to go out." A pause. "What's wrong with him?"

Sylvain's voice, also off-camera: "There's nothing wrong with him."

Gino: "He's blind, isn't he?"

Annette turns to face the camera. "Turn that thing off, Sylvain," she says. "He knows it's on. He can tell. I swear he can tell."

Here's another reel. Sylvain shot this film of Annette. It was probably going to be part of her documentary.

"We are on the interior road. It's a dead end that winds past the towns of Urraca and Iracundo, which we've just passed, and goes farther up the slope of the volcano. Up there, just a couple more miles away, is the town of Jaula, which is Spanish for *cage*. It literally is. It's totally secluded. Only a few stone houses wedged in primeval jungle. The road is narrow, and during storms it turns to an impassable torrent of mud. Look, you can see that island from here. Sampetro. The water looks so placid . . . motionless . . . unreal . . . No, keep shooting, I'm all right. Do you see these vines? They dangle from branches so high you can't even see where they come from. Vines are clever parasites. They use these trees to crawl to the light. They wrap themselves around the trunk and form a lattice, trapping the tree in a cage, and finally smothering it. Some of these trunks are hollow. The trees that once held them up have long withered away. Everything must find a way to survive. Listen, can you hear that? It's the sound of women reciting the Passion. It's coming from that hut over there, can you see? This place is still largely animist, and like the vines, local superstitions have wrapped themselves around religion in order to survive. They say everything here is watched by the invisibles. The invisibles demand that in order to receive something, you must first give something up. Everyone lives by their rules. They live all their lives paying for the privilege of inhabiting the world of the invisibles."

In this clip, you can see fog hovering over the surface of the water. You can hear the chopping of the oars in the water. Sylvain is rowing a small canoe. This is one long uninterrupted shot, where, for quite a time, no words are spoken. He seems adrift in an endless mist, a dream. Then, after a while, you can hear Annette's voice behind the camera: "How do you know which way to go in this fog?"

"Instinct," says Sylvain. He lays the oars down and buttons his jacket and turns the collar up.

"Are we okay?"

"Yes," he says. "We're doing all right. We're right in the middle of three bodies of water."

"Right at this very spot?"

"The South China Sea, the Philippine Sea, and the Pacific Ocean."

"You should have brought a cap."

Sylvain doesn't seem to hear her. He peers out at the endless distance, at nothing.

Annette says, "Are we still okay? Is everything all right?"

Another reel. Annette is walking along the crags, oblivious to the tumult of waves crashing close beside her. Drops of water splatter on her dress and dry as quickly in the sun. Her skin burns easily; even in a clip as faded as this, her color is vivid and burnt. She's wearing a wide-brimmed hat, which makes her stand out among the women of the island. They wear huge wigs of straw to protect themselves from the sun and rain, the way their forebears did. She walks among them absently, unaware of the curious, sometimes reproving glances.

Jump cut, hours later. She's at the plaza, sitting on a stone bench, rubbing the soles of her feet. Behind her the weathered church looms, whitewashed, clean as a shell. The bell tolls. It's late afternoon, the hour of the Angelus. Around her, people stand up to face the church and pray. She remains sitting, uncomfortably, then stands up to face the church as well, but quickly decides she doesn't have to, and sits down again. The tolling stops. She sits there for a while, not moving as the island resumes its normal routine. Children stream past her. The women at the market have packed up and are heading home. For the first time she looks at the camera. She wasn't aware that all this time it's been following her. Her smile is wan, though not without affection, and not without sadness. The camera zooms in. Sylvain's voice-over, a mere whisper, can hardly be heard: he's speaking to himself more than to her. *I wish I could bring back her joy, but I know I never will.*

Another reel. The local police chief of San Crisostomo interrogates Sylvain and Annette. It's Annette who speaks on behalf of the couple (this footage was obviously shot by Sylvain).

"You wanted to take the boy to Sampetro?"

"We wanted to take a look at it, yes. To see what those stories are all about."

"You know it's risky to go there, right? No harbor to shelter in. And the waves crush anything so fragile as the canoes we have around here. Only army boats are allowed there. It's off-limits to anyone else."

"Why?"

"If you missed a step coming on to shore, you'd plunge straight to the bottom. You would never be seen again. We can't be responsible for you."

"And the stories about it?"

"Healers, shamans—all hearsay, colorful tales, elaborate lies. Only one person can heal, Mrs. Aubert. Only Christ can heal."

"Oh, for crying out loud."

"We'd like to ask you to stay awhile longer. Until we finish the search."

"How much longer?"

"A week. Maybe two."

You can't hear much from here on. The camera zooms out and reveals that they're at the airport. A turboprop has just landed. People are already crowding in. The scene is one of total mayhem. Annette's in the frame again, dragging her suitcase away from the rabble. "He says people have seen us on the beach. He says it's not right. To be seen walking around like that. What's that supposed to mean? I don't know what's wrong with these people, Sylvain. I don't know what they expect us to do."

From the plane, you can see the island down below, a monochromatic blur, dull as khaki, devoid of vegetation. Annette's soft voice: *It seems so close one could easily imagine just swimming to it.* Her face appears in the frame. *Turn it off, Sylvain. I don't want to remember any of this.*

I'm looking at that clip again, the first one I ever saw of the boy. It's the one with the birthday cake, the candles drifting across the frame in a hazy, ethereal ribbon of light. The little boy finally comes into frame, holding a toy gun, the brim of his party hat falling over his eyes. He realizes the camera is on, and, on some instinct, he is drawn to the whir of it.

I freeze-frame right there.

The boy is looking straight at the camera, at me, at something he can barely see. He's smiling. It's the smile of the innocent, unaware of what the world is, and what it's going to be. It is an image both hopeful and tragic. It's the image I want to remember when I finally burn these reels.

I can hear, faintly, the murmuring sea. A distant rumor of

waves, a mere fraction of sound, an invisible but certain presence—present but not threatening. I stand by the window and look out. The sky is wide, an infinite, cloud-less canopy of blue. The house hasn't changed, which surprises me, because I demand that the world change with me, and for it to remain unchanged is to be indifferent to the passage of time that has forever altered me.

The door is still unlocked, its chain still looped through holes where the lock had been. The only thing that's different is the rusting crucifix, one end of which has become unhinged so that the weathered Christ embossed on it dangles from one wrist, the wind swaying it like a pendulum. Without anything to remind me of her, this is mere space, its emptiness magnified by an unbearable, unnerving quiet.

The silence is soon disturbed by the sound of feet pattering up the road. I walk out to see who it is. I catch her running past, breathlessly heading out to sea. *Well, are we going to the water?* I follow her out to the crag. I can see, from here, how the light reflected from the water below seems to have sought her out alone.

But by the time I get there she's no longer around. I glance down at the churning waves. I can see two people, a man and a woman, standing at the edge of the crag, looking out, not speaking, not moving for a long time. Their clothes are soaked, their arms and legs streaked with bloody cuts. The waves are thrashing, the sound of its roar like that of an animal made violent by its own fear.

I don't know how long they stare at the water, or what they're waiting for. Then a thought courses through my mind. It's a thought so strong, so solid, I feel it rip into my brain, and I know what they're thinking as though they've already articulated it. In a while they'll scramble back to the jeep that's parked by the road. He will drive as fast as he can, and even before they reach the plaza, as soon as he sees people in the distance, he will jam his hand on the horn and, in a voice full of horror and pain, he will finally cry out for help.

Images, lost in the sea of time.

Among her things I find a letter from the professor. On the envelope I recognize her tiny scrawl. There's a note she had scribbled.

Step 1: Give to M on first anniversary.
Step 2: Watch M's reaction and videotape if possible.

Inside, there's a brief letter from the professor, and a photocopy of a handwritten document that's so faded the words seem almost ghostly.

Here is the letter I promised you. He left it with me, but told me never to share it with anyone, only to those who will understand. Didn't know what that meant, but I have never shown it to anyone before. I've read it again and again, of course. I don't really know who he wrote it for, but he said when the time comes I will know. For the last 30 years I thought he wrote it for me. But now I know, and I would like you to have it.
Always glad to be of help,
Victor

Watch M's reaction.

You won't see it. But you will see what I'm doing now. I am not the one he wrote this for. This was not my quest. My quest was for the lost boy. But I know of someone who needs it the most.

"What are we looking at now?"
"It's the stuff that I shot in San Crisostomo."
"But it's all images of water."
"It's a dream I had while we were there."
"How are you going to explain that to Phil?"
"Phil will never see this film. But I want you to look at it. Since I couldn't film the dream itself, I'll have to tell you what it was about."
"All right, tell me."

There's a man in the dream, and I think it's me. He's standing on the crag, looking out at the water. It's turning deep blue in the morning light. He stands there for what seems like an eternity. *At some point I'll have to do it*, he tells himself. He pulls his shirt and jeans off, takes a deep breath, and dives into the water.

The crag doesn't slope gradually out, but plunges straight into the deep. It's hardened volcanic rock, with sharp, jagged edges. Schools of tropical fish flicker around him. The light from the surface shoots arrows that grow diffuse in the roiling water. He's amazed that he doesn't sense fear, but fascination. He finds a wooden shard wedged inside the rock ledge. It's about as big as a surfboard: old, rotting wood, flecks of paint peeling like fish scales. He tries to pry it loose. It doesn't budge. It's been pushed into the rock by years of pressure from the sea.

Suddenly he's being pulled under. Kelp and seaweed

coil around his legs. Something's holding on to him. His heart races. He's running out of air. He treads toward the surface, but the undertow keeps pulling him down.

Just when he thinks he's going to drown, the undertow slackens and swells up. It pushes him up so strongly he hits the edge of the crag. He struggles with it, against it, his arms and legs scraping against the jagged ledge. Ribbons of blood ooze from his ripped skin. The force keeps welling up. Finally he can see the light rushing toward him. He breaks through the surface, gasping for air.

the little toil of love

To: jordan.yeats@gmail.com
Reply-to: masquedefer@gmail.com
Re: Janya wanted you to have this

There's a saying from Confucius that I love & am trying so hard to remember: At this point in my life, I have learned the will of heaven; in ten years I might even learn to accept it.

That's not exactly how it goes but I've grown to love my version anyway & I want to quote it now, imperfect as it is, because it's the only way I can say what I'm trying so damn hard to say. In just a couple of hours I am going somewhere I don't want to be & I won't have much time to tell anybody anything. I don't know who you are & you don't know who I am & I'm afraid anything I tell you will only come out presumptuous & therefore useless. So all I will say is this.

In letting you go, I think I did the right thing. You would have become like the young that I've seen here. Carefree & innocent, oblivious to the suffering that is soon going to devour them. I am afraid for them, I am afraid because there is nothing I can do.

I am here in that part of the world where you were born. I am here because I believed what everyone told me, that I could change the world. I sure damn hope I have made it better for you. I tried to save you; your happiness is what will save me. For the sake of this reckless man, you must be happy.

If only you could see what I see. The full moon hovers above me, such majesty & such soft light, gently shining over this earth so wretched & desolate. I can't stop looking at it. Up there, we have just dug up the Descartes Highlands. We have left our tracks on its surface & they will stay there for a million years, evidence that we were once here & we were so full of wonder.

We must be living in glorious times then, though some of us are a little unhappy & others have lost their way. Seek those who are not afraid to be joyful & full of love. They are so few, but they will give you strength. Because only those who truly love us can forgive our necessary betrayals.

Maybe someday I can tell you all about it, what the will of heaven was, my ramshackle history, secret & pitiable. Maybe I don't even have to. Look up some clear night & imagine how the Descartes Highlands has our imprint, yours & mine. No matter what our lives have been, this magnificence is all that will be remembered of us. We are all immortal.